Drama Unsung

Jennifer Jamelli

Drama Unsung. Copyright © 2014 by Jennifer Jamelli.

Cover design by Ravven.

Printed by CreateSpace.

ISBN-13: 978-1500879792

ISBN-10: 1500879797

To Francie Eyer, an awesome music director (and mother☺)

AND

To my past, present, and future Drama Club students

Prologue

"I Dreamed a Dream"

Cosette. I've wanted to be her since the very first time I saw *Les Misérables* on Broadway. After the curtain closed that night, I got to work right away. I started to memorize her lines, sing her songs. I was only eight years old, but I had a plan. A hope. A dream.

Now, at eighteen, I'm in the dressing room getting ready for my opening night performance of *Les Mis*.

But I'm not Cosette.

And I wish I had known ten years ago—or at least during auditions a couple of months ago—that not getting to be her would lead me to my real dream come true...

Chapter 1

"Do You Hear the People Sing?"

It's my turn. My callback. My only chance to be Cosette. Well, unless I'm somehow offered the role on Broadway someday...but really, like that will ever happen.

So this is it. And I can't mess up. I know if I do—

"Alexa. Alexa? Do you want me to play the intro again?"

Great. I messed up.

"Oh...yes, please. I'm so sorry."

Okay. Concentrate, Lexi.

My intro begins...again, apparently. A girl in the front row—the one with all of the shiny blonde hair—is whispering to the less shiny girl beside her. Her perfectly pink lips form the words "new girl." The guy on the other side of her, the one who looks more like a football player than a member of Drama Club, whispers back. Then the girl snaps her golden head around with a murderous look, saying—

Wait. My opening note. Gotta sing.

I begin the opening verse of "A Heart Full of Love," singing words and notes I've sung at least a thousand times before. And it's not bad. My voice is a tiny bit shaky from nerves, maybe, but otherwise, not bad.

Nonetheless, there are no more than a few polite claps of applause (from a guy in a bright purple shirt who is sitting in the second row) as I leave the stage and sit back in the auditorium with the other auditioners. Once I get back to my seat, no one really acknowledges me at all.

A tiny little girl, another blonde, from the second row is up next. Same song. She doesn't miss her intro, though. And she's not shaky. She's really good. I don't know how the director will even dec—

"Hey. Alexa, right?"

Tight jeans. Bright purple shirt with the word DIVA spelled across the chest. The guy from the second row who clapped for me.

"Um, yeah...uh, Lexi." I give him a small smile.

"Eric," he says, holding out his hand.

Even though I am a little surprised by his formality, I give him my hand. I don't want to be rude. He is, after all, the only person who has thought to talk to me.

He doesn't shake my hand. He flips it over and smacks a kiss right on top.

"Enchanté, Mademoiselle." He speaks with an exaggerated, thick accent—much like the one Madame Yeux uses in French class.

I can't help myself. "Enchanté, Monsieur."

And we smile. Like we get each other. Like maybe I've actually found a friend after a few weeks of walking through the hallways of school by myself.

"Eric, you are up." Mrs. Leonard calls him to go next, and my one and only prospect for a friend smiles, lets go of my hand, and bounces up to the stage.

The opening bars of "Master of the House" ring throughout the auditorium. He must be called back for Thénardier. Not surprising. He doesn't exactly fit the mold for the romantic lead.

As the song starts, he looks right at me and winks. Then he pulls the microphone off of its stand and begins moving around as he sings. He saunters around, lost in the character...so lost that he even makes some rather vulgar dance movements.

I look back at Mrs. Leonard for her reaction. She's delighted.

"Lovely, Eric. Well done. Brilliant."

Eric gives a little curtsy before exiting the stage, and the other students clap and cheer him on. He smiles at the clump of his admirers but then plops down in the seat right next to me.

"Nice choreography." I smile over at him.

He smiles back. "Oh, I know. I've been told it was quite brilliant."

Next up is the girl from the front row, the shiny blonde. As Mrs. Leonard calls her name, she, um...Addison, leans over and kisses the quarterback-looking guy sitting next to her. Right on the lips. Then she stands up and freezes, her neck bent back and her head looking up (I guess to God or something).

"Come on, Miss Thing. This isn't the *Tony Awards*." This comes from right beside me. Eric.

I scrunch down a little in my seat. Just what I need...to be involved in making fun of—

Unbelievable. She starts to laugh. So does everyone else.

"Just practicing for when it is, Eric." She smiles and walks up to the stage. Then she sings yet another rendition of "A Heart Full of Love." And she's not bad. Her voice is light, airy—pretty fitting for the young Cosette.

Her face is blank, though. No emotion. No acting. She's just a doll with notes and words slipping through her lips.

I take a second to glance at the boy, the one who looks like he should be at some sort of athletic practice instead of here. He's focused on Addison, smiling encouragingly as she finishes her song. When she sings her final notes, he joins everyone else in applauding her back down to her seat. Her applause is by far the loudest I've heard so far today.

Soon, Eric stops clapping and leans over to whisper to me. "It's best to stay on her good side." Then he pauses and leans in even closer. "Want to know her *Days of Our Lives* storyline?"

"Um...sure."

"We all have them, of course, but hers is pretty essential to know if you're gonna be in the show. Plus, hers is one of the more interesting ones around here. Not more interesting than mine, of course, but mine is too racy for *Days of Our Lives*." He smiles and does this thing where he licks his tongue over his top teeth.

He then begins his storytelling, nodding his eyes to where Addison and that guy are now cuddling. "Those two are the Drama Club. Every year they try out, get called back for main roles, and then get cast as the leading romantic couple."

I feel my eyes widening in surprise. "Every year? What?"

Eric nods. "I know. It's crazy, right?"

I nod my head slowly, still trying to process what he's saying. "Yeah...but, really? How? Why?"

Another girl is called up to the stage. A redhead with crazy polka-dotted knee high socks and a miniskirt.

Eric yells, "You've got this, Sam," before leaning back, smoothing his shirt down over his flat stomach, and continuing his story.

"Well, this used to be kept a secret, but pretty much everyone knows or suspects now. Mrs. Leonard still tries to pretend that no one is aware of the whole situation, though."

I just nod and wait to hear the rest.

"We're all pretty sure that Addison's father basically funds our show each year. We've all heard many times that Drama Club has very little money...so it's kind of suspicious that we somehow manage to produce pretty huge shows year after year...and it's never been a secret that Addison's father is really wealthy...and somehow Addison is cast as a lead every year. It all kind of adds up."

I nod. Yeah, it does. But that means that I've already lost the chance to play Cos—

"But most of us don't really worry about it all that much."

I look at him in surprise.

"We get to do pretty awesome shows...and, really, that's not our only benefit."

"What else?" I ask in a whisper, trying to wrap my head around the fact that so many people sacrifice the chance to play the romantic leads each year.

"Collin. The boyfriend." He nods his head in the direction of the first row of auditorium seats. "The hot hetero." The one who looks like a football player. What about him?

"He only started trying out because she made him three years ago when we did *Footloose*. And now she makes him do it every year...well, I secretly suspect that he kind of likes doing it now, but I don't know that he'd try out without her." He pauses and grabs my hand. "But, Lexi, he can sing. And dance. And act." He does that tongue on teeth thing again. "And did I mention that he's freaking adorable?"

"Yes—you did make that pretty clear." I smile as much as I can manage given the fact that I'm being told I don't even have a slight chance of playing my dream role. "Okay. But you see all of that as a benefit? Really? He's competition."

"We need him," he says simply. He then looks around the room a little. "As you can see, not many guys go out for Drama Club here. And straight ones are almost unheard of... unfortunately, so are ones that are even remotely cute."

He has a point. The two other called-back boys are both at least one step out of the closet. They haven't gotten far enough into being gay to worry about their appearances, though. I think one is even wearing sweatpants.

Eric continues. "And Leonard can get male teachers to play some parts, like Jean Valjean this year, but she can't put teachers opposite high school girls for the romantic roles...obviously. So Collin's what we have." His tongue is on his teeth again. "And he sings like a young Michael Crawford. Minus the charming British accent, of course."

As though on cue, Mrs. Leonard calls on Collin to sing next. Addison kisses his cheek rather loudly—I can even hear the smack of her lips against his skin, and I'm rows away—and then he heads up to the microphone.

Eric settles back into his chair to listen, closing his eyes and resting his hands on his lap.

I lean back too. And I listen.

And it's amazing. He's amazing. His somewhat husky voice paired with the agony in his eyes makes him the perfect Act II grieving Marius.

When the students in the crowd begin their cheering at the end of his song, he smiles and runs his hand through his dark, tousled hair before going back to his seat.

Eric and I clap with the others. Then Eric leans forward in his chair and faces me. "What a waste. That voice, that body, on a heterosexual male." He shakes his head. "When are Sparkles #1 and Sparkles #2 gonna step it up?" He nods over to the only other two boys who are here.

I don't know if it's Sparkles #1 or #2, but one of them gets up as "Justin" is called to go next.

Eric keeps talking. "So, obviously, Collin is perfect for Marius, just like he was perfect for Tony in *West Side Story* last year and Captain von Trapp in *The Sound of Music* the year before that and—"

"Okay. So he gets a lead every year, and he deserves to every year. I get it. But—"

"But Addison can't act." He just says it. Flat out. I would've tried to dance around the subject a little, but he just puts it right out there.

I look him in the eye and nod. "Right."

He shrugs his shoulders slowly as he speaks. "So what is Leonard going to do? Put another girl in the role opposite Collin and let her dance and sing with him and—" He stops to gasp dramatically. "Kiss him right in front of Addison?"

Oh. Got it.

"And then Addison would probably quit and pull Collin out the door behind her, leaving us with, what, a no-name one act show and this guy as our romantic hero." He nods up to the stage.

I laugh. "This guy," Justin apparently, is terrible. I think he's only hit the correct pitch for one note so far. And I'm pretty sure that was an accident.

Still...this is awful. Really. Awful. Cosette is slipping through my fingers. Splattering through.

"So why even have auditions and callbacks for these parts?"

Eric smirks. "Oh, Leonard would never break from the traditional process. You have auditions, then a callback list, then callbacks, and, finally, a cast list. That's the way she auditioned back when she was in high school. Like in 1930."

"But—"

"It's not fair. At all. I know. It's also not fair that Addison is somehow involved in the show picking process."

I look up at him, surprise, I'm sure, registering on my face.

"Right after Addison saw the *Les Mis* movie, she became obsessed, talking about how she was just like Amanda Seyfried."

"Well, she is really pretty." And she does have straight, long blonde hair.

"But she can't act." Eric sings the words to the opening of Beethoven's 5th.

This is unbelievable. I can't believe that this has been going on for four years.

Eric seems to read my mind. "Believe me, you aren't the only one irritated by this whole setup. But no one is gonna tell Leonard that it's unfair. And no one is gonna tell Addison that she can't act. Why rock the boat? When else are we ever gonna get to do a show as big as *Les Mis*?" He pauses, shrugging again. "And besides that, we all know that we need Collin in the cast."

"But why couldn't you do the romantic male lead? You had a great audition today. Brilliant, if I remember correctly." I nudge him and smile.

"Well, I used to think about that too. Obsess about it, really." He smiles and raises his eyebrows toward me. "I'd even practice trying to woo the ladies every night with a mirror."

"You just couldn't stomach touching a girl without heaving your lunch all over the place?"

"Nah—I could do that. I think it'd be pretty believable too." He laughs. "Seriously, Lexi, if gay guys couldn't pretend to be in love with women, Broadway would probably have to block off its streets forever."

"True. Okay. So what's the deal, then?"

"I know he's better than I am. His voice is better. So is his acting. I get that. It took me a long time to accept that, but I do get it now. And besides, if I wasn't available for the supporting, comic-relief-providing, male roles, who the hell would play them? This guy?"

He again nods up to the stage, where the other Sparkles is now singing "Stars." He can sing at least. Pretty well even. But he has no expression on his face. Zero. Like he's singing about sharpening a pencil.

Eric leans over. "I wonder what Leonard is writing in her notes for his acting right now." He pauses. "Perhaps, this SSSSUUUCCCKKKSS!"

"Why did he get a callback then?"

"Well, he's probably gonna get a part since he can at least sing. Leonard doesn't ever really have the luxury of being picky with guys. She has to use them all, the few that try out. So, really, all the boys get a callback each year."

Oh. Another tradition.

"And why did I get one?"

"Cause you are good. Really good." Eric smiles. "And there are other leading parts you might get."

Just not Cosette. Got it...

Mrs. Leonard puts an end to our conversation as she rings a little bell and heads up to the stage. She moves pretty fast. Maybe she's younger than she looks. I decide to ask Eric.

"Well, that's tricky." He responds in a whisper, a pensive look on his face. "She looks ancient, but she's got a lot of spunk." He pauses. "Maybe she just doesn't know about hair dye. Or makeup."

Mrs. Leonard begins to speak from the center of the stage. "All right. Thanks for coming out today. You are all shining stars."

"Blech. I think I can taste the pizza I had for lunch coming back up into my mouth," Eric whispers quickly and then closes his lips tightly as he tries not to laugh. I look away so we don't both start giggling.

Mrs. Leonard tells us to check the cast list tomorrow morning.

Tomorrow morning? I lean back over to Eric. "At my old school, my teacher always posted the list online the night of auditions. Much less waiting."

He smiles again. "Maybe Mrs. Leonard doesn't know about the internet either."

I smile back and grab my bookbag before we both walk up to get Eric's stuff. When we get to his old seat, he introduces me to the tiny blonde who auditioned after me. Who auditioned really well.

I guess she already knows that she won't be getting the part of Cosette, though.

Her name is Sarah. She's a junior. She seems nice, and I think she's actually interested when she asks me about my old school and then about my parents' new law firm.

While we are talking, the redhead with the polka-dotted socks comes up and wraps her arms around Eric from behind. He holds her hands as they rest on his stomach, and she puts her chin on his shoulder, saying, "Think I'll get to play your wife?"

So she already knows that she also won't be putting on Cosette's ringleted wig...

"I hope so, darling," Eric replies.

She lets go of him and picks up her sparkly bookbag, saying, "I don't know if I can learn all of your 'brilliant' moves, though..."

"I'll teach you." Eric smiles. "Hey, Sam, this is Lexi. You know, the new girl."

Sam throws her arms right around me, squeezing rather tightly for such a small girl. "Welcome to Drama Club, Lex," she says. "You sounded pretty awesome up there."

"Thanks."

She lets go of me, hugs Eric and, um, Sarah, and she is off.

Sarah leaves too. Eric and I start to follow behind, and soon we pass Addison and Collin. Cosette and Marius. The guaranteed leading couple. They are now sitting in the middle of the auditorium, holding hands and talking. Or maybe they're running their lines already. Who knows.

As Eric does the introductions, Collin puts his Marius eyes on me. My black Mary Janes stop walking.

"You sounded great up there today." His slightly husky voice. Guess he doesn't just use it for Marius.

"Um, well, I don't know about great. But, thanks." I give him a small smile.

He returns it, his deep brown eyes shining. And I have to disagree with Eric. I'm so glad that such a perfect smile belongs to a straight guy.

"Sweetie, I'm hungry now." She, Addison, interrupts our smiling and puts her head on Collin's shoulder.

"Well, okay, um," I try (unsuccessfully) to find a graceful way to leave.

"Hey, Lex—hop on." Eric leans down so I can jump up on his back. I climb on, and he bolts up the aisle of the auditorium as my bookbag bounces up and down on my back.

He puts me down when we reach the lobby outside of the auditorium, and he then spins around to face me. "If those two somehow don't end up married with two kids...if they ever actually break up, he's mine first. Sorry." Eric puts his tongue back on his teeth mischievously. "I've got a plan to turn him to the other side. The better side."

"Fine with me. I won't be interested."

Eric raises his eyebrows and walks ahead of me.

"I'm not interested." I talk to his back.

"Sure." He doesn't even turn around.

I hit him on the back of his bright purple shoulder. "I'm not."

He turns around so fast that I step on his shoe. He doesn't even flinch before he puts his face right next to mine. Almost nose to nose.

"Too bad. I'm pretty sure he's part of your storyline."

"My—" Oh, right. The *Days of Our Lives* thing. I move my face from his and walk ahead toward the parking lot. "I don't have a storyline."

"I've already told you that everyone has one." He comes up beside me and grabs my hand, swinging it back and forth as we take our final steps to the parking lot. "You'll see, Lex. You'll be on the cover of *Soap Opera Digest* in no time."

He stops abruptly, and our hands finish swinging a second later. "This is me."

The shiniest (or maybe only) purple car I've ever seen. I smile over at him. "Of course this is you. What else would you drive when you're wearing that shirt?"

He smiles too as he clicks open his doors and ditches his bookbag in the back seat. Then he looks back at me. "You're pretty fabulous, you know."

"Of course I know."

"I almost suspect that you've done this hag thing before."

"I hate that word. Can't you just refer to me as, I don't know, a friend or something?"

"Nope." He kisses me on the cheek and opens the driver's door. "That's not how it works, Lex." He smiles and gets into the car. "Meet you by the cast list tomorrow morning?"

I shrug. "What's the point?"

Pointless or not, I wait anxiously for the school doors to be opened so I can see the list. Eric joins me after I've been waiting for only about two minutes. We stand together in nervous silence. I stare into the eyes of the little gummy bear that is pictured in the middle of his orange t-shirt.

Soon, Sarah and Sam join us as well, and the Sparkles duo isn't far behind them.

Addison and Collin don't show up until a minute before the doors are supposed to open...and Addison is crying. Collin has one arm around her, and his other arm is full of books—presumably his and hers.

"Addie, you were fine. You didn't miss a note."

"But I—" She starts to whine. And she still is whining...but I can't hear it anymore because *he* has caught my eyes.

He looks, hmm...well, gorgeous, with his dark brown, eye-matching thermal tee, but he looks more than that. Frustrated. Irritated? Maybe even a little bit embarrassed.

I shrug and give him a tiny smile.

He blinks his eyes softly and smiles back—for like a second—and then Addison turns up her head to look at him. His eyes leave mine in a mega-fast second, and he gives her what he must think is a reassuring look. His mouth looks reassuring. But his eyes are again a bit annoyed.

Doesn't matter. She buys it.

"Thanks, honey. I'm so lucky to have such a supportive—" She begins.

"Doors are open," Sarah interrupts, and Addison's gushy speech is forgotten.

We don't exactly run to Mrs. Leonard's room. If we did, some wide awake and ready-to-yell teacher would definitely stop us and lecture us and ultimately slow us down. So we don't run...but we don't quite walk either. Something in between.

We make it to the second floor. Room 204. Only a few steps away. And I can already see a blur of typing on the white sheet hanging in the doorway.

Addison runs ahead so she gets to the door first. After shrieking, "I got it," she turns around and kisses Collin on the cheek before running into Mrs. Leonard's room to—

I don't know. Hug her? Thank her for accepting her father's money in exchange for looking past her mediocre acting skills once again?

Eric nudges me. It's our turn to look. I nod to tell him to look first. He walks up beside Collin to study the list.

"Monsieur Thénardier." Eric's head starts to nod up and down. "It's clear that my moves really were brilliant." He smiles back at me and then puts his hand on Collin's muscular shoulder. "Way to go, man. You'll make a great Marius."

Collin mumbles a thank you.

As Eric turns away and walks back to me, I can't help myself.

I whisper. "*Way to go, man.* Is that what the straight guys are saying nowadays? Or is that phrase only used by gay guys who are looking for an excuse to initiate physical contact with a—"

"Hey!" He cuts me off and smiles. "Shut up so I can tell you what part you got."

I shut up and listen.

He takes both of my hands in his, excitedly saying, "You're my daughter—Éponine!" He spins me around in a little dance.

Éponine. Okay...not bad. Not Cosette, but not bad. Éponine's song might be a little bit low for me...but at least I *have* a song.

Eric suddenly stops spinning and leans over to whisper in my ear. "You're also the girl who secretly wants to come between Cosette and Marius. It's perfect!"

Yeah. Perfect.

Chapter 2

"At the End of the Day"

The 3:00 bell rings, and it's time for rehearsal. First practice. Full cast.

Eric meets me by my locker and we head to the auditorium together. It turns out that we actually have two classes together. French and English. I'm kind of shocked I didn't notice him during the first weeks of school—I must've been too busy trying not to do anything stupid during my first classes as "the new girl."

It'll be nice to have someone to sit with in class now, though. And someone to walk with in the halls. I'm really glad he's with me now as we enter the back of the auditorium for our first practice. He opens the door and holds it so I can go in first.

I am not prepared for what awaits me inside.

Addison and Collin are kneeling downstage, holding hands and looking straight ahead. Addison is holding a letter in her non-Collin-occupied hand.

Hmm...the exact location for Cosette and Marius during the traditional finale of *Les Mis*.

Mrs. Leonard is nowhere to be seen, so this clearly isn't part of rehearsal (it would be odd even then—why would they be rehearsing the final scene of the show during the first night of practice anyway?) Stranger yet, no one is around. Anywhere. The auditorium is silent and dark except for a dim light on the stage.

What is going—

"Oh. I should have warned you," Eric whispers from right behind me. "I just figured they'd be done by the time we got down here."

"Done with what, exactly?" I whisper back as he moves to stand beside me against the back auditorium wall. I hope we can't be seen from the stage.

"Their stupid little first rehearsal ritual." I can tell from the tone of his voice that he's probably rolling his eyes. "Addison likes to act out the final scene before she even begins playing a character. She says it helps her to visualize where her character is going to end up before she can think how to best act out her—"

"But she can't act." The words just tumble out of my mouth, thankfully in a whisper.

"I know. That's why this particular routine is really stupid."

"This particular—" I begin to ask.

"Oh—they have many more obvious traditions. You'll see."

I open my mouth to ask about seven million questions, but then I snap it back shut.

"I know what you're thinking," Eric begins. "Why doesn't someone just tell her that her routines are dumb? Or that she doesn't really even deserve the parts she gets?" He pauses and then answers his own questions. "Well, because then she'd just go whining to Leonard about it, and in no time, the truth-teller would be cut from the show for some Addison-created reason...or just treated so terribly that he or she would want to drop out anyway."

"Seriously? She has that much power?"

"Seriously, Lex. You don't even know the start of it. I'll save all of that for a gossip night down the road. For now, try to swallow this." He takes a breath and then continues. "One girl tried to tell Addison the truth last year during auditions." He pauses again. "That girl didn't get a role—and she sang 'I Feel Pretty' better than anyone else."

Unbelievable.

"It's best not to mess with Miss Addison."

I focus again on the stage where she and Collin are still staring straight ahead in silence. There really isn't anything else I can do at this point. It would be really odd to walk to the front of the auditorium right now.

So I stare ahead at them and wait. And wait. Eric does the same.

About seven months later, Mrs. Leonard strolls onto the stage behind them. She speaks loudly.

"Hello, my darlings. How are we already beginning your final season? And what am I ever going to do next year?"

Eric leans over to whisper again. "What she means is, what is she ever going to do without Addison's father and his money next year?" He laughs quietly.

Addison gets up to hug Mrs. Leonard. Collin keeps staring ahead, but he drops back from his kneeling position, now sitting on his feet. He looks uncomfortable. And bored. And...embarrassed? Maybe. It's hard to tell from back here.

At least he can't see—

The auditorium doors beside us are opening, and light is starting to stream in as cast members begin to enter.

"Hey—what are you guys doing? Making out back here in the dark?"

I recognize the voice. The redhead. Sam. Madame Thénardier.

She grabs Eric's hand and looks at me with mock horror. "He's my husband now. At least until the play is over." She smiles and continues. "You know he's gay, right?"

I smile back. "I was starting to suspect...the flashy purple car kind of gave it away."

Sam pulls Eric closer and rests her pigtailed head on his shoulder. "So you have to settle for being yet another hag."

"Lexi doesn't like that word." Eric looks over at me with gleaming eyes, yet again licking his teeth with his tongue. "Even though it's what she is."

I hit him quickly on his non-Sam-resting shoulder.

"And I've really been in search of another one. It's so hard to find a good hag these days." He pauses and sighs. "I thought Sarah had potential, but she's just too busy with her over 4.00 GPA and now with being an understudy for the show." Sam lifts her head and Eric turns to look at her. "I was just kind of hoping that Lexi would step up to the plate." Then he leans over to me and whispers, "And by step up to the plate, I mean be my hag."

I shake my head and roll my eyes, and that is really all I have time for because the auditorium lights are slowly fading on. It looks like rehearsal is about to begin. Everyone seems to be congregating in the front of the auditorium. Mrs.

Leonard is walking around the stage, yelling out and encouraging cast members to come up and sit in a big circle on the floor.

"Let's do this." Eric takes Sam's hand and mine, and the three of us skip down the aisle to join everyone else. After ditching our bookbags in auditorium seats, we climb onto the stage and sit side by side in Mrs. Leonard's circle. Eric plops down between Sam and me, and, for now, the space on the other side of me is empty. A bunch of people still haven't sat down yet. Instead, they are crowded around some girl who is all sad and weeping.

Yep. It looks like this Drama Club is just like the one back at my old school. More drama offstage than on...must be pretty universal.

Based on what I can hear from my spot, these tears seem to simply be leftovers from this morning's posting of the cast list. Most people get over their disappointment enough after a few hours that they can at least fake being okay during the first practice. But there is always one...

There are about five people surrounding the crying girl, offering their support or whatever, but it seems that the main grief counselor is Addison. She's holding the girl so close to her chest that I can't even see the girl's face. I have no idea who she is...not that I can possibly remember all sixty or so people that I saw for the first time at auditions this week anyway.

Addison has now turned her own head, and I can see her lips moving. "It's not fair." She seems to be repeating the phrase over and over again.

"Just another day in Drama Club," Eric whispers beside me. "But don't worry about it, Lex. Really. You totally deserve your part."

What?

I tear my eyes from the little weepy clump of people and ask him what he's talking about.

"Éponine." He says it as though I should already understand what he's going to say. "You earned her."

"Okay...thanks, I guess."

"No problem. Casey gets like this at some point every year anyway. About a boy. Or a key change. Always something. For a junior, she's pretty immat—"

"Wait." I spin completely around so we are facing each other Indian-style, knees to knees. "All of that crying over there is about Éponine? About me?"

"Sorry, Nancy Drew. It is." He scrunches up his eyes a little. "I thought you knew that."

Sam leans over Eric to join in. "Remember on the first day of auditions? She said that she spent her entire summer watching and re-watching the movie to memorize Éponine's lines, her facial expressions..." Sam drifts off and leans back to her original sitting place.

Hmm...I do vaguely remember now. But that was on the first day of auditions...back when I wanted to be Cosette. Back when I thought that there were actual auditions for Cosette. I wouldn't have paid much attention at that point if someone wanted to be Éponine.

"So wait," I begin to verbalize my thoughts. "When Addison keeps saying that it isn't fair..."

Eric's hands are all of a sudden on my shoulders, holding me down as though he thinks I'm going to get up and confront Addison or something. Like I'd ever have the nerve to—

"Lex—of course you getting this part was fair. If we are going to talk about fair..." He nods over to where Addison is standing.

"All right, my shining stars. Let's circle up." Mrs. Leonard ends our conversation. For now. She is ready to begin, standing in the center of what will be her circle after people sit down and fill it in.

Eric looks me sternly in the eyes and then removes his hands from my shoulders. I keep my eyes away from Addison and Casey and try not to think about what they're saying about me.

Sam leans over, laughing. "What did he think you were going to do exactly? Punch someone? Cut someone?" She shakes her head at Eric. "You have such a violent view of heteros."

Eric giggles a little as we all move to face in toward the circle, in toward Mrs. Leonard, who is starting to speak even though people are still slowly coming to sit down.

"Okay, my dear, dear cast members, let's begin introductions." She pushes some stray strands of gray hair from her face and then closes her eyes. "Let's all close our eyes so we can concentrate on each other and our words."

I look around, and those already sitting begin to close their eyes. When my gaze lands on Eric, he winks, nods, and shuts his eyes—holding his face up like he's some sort of Greek god...or goddess, rather.

Sam has also already shut her eyes. So have all of the people directly across from me. And there is no one beside me on the other side, so there really isn't anywhere else to look.

So I close my eyes and wait for the introductions to begin.

Eric's rather soft hand grabs my left hand and drags it to the stage floor between us. He squeezes my hand. Really hard. Instead of yelping out loud, I flip open my eyes to look at him. He has a smirk on his face. His eyes are still closed, though. I pinch his hand, watch his face scrunch up a little in closed-eyed pain, and then shut my lids once again.

Mrs. Leonard is beginning to introduce herself. As a director, teacher, nurturer to us all.

When she says the word "nurturer," Eric squeezes my hand just a little. I'm pretty sure he's trying not to laugh.

Now we are supposed to go around the circle, introducing ourselves, our characters, and our feelings (as Mrs. Leonard puts it anyway...I'm not really sure how we are supposed to "introduce" our feelings. Hopefully, I don't have to go first). After we speak, we are supposed to squeeze the hand of the person to the right of us. Then it will be that person's turn. Great. I guess Eric has just been given permission to assault my hand again soon.

The circle introductions begin. Our first speaker is Mr. Fiero. My English teacher. Number 24601 himself. It sounds like he is pretty far away from me. Good. It won't be my turn for a long time.

"So, as you already know," Mr. Fiero begins in his slightly scratchy, compassionate (perfect for his role) voice, "Mrs. Leonard has asked me to play Jean Valjean. I love this show, so I'm pretty excited."

That's it. I guess by saying that he is "excited," he has sufficiently introduced his feelings. Not too bad.

The next voice belongs to a journalism teacher. Miss Price. She will be playing Fantine. From what I've heard, this is the first time Mrs. Leonard has used a female teacher for a role. Apparently she thought it was necessary for the emotional depth of the part or something. That's what Eric heard anyway. I guess that makes—

I feel someone sitting down beside me. *Please don't be that Casey girl. Or Addi—*

It's not either of them. I smell cologne. A rich, intoxicating cologne. Not a girl's scent. Not a gay scent either. Too clean and not-designer smelling.

That leaves only one option.

Until Mrs. Leonard completes her yearly task of badgering extra male students to join her cast, there is only one person not over the age of eighteen who could be wearing that cologne...

I'm sort of surprised that he is allowed to sit by me. Or by any other girl. I hope Addison doesn't try to dropkick me or something later. It's not like I chose to sit beside him.

I can't say that I'm too upset about it, though. It's been many months since I've sat so close to a guy...well, a guy who doesn't buy cologne for other guys...

"And as for what I'm feeling," Miss Price is still talking in her slightly annoying nasal voice, "I'm feeling like I'll throw up if I'm backstage with you guys and I have to see you all making out with each other."

A little laughter comes from somewhere in the group.

"You've been warned." She finishes with a little giggle. I don't think she has much to worry about just yet. Not until Mrs. Leonard imports some of the boys from her English classes. Until then, she really only needs to avoid Collin and Addison.

Addison.

Where is she sitting, I wonder? Is she on the other side of Collin?

The introductions continue. All of the new names and voices start to blur together. The female ninth grader playing the male part of Gavroche. Sarah, who is understudying for both Addison and me. Zach, who sounds like he must be

Sparkles #2. He will be playing Javert. Makes sense. He'll at least be able to sing the part. Just with no emotion.

After him is Sparkles #1 (for sure—I remember that he was introduced at callbacks as Justin). So the two of them are sitting together yet again. Interesting. Maybe Miss Price has more to worry about backstage than I predicted...

More names, more notes, more voices go by. I can't keep track of it all. It'd be helpful if I could open my eyes. I guess I could, but Mrs. Leonard already called out one person for doing that while Sarah was speaking. We are only supposed to open them for a moment when we end our intros and reach over to squeeze a neighbor's hand.

I hope my hand isn't sweaty when I—

"Hi." Eric. It's Eric's turn. That means I'm next.

Eric introduces himself using only his first name (he told me earlier that he does this in honor of Madonna...and Cher...and Björk). After singing a few lines of "Master of the House," he says, "As for my feelings," and then pauses for a ridiculous period of time. Most people have skipped over the feeling part of the introductions...but not Eric.

He takes a final deep breath before starting to speak again. "Well, I'm feeling many things. I feel the anticipation of starting a new show, a new role. I feel peaceful as I sit in this circle of friends. Unfortunately, I also feel as though my hands are beginning to perspire, so I feel bad for those next to me. Hmm...I'm starting to feel slightly hungry since I skipped lunch in order to meet with my math peer tutor...who I feel is pretty hot, but unfortunately taken...by a female. Oh, I guess it's also important to note that I've been feeling confused about my math homework—hence the peer tutor." Another deep breath. This time, he raises his hand (and mine—and probably Sam's too) in a yoga-style inhale and exhale.

When he finally puts our hands back down, he squeezes my hand. Pretty hard again. I pinch back again. And then I get ready to speak.

Here goes. "I'm Alexa Grace. And I've been cast as Éponine, and—"

"Which is ridiculous." I hear it. A whisper. From a person over on the right side of the room.

I feel myself tense up. My hand goes limp in Eric's grasp. He gives my hand a couple of soft squeezes. He's not joking around this time, though. I know he's trying to help.

Why did I say "and"? If I hadn't, I could just pretend I was done talking, and then we wouldn't be sitting here in silence...waiting for me to think of something to say...about my feelings.

Well...hmm...I feel tense all over, a little like yelling, and a lot like crying.

I'm still not talking. Oh my God. This is so awkward. I'm sort of grateful that my eyes are closed for this.

Okay. TALK.

"And..." I don't know what words to put next. "And..."

And his hand is on mine. On my right hand. On my lap.

Collin's hand.

Warm. Strong. Squeezing so gently.

My stomach starts jumping around a little. And—and now someone is giggling quietly. It's coming from the same direction as the mean whisperer.

Collin squeezes my hand again, and I force my mouth open. "And I'm really excited to get to work with all of you."

LAME. But done.

I squeeze Collin's hand softly. To thank him...and to let him know that it's his turn.

"Hello. I'm Collin." He rubs his thumb back and forth over my fingers and gives my hand one more squeeze before releasing his grasp. "Collin Mitchell."

Wow.

My stomach is even jumpier now. And my head is just one big jumble of blur.

Eric, who must've just strung enough information together to realize that Collin is sitting on the other side of me, starts squeezing my hand over and over again.

He's all excited.

And he doesn't even know...

Collin finishes talking and Addison goes next, saying she's humbled to have earned such an important role.

After her is Casey.

Either one of them could have been the mean whisperer...

Casey is playing several minor roles as a member of the chorus. She whines a little about the fact that she'll have to play a male for the opening prison number.

So will all of us. With only four boys trying out, I kind of just expected that would happen.

The introductions continue, and Eric begins rocking our hands back and forth and back and forth on the stage between us. I'm guessing he's getting bored.

This has been going on a long time. I'm not sure that I would call it boring, though. I don't know what to call it.

Eventually, the last person finishes speaking. We are still supposed to keep our eyes closed, though. Mrs. Leonard wants us to remain in our circle as we sing the refrain to "Do

You Hear the People Sing?" From the way that she announces it, it's pretty clear that this is some opening rehearsal tradition.

Mrs. Leonard begins in her over-the-top vibrato, and then the rest of us jump in. Eric drops my hand so he can drum along with his hands as he sings. Collin sounds amazing yet again. He probably could've played Jean Valjean...if Addison would've given him permission to audition for the role.

The sound overall is pretty awesome...all of these powerful voices in such a condensed area...bouncing all around in a circle. Definitely overwhelming.

As we end in spontaneous harmony, I feel my mouth succumbing to a smile.

A couple of seconds later, Mrs. Leonard tells us to open our eyes. When I do, I can feel him looking at me. Collin.

So I look at him, and I see his eyebrows scrunched down in concern for a beat before he sees the smile still decorating my face.

And he smiles back...and it's adorable. And—

"Sweetie." No. "Sssweeettiiee." As if the word has like eighteen syllables.

Addison.

Collin turns away from me around the second syllable, and I quickly drop my eyes to my lap. To my hand. The one he was holding only minutes ago...

I wonder if it smells like his—

"Will you go get my script? Oh—and my sweater from my locker? My leg is asleep."

I hear every word Addison says. Her voice is loud. And annoying.

Collin gets right up and heads to stage left where Mrs. Leonard is signing out the scripts.

I guess I should go get mine too. After Collin gets his, of course.

I hear him thank Mrs. Leonard before I lift my head to ask Eric and Sam to go over to the script table with me.

"Maybe Mrs. Leonard needs to use a hearing aid during auditions." The mean whispering has resumed. It's too loud to be classified as whispering though, really.

I push my head right back down and continue to stare at my lap.

"Or perhaps she was bribed." A second mean voice. I'm pretty sure Casey is whisperer number one, which makes Addison whisperer number two.

Number two continues, "Or blackmailed to—"

"Lex—scripts. Now." Eric. He has finished his conversation with the girl on the other side of Sam. He jumps up and holds out both of his hands, one for me and one for Sam.

"C'mon, hags."

For once not minding Eric's terminology, I grab his hand, stand up, and get as far away from the duo of mean as possible.

Chapter 3

"Red and Black"

First scene rehearsal. Not Éponine today. Just one of the members of Jean Valjean's chain gang. And there are a lot of us. Mrs. Leonard is making all of the girls in the cast pretend to be men for the beginning. She wants the chain gang to fill the stage—to show an overwhelming number of miserable people as soon as the curtain opens. Or something like that. She explained it yesterday, but Eric was whispering to me at the same time. In French. He was trying to see if we could carry on an actual conversation in French (not just "What is your name?" or "I'll go to the bakery for some bread") without messing it up. Needless to say, we couldn't do it.

I wish he was here now, though. But Mrs. Leonard isn't making any of the original four male high school cast members participate in this song. I don't think she believes that they'll be able to change costumes for their other roles quickly enough.

The girls, however, have to change costumes, hair, makeup...and gender (except, I guess, for some of the girls playing bit male parts). Even Addison has to do all of this. She is surprisingly not upset by it, though. She and Casey are sitting right beside the piano bench and singing loudly. Almost obnoxiously. At least they aren't whispering.

Well, I haven't heard them whispering anything, but I am sitting far away from them beside Sam and Sarah.

As we sing the opening number again and again, I'm rather amazed by the number of new cast members sitting in the chairs surrounding the piano. There have to be at least ten new male faces. Straight faces. I wonder how Mrs. Leonard convinced them to join the show. How she manages to do this every year. Sam thinks that she tells the guys that there are a lot of girls, potential girlfriends or prom dates or whatever, in the cast.

I don't know how attractive the girls seem right now, though, as we all sit here and pretend to be men, singing in low, less than comfortable voices. It's a good thing we can hit the notes, though, because most of these bribed boys don't really seem to be singers.

After we sing the opening song for like the forty-fifth time, Mr. Thoms, our music director and also the music teacher here at school, seems to be satisfied.

"Okay, Mrs. Leonard, they're all yours." Mr. Thoms dismisses us with a wave of his hand, sending us up to the stage to report to Mrs. Leonard.

I grab a seat next to Sam as we once again sit in a circle on the stage floor.

Mrs. Leonard stands in the center of our circle, looking around at all of us as she speaks. "Now, if I had to guess, I would bet that none of you have worked in a chain gang before." She's smiling, delighted by her little supposition. "Well, today we are going to change that. We need to practice being together, working together, moving together."

She holds up a LONG piece of rope. Attached to it are weird ankle cuff strappy things every few feet. I guess we really are all going to be tied together.

"Now, I'm going to place you in order so you know where I want you to stand." She starts to read a list from the clipboard she's holding.

And I get my position in line. I'm not by Sam. Or Sarah. Or even by one of the new straight boys or one of the countless kind-looking female chorus members. Nope. I'm behind Casey, who is behind Addison. And the girl on the other side of me is already talking past me to converse with them.

I look over at Sam, who is about fifteen people away from me. She shakes her head and gives me a sympathetic look. I just give her a shrug back. What else can I do?

When we are instructed, I strap my right ankle to the rope. The others around me seem to be doing the same thing, only they do it as they discuss their weekend plans. I try to politely stay out of the conversation between Casey, Addison, and the girl on the other side of me.

Once it appears that we are all strapped in, Mrs. Leonard claps her hands and asks us to now form a gigantic (connected) circle on the stage. It takes us a bit to get into a workable rhythm to move together. But we manage.

"Good. Good. Lovely." Mrs. Leonard is in the middle of our new circle, ready to give further directions.

"While we aren't going to learn all of the official choreography today, we are going to practice moving in step to the music for this scene." She laughs. "I'm pretty sure you know your singing parts by now."

Mr. Thoms soon begins playing the beginning notes for "Look Down," and we start singing. And moving—but slowly. We make it around the large circle about two times during our first run of the song. Mrs. Leonard is impressed. Next, she wants us to walk throughout the auditorium.

It takes some more concentrated effort to start moving together across the stage and down the staircase. I follow Casey's steps exactly—careful not to give her a reason to turn around and look at me.

The girl behind me (Katie?) isn't being quite so vigilant. I can feel some resistance each time I move my right foot forward. She just can't quite get in step, but I'm not turning around to correct her. She'll get it eventually.

"Beautiful. Beautiful." Mrs. Leonard has to yell over the piano, over our singing, and over the marching of our feet.

We have made it to the back of the auditorium—back by the doors where Eric and I stood and watched Addison and Collin's little routine only yesterday.

Now we're supposed to continue the whole way back up to the front, back up the stage left steps, and into our original circle. The song starts yet again, and we move, my eyes still cemented to Casey's feet. Without looking up, I can tell that Casey is no longer singing. I can hear her laughter—even over the sound of my own voice.

I sing a bit softer to try to hear what she is saying, presumably to Addison. I can't catch any actual words, though. Just laughter. I try to convince myself that maybe it's not about me this time, but I have a hard time concentrating on my thoughts with the loud music, the laughter, and Katie's foot pulling along behind me. I have no idea how I'm going to drag Katie's foot up the—

And then it happens. An extra tug, an out of rhythm pull on my right foot, and I hit the stairs. Hard. My chin slams on one of the steps as my legs slip out behind me.

Katie falls forward a little too, but gracefully, I guess, because I don't hear any new loud bumps.

"STOP." Mrs. Leonard is screaming and coming closer. At least it sounds like she is coming closer. My eyes are closed.

If I open them, I just know that some tears might slip out. Tears built up from the throbbing pain in my chin. Tears from the initial shock of my fall. From...

"What happened?" Mrs. Leonard's here now. Right beside me, it sounds.

"Oh—I guess I should've been going slower. I figured that she should have finally gotten the hang of this since we'd almost finished our entire tour of the auditorium. I guess I was wrong." Casey.

She's not done. "I'm so sorry, Alexa. I should have tried to help you more."

What? What is she—

"Are you okay, Alexa? Should we go to the emergency room or something?" Addison. She can't act even when she's playing herself; her overly concerned voice is still dripping with nastiness.

Mrs. Leonard doesn't seem to hear it, though. "Addie— that just might be what we need to do. But first, why don't you unbuckle your ankle and then run to get the nurse?"

"Of course, Mrs. Leonard."

"I'll go with her, Mrs. Leonard," Casey chimes in. Nothing but helpful, these two.

The next thing I hear is Mrs. Leonard telling everyone to remove themselves from the rope. Everyone but me, of course.

I hear students moving around me, climbing into the auditorium seats. I try to move my legs to a seated position on the stairs.

It hurts.

I can tell my legs are scraped and bleeding. I can also feel air, so I'm guessing that I now have holes in my favorite jeans.

I try to move my head a little to check. Not a good idea. Now the aching in my chin is matched by a pounding headache. Head back down, resting on the stairs. Eyes still closed.

"LEX—are you okay? Can we get you some ice or Band-Aids or something?" Sam is here. And I'm guessing the "we" means that Sarah is with her.

I try to smile even as the right side of my mouth is smashed up against the step.

Another bad (and painful) idea.

Before I can even attempt to produce some sort of language (which seems like the next logical move), a new voice enters the scene. A rather loud voice. The nurse?

"Everybody move, please."

Sam and Sarah say that they will talk to me in a few minutes, and the nurse then takes over, slipping the cuff off of my ankle and beginning to wipe at my face.

Is my face cut? Bruised? I don't know. She does seem to be spending a lot of time on my chin, though.

When she asks me to open my eyes, I listen, and she brushes away the few tears that slip out before they even reach my nose.

"Thank you," I whisper.

The smile she gives me stretches from her mouth to her soft brown eyes. "Sure. Now let's get you up and checked out." She places her hands under my head and then helps me lift myself up to a seated position.

My head is still pounding, but now is not the time to complain about that. Now is the time to stand up and get out of the auditorium and away from the little audience in front of me.

The nurse takes my arm to help me stand, but really, I don't need the assistance. My knees hurt, but I can walk just fine. I can tell that nothing is broken. I'm sure that the nurse knows that now too, but she still keeps holding onto my arm as we walk out of the auditorium, past all of the cast members. Past Addison and Casey, who give me little smirks as I walk by...I guess just to make sure that I understand what they did. And probably to make sure that I realize that Mrs. Leonard will never believe me if I say anything...

When I get to her office, the nurse, um, who just said her name is Mrs. Trevo, shines a light in my eyes and cleans my knees through the holes that are on both sides of my jeans. When she asks me to roll up or take off my jeans so she can bandage my bruises, I just have her tear bigger holes to give her access to the cuts. It's not like I'm going to keep the jeans. The holes would be okay, but the blood stains are probably less than in style.

Besides that, I don't really want to keep a souvenir from this day.

Mrs. Trevo asks me to call my parents, but I insist that this isn't necessary. They told me last night that they set up some new client meetings for today. They seemed really pumped about them. I'm not ruining that. I convince Mrs. Trevo that I'll be okay to drive home after rehearsal. I then also have to assure her that I'll be okay to go back to rehearsal, that the pain is starting to subside and that I can easily handle the hour that is left.

If I don't go back, I'm going to miss some of the general moves for the opening number. On top of that, I'm giving Sam a ride home afterwards. I have to stay.

Before I can leave the office, Mrs. Trevo tries to put bandages over the cuts on my chin. I politely (but firmly) refuse them, and I make my way back to the auditorium.

When I arrive, everyone is all chained together again, but now there is no space between Katie and Casey. No place left for me.

I head right up to Mrs. Leonard, who is once again in the middle of the stage. I ignore the whispers that accompany my journey up the stage right staircase.

"Where do you want me to jump in?" I waste no time when I reach Mrs. Leonard.

She looks at me with surprise. And then with...pity? "Oh, Alexa, honey, I think it would be best if you just step out of this number. The rhythms for the actual movements are much more difficult than what you had to do when you were just walking around the auditorium. And with the troubles you—"

"I wasn't having trouble following." I blurt this out. I know I shouldn't interrupt, but I can't hold it back. I. am. so. angry.

Mrs. Leonard's look of pity is now joined with a tinge of impatience.

"This will make it easier for you to get into your costume and makeup for the young Éponine anyway. And you won't have to pull your focus from your role." She pauses and lowers her voice, as though my whole situation is somehow now private. "Focus on Éponine. I know you're going to sing her beautifully. And since she doesn't really dance, you are just, well, perfectly suited—"

My mind shuts her off here and focuses instead on the years of dance lessons I took back in Ohio...the annual recitals...the nightly practices for my ballet solos. But there is no place for that information in this clearly almost over conversation. Just like Mrs. Leonard didn't feel there was a place for a separate dance audition for this show.

So she never let me dance for her. And now I never will.

I don't look up as I walk off stage left. I don't want to see those smirks again, and I don't know what to do with the concerned looks that are probably on Sam and Sarah's faces.

Once I make it backstage, I find a little prop storage closet tucked into the side of the stage wing. It's unlocked, so I sink into it, closing the door behind me. I don't bother to find out where the light switch is (if there even is one). I just sit on the floor, lean against the wall, and close my eyes.

And then my phone buzzes in my front pocket. I reach for it in the darkness.

A text from Eric.

You okay?

Sam must've texted him while I was with the nurse. I write back.

Yeah—I'll be fine.

My phone buzzes again before my response even goes through. Eric again.

Those bitches won't get away with this. Karma is gonna get them.

I write back to him.

Wait. What?

How can he possibly have figured all of this out? No one else even—

My phone buzzes again. A picture this time.

I open up a captured image from Instagram. A captured image from only about a half hour ago. Me on the stairs. The photo is captioned "The Fall of Éponine...several scenes ahead of schedule."

Seriously? I don't really need to check who made the post. The shot was clearly taken from right above me, and only two people would've had that vantage point. Out of curiosity, however, I still check to see which one posted it. Casey.

Before I close the image, I see that eleven people have already "liked" the photo.

Great.

All of that anger from minutes ago comes rushing back.

My face is burning, red with anger and frustration.

Red.

Oh—and black and blue.

Chapter 4

"Look Down"

I walk into school with my head down, hoping not to see anyone who witnessed my "fall" yesterday. I make it to my locker. Eric is beside me before I can even start to enter the combination for my lock.

"I brought you this." He's holding a tube of concealer. "I worried that your chin would look even worse once you slept on it."

I turn from my locker to face him. Based on his expression, I'm pretty sure his worries are justified. And I even tried to cover up the bruise with my own makeup before I drove to school this morning.

Eric opens the tube of concealer and starts vigorously dabbing my chin. I let him go at it, even though it's sort of painful.

As I'm standing there, I peek down at his shirt. And I laugh. White, short-sleeved today. A little red cross in the middle of his chest.

"For you," he smiles and then whispers, "my broken little hag."

Before I can say anything, he scrunches up his nose and pulls back to study my face.

"I think we're gonna need some water. Hold on." He shoves the tube of concealer into my right hand and bolts toward the guys' bathroom.

I use the little makeover break to get into my locker, but I don't get past opening the door.

"I wanted to call last night to see if you were okay, but I don't have your number."

My stomach tenses, and my head gets a little fuzzy.

A melodic, husky voice. Just as beautiful in speaking as it is in singing.

Collin.

I turn around slowly, trying to casually place the palm of my hand on my chin. I'm not sure why Eric said he needs water. Did he use too much concealer? Did it turn my skin green?

I don't quite meet his eyes. "Oh, I'm fine. But thanks."

"Are you, though?"

He slowly brings his fingers up to my face and pulls my hand down from my chin.

More than a little shaken by the heat of his hand, I lift my eyes to meet his. Deep brown eyes. Crinkled now in a small smile. He blinks and moves his focus to my now-exposed chin.

He gently drops my hand at my side and reaches up to touch the side of my face.

"You're bleeding." His eyes aren't smiling anymore.

"Oh, I—"

"Got the—" Eric loudly comes around the corner, stopping abruptly when he sees us...sees Collin's hand on my face. "Water," he finishes slowly, holding up some wet paper towels.

"Good." Collin takes his hand...and the pulsing warmth...from my face and turns to Eric. "Do you need me to get anything else? A Band-Aid or something?"

"Nah. I got this."

"Well, okay then, I guess..." he looks back at me. "I'll see you later."

I smile. He smiles. And he's off.

Before I even have the chance to look back at Eric, he's humming the *Days of Our Lives* theme song in my ear. I roll my eyes as I turn back to give him access to my chin. His eyes are all glisteny.

"Told you you'd get a storyline."

I just shake my head and let him get back to work on my face.

He talks nonstop as he works. About Collin. About the fact that "only a hetero male" would think it would be acceptable to cover a bruised chin with a Band-Aid. About Addison and yesterday.

Apparently, this is new behavior for Addison.

"We've tolerated her lack of acting talent almost wordlessly for years," Eric exclaims as he closes the concealer tube and intently studies my chin. "She doesn't get to do this too."

He can say that, but really, what can he do to stop her?

"I just don't see what she's got against you." He smiles. "You are pretty harmless—like most H—A—G—S."

I swat his arm just as the warning bell rings. Time for this school day to begin.

Not a good day. Every person in this school must follow Casey on Instagram. So some people giggle when I walk down the hall. Others just stare a little at my chin. A few here and there ask me how I'm doing.

I just try to keep my eyes down, head down, everything but my guard down.

It isn't until late afternoon that I hear the fake sweet, annoying voice that co-sponsored my horrible day.

"Oh, I'm so glad you are here today." Addison walks over to my locker, dragging Collin by the hand. "We were so worried." She places her other hand on Collin's shoulder to emphasize the word "we" as she speaks.

Collin sort of smiles, but he looks uncomfortable in general.

She's not done with her speech.

"I'm so thankful that Mrs. Leonard isn't going to make you try to do that chain gang thing anymore." She smiles. "She really should've had us do dance auditions before assigning scenes and musical numbers."

I don't know what to say. Luckily, Eric and his little Red Cross badge are back to my rescue.

"It *is* too bad there weren't dance auditions, Addison." Eric cuts into the conversation as he comes up behind me. "But you should be really *thankful*" (he says it the same way Addison used the word only seconds ago) "that Mrs. Leonard didn't make us do them, especially with your limited background in dance." He puts his arm around my waist.

"Funny that Alexa was the one who *misstepped and fell* when she's the one with like a decade of dance experience."

Eric squeezes my waist and smiles over at me. I give him a small smile back, entertained by the fact that he has only known about my background in dance since yesterday when I was venting during our late night phone call...so like for fourteen hours...yet he talks like he's been following me on a national tour or something.

Addison looks like she's trying to hide the surprise on her face, but she's not really doing a good job.

"Well, I've got to get to chain gang practice." She waves her fingers a little at us and pulls Collin away. He looks back out of the corner of his eye and blinks me a tiny smile before turning to follow her.

As Eric begins the *Days of Our Lives* theme song again, I interrupt by thanking him and then grabbing his hand so we can head out to the parking lot together.

We stop at his car to say goodbye.

"Well, try to enjoy your afternoon now that you don't get to spend hours at practice pretending to be a boy." He smiles and licks his teeth. "It's overrated anyway—being a girl seems like so much more fun. You get access to many more hot guys..."

I shake my head, give him a quick hug, and turn to find my little gray car.

"Hey!" Eric stops me after a few steps, and I look back over my shoulder.

"Keep your chin up, girl—don't hide my masterpiece!" He grins. "I put a lot of work into that face today."

With a quick smile and a roll of my eyes, I turn back toward my car and head home.

By the time I have rehearsal again, my face has healed.

Today, we're blocking for the young Éponine scenes. I didn't even expect to play the young form of Éponine. It's kind of a strange concept since there is such an age gap between her and the older Éponine.

Sam and Eric think that things are this way because the older Cosette insisted upon playing the younger Cosette...

It makes sense.

So that we appear somewhat smaller, Mrs. Leonard has Addison and me sitting on the floor most of the time. She says she's also going to mess with our makeup and work on finding costumes to make us look younger.

I don't have a whole lot to do. I sit on the floor playing with toys while Sam and Eric fawn over me, playing my doting parents. Eric keeps petting my hair as he says his lines. I lean my head back on his knee and go with it.

When Mrs. Leonard has Cosette do some extra work on "Castle on a Cloud" with Mr. Thoms, Eric, Sam, and I go to sit in the auditorium.

And we watch.

And she does sound good, but she looks bored. Not like she's the young Cosette, who is being emotionally abused and worked to death.

Mrs. Leonard says nothing, though. She claps when Addison sings her final note and then says she's ready to move on to "Master of the House." That's Eric's cue. And Sam's. They go onstage and are joined by some members of the chorus—some girls (not Casey—thankfully, she's not here today) and all ten or so males who were bribed to join the cast.

I start to pray that Addison doesn't come sit in the audience, but I stop when I realize it isn't necessary. Addison pulls up a chair beside Mrs. Leonard, who is sitting right below the stage in what will be the orchestra pit. They look together at Mrs. Leonard's script for a bit...and then Addison stands up and starts giving directions to the students on the stage.

WHAT?

The people onstage don't seem to be finding this strange. And they're listening to her. Eric and Sam are even paying close attention to whatever she's telling them.

Wow. This...she...really is unbelievable. Even more so than I thought...

Eric hinted that there was more to know about the Addison situation. This has to be what he was talking about.

At first it seems like Addison is just reading the cues and movements written in Mrs. Leonard's script. Enter stage left. Sit down in the chair behind the bar table. Hold hands with your wife. Exit up stage right.

Once they get all of that down, though, she joins them on the stage, leaving Mrs. Leonard's script behind. She moves around to the different characters, giving various directions. I can only catch a few words here and there.

I do hear one phrase over and over again, though.

"You know—like they did in the movie." She has said this at least eight times already.

My mind flips to one of the first conversations I had with Eric—when he told me about her obsession with the *Les Mis* movie. I just didn't—

Wait. She is now sitting on some tall (straight) guy's lap while she's watching Eric and Sam do the beginning of the song. She's not really watching them, though. She keeps laughing and sliding her arms further around the guy's neck.

When Eric and Sam finish their part, Addison nuzzles her blonde head under the guy's neck for a hug and then slowly gets up and back to work.

Collin's brown eyes pop into my head. I know that this...the hugging, the touching, even the lap sitting...is really not abnormal behavior for Drama Club...but still...it seems odd for someone who's been seeing one guy for so many years...

But what do I know? I've not had a rehearsal with both of them yet. Maybe Collin is all snuggly with other cast members too.

Something about that thought doesn't settle well with me, though...

"Hey—wake up!" Eric's back. I sit up in my seat and turn to him.

"You didn't tell me that Addison is like an assistant director or something."

Eric scrunches up his nose a little and frowns. "I know— we never did get to have that gossip session I promised. Maybe this weekend?"

"Maybe." I can't let it all wait until then, though. "So she gets to tell the students to do whatever blocking she comes up with?"

Eric smiles. "I wouldn't go that far. She doesn't *come up* with anything." He laughs. "She just tries to have us copy her favorite parts of the movie." He pauses to sing the words "SO DUMB" on an unusually high pitch.

"But why is she allowed?"

He raises his eyebrows in a "you should know this already, but I'll tell you anyway" look. "Addison is Leonard's star, her prodigy child." He stops and whispers, "her bank roll for the show."

"Okay...but if she has this much power, why didn't she just tell Mrs. Leonard to not put me in the opening scene? Why bother to make me fall?"

Eric puts his arm around my back and pushes my head down on his shoulder.

"Oh sweet baby girl. You are yet too naïve." He rests his head on top of mine. "Think about it—her little falling blocking, which, by the way, was surprisingly something not from the movie as far as I know, did so much more than get you out of the number." He pauses and says the next part gently. "It made you look incompetent in front of Mrs. Leonard—who obviously liked you enough to cast you as Éponine—and in front of the other students...which pleases her since she doesn't like you."

I push up both of our heads so I can look at Eric.

"Well...I kind of figured all of that, unfortunately. But what is the deal? What did I do to make her so against me? It can't just be because Casey wanted my part. Can it?"

Eric shakes his head. "No. I don't think that's it. She's too selfish to be this mean on Casey's...or anyone else's behalf. It's not like you got *her* part."

"Then why all of the hatred toward me?"

Eric pushes his mouth to one side in thought. "That, I don't know yet, my darling hag."

I give him a disgusted face and put my head back on his shoulder. Then I look back up to the stage to find Addison.

And there she is, standing by the same guy (Michael, I think) she was sitting on before. Now she's leaning over and whispering something in his ear...which would be fine...standard Drama Club conduct...if Michael wasn't rubbing his hand back and forth over her knee...

Before Addison can look up and catch me staring and probably then just find one more reason to hate me, I slide my eyes down to my lap.

It's none of my business.

Chapter 5

"On My Own"

Today is the day I've been dreading. It's time to block the Cosette, Marius, and Éponine scenes. My first rehearsal with Addison and Collin together (well, it's my first blocking rehearsal with Collin in general). And the Thénardiers aren't on the schedule...so no Eric and Sam today. I'm sure that Sarah will be here, but I know she'll be busy copying down our blocking and, you know, memorizing two roles.

Eric drops me off at the auditorium before heading home. A hug, a kiss on the cheek, a wish of good luck, and his bright yellow t-shirt disappears into the mass of students exiting the school.

Okay. I can do this.

I turn to the auditorium door, but before I can even touch it, it slams open.

"There you are." Addison. All dressed up today in a little pink dress. "Great. You're going to need to help with the hunt this year." I'm pretty sure I give her a blank look, but she doesn't stop to explain. She hastily grabs my hand and shoves a blue envelope in my fingers.

"Don't forget to hide it until he asks for it." She motions for me to put the envelope into the pocket of my jeans, and then she bolts back up to the front of the auditorium.

I am left holding the door open in one hand and the blue envelope in the other. I'm not quite sure what to do, so I just do what seems easiest for now. I put the blue envelope in my pocket and head slowly down the aisle to the stage.

Rehearsal is going to be pretty male-heavy today. I don't see any other girls—just Addison, Sarah, and me. Well, and Mrs. Leonard, I guess.

Otherwise, there are guys. Most of them are clumped together on the left side of the auditorium. The bribed boys for the most part. And half of the Sparkles duo. Oh, and Mr. Fiero, who has started to grow a Valjean beard.

As I decide not to go over there to sit, my eyes are drawn to the other side of the auditorium where Addison is seated.

With Collin.

She is playfully running her fingers through his hair and talking nonstop. He...well, *wait*...he is holding several blue envelopes. *Okay...*

I take a seat next to Sarah in the otherwise completely empty middle section of the auditorium. And I try not to look over to my right...but I really want to know what is going on with those envelopes...

I don't see how they could have something to do with today's blocking or—

"All right, beautiful faces. Let's begin." Mrs. Leonard assigns us places to start—some of us on the stage with her, some of us at the piano with Mr. Thoms. I'm in the second group...with Addison and Collin. Just the three of us.

After saying goodbye to Sarah, who is scheduled to run some Cosette blocking on the stage, I grab my script and head over to the piano...without looking over at Addison and Collin.

Here we go.

My back is turned when they come up behind me.

"Hey, Éponine." Collin greets me just as he does when we pass each other in the hall. Well, except he normally uses my real name. And normally Addison pulls him away seconds later.

I turn around to a warm smile on his face. And a second later, Addison moves closer to him, slips her arms around his waist, and starts to whisper in his ear.

I swear I see a little irritation in his eyes...just a trace of it. I give him a small smile and then turn my head quickly— so quickly that my dark brown ponytail swats me on the cheek.

And then I plant my face in my score as we start to sing with the piano. I don't look up. Even though Collin is standing only inches from me...so close that I breathe in his familiar cologne...I keep my head down. I don't want to see Addison glaring at me from the other side of him. And I don't want to see them looking at each other all lovingly.

And I especially don't want to see her catching me looking at him.

When we sing and it's only the two of us singing, Marius and Éponine hold an entire conversation through our song, but I don't even glance at Collin.

When the song ends, Addison gushes a little over Collin's singing before asking him to go grab her a snack from the vending machine.

And then all of a sudden, she's right beside me.

"Try not to lose that envelope when you're learning your moves for the next scene. Don't screw this up for me."

I just stare at her.

Right after she walks away, I run to the prop closet, my prop closet. I get my phone out and start a text to Eric as soon as I'm seated in my dark, quiet spot against the wall.

What is "The Hunt"?

I peek my head out of the closet as I wait for a response. It looks like Mrs. Leonard is going to do some work with Cosette and Jean Valjean before my next scene, so I have some time. Time to get some information from Eric.

He writes back pretty quickly.

Oh, God. Don't tell me she gave you a blue envelope.

I hit reply.

Um...yep.

He writes back a second later.

She is ridiculous. I can't believe she's involving you in this.

And "this" is?

Another dumb ritual. A scavenger hunt thing to celebrate their anniversary—they first met or something on this day in 7th grade.

Oh.

This anniversary always hits during musical season...so most of us have been given a blue envelope at some point or another.

So what do I have to do?

Just wait for Collin to come ask you for the envelope.

So she is essentially sending him to come talk to me...something doesn't seem quite right with that...

My phone buzzes again.

Which number did you get?

Huh?

What number is on the envelope?

Oh. I straighten out my legs and slide the envelope out of my pocket. Using the flashlight function on my phone, I examine the front of it. Then I hit reply.

It's number 10.

Wow. The last clue. Pretty prestigious.

Another buzz.

Did you open it?

No. Should I?

Well, don't you want to know what you're giving him? What if it says he should punch you in the face or something?

I guess he has a point. I run my fingers along the seal of the envelope...well, what should be the seal of the envelope. It isn't sealed. The flap is just tucked in.

Why not.

I carefully lift the flap, pull out the half sheet of paper inside, and turn my phone back into a flashlight.

The words are written in big, flowery cursive.

Opening Night
Casey's
After
Me (Finally!)

Before I can ask Eric what it means, I hear Mrs. Leonard ringing her little bell. Must be time for the next scene.

I slide the cryptic little clue back into its envelope, retuck the flap, put the envelope in my left pocket and my phone in the other, and leave my little hiding place.

And our scene work goes really well. Marius encourages Éponine to help him get Cosette, and Cosette and Marius declare their love for each other while Éponine watches in the background. Collin reassumes his intense Marius eyes from auditions, and I match them with Éponine's desperate and heartbroken glances.

It's good. It's powerful—I can feel it. Even Addison's lack of acting doesn't mess it up. Her overall blank face is still, I have to admit, beautiful, so she looks the part of the stunning girl Marius can't get out of his head. And her blatantly absent emotion somehow makes her seem timid, childlike, innocent...and it kind of works. It just all somehow works.

Mrs. Leonard seems to agree. As we stop for a break, she can't stop gushing about the "electricity" on the stage. Addison goes over to her to further discuss the scenes, saying something about the way Amanda Seyfried did it or something, and I run back to my closet to text Eric.

As soon as I sit down in my spot against the wall, I jump back up to a standing position.

I am not alone. I definitely just brushed up against someone.

"Oh. Sorry. Are you okay?"

That perfect voice. Collin.

I remain standing, realizing my heart is actually somehow beating even faster now that I've identified my unexpected guest.

"It's Collin. Sorry I scared you." He pauses and sort of laughs. "In all the years I've been hanging out in here, no one else has ever come in."

Sounds like I'm the one who is the unexpected guest.

I try to regulate my breathing so I can talk normally.

"Sorry—I just have always been by myself when I've come here too."

"Alexa?"

"Yeah."

"Oh. Hi." A pause. "There's plenty of room for both of us in here. No need for either of us to have to suffer through all of the extra gossip and melodrama out there." I smile. And then I realize that he can't see it.

"Here—I'll move over a little so you can sit."

I hear him sliding against the wall...sliding until there is a little bump and a rattling noise.

"Well, I guess that's as far as I can go if I don't want to join all of the hats, and dishes, and weapons, and whatever else is on this shelf."

I smile in the dark yet again.

"Here—take my hand so you don't fall."

I breathe. And then I lower my right hand into the darkness, fumbling around a little to find him.

"Got it," he whispers. He grabs my hand and pulls me down beside him.

We sit side by side, shoulder to shoulder. And he still has my hand—it's resting with his on top of his bent knees.

We start to breathe in sync, shoulders slightly lifting and dropping together. Quiet. Still. Serene.

Nothing like the sideshow that is going on in my stomach right now.

"Oh, um, sorry." He breaks our silence, carries my hand over to my own bent knees, and then lets go.

"Don't worry about it." I smile toward him yet again...yet again in the dark.

"So what do you normally do in here?"

"Well, text. Play games on my phone. Run my lines quietly...and without accompaniment, obviously."

He laughs. "The super quiet a cappella closet rehearsals. I have them too."

"So you must also have those late night panic attacks where you keep picturing yourself messing up your lines or pitches on a show night."

"Of course." He pauses. "But that isn't the only reason I rehearse in here." Another pause. "I think it's easier to get the emotion right in here."

I wait for him to explain.

"Out there, Mrs. Leonard's right on top of us, trying to make sure we move at the right time—lift an arm here, turn around there, you know. And all of the others are in the audience doing stupid stuff."

I nod. It's eaten up in the darkness just like my smiles.

"It makes it hard to get into the intensity of the scenes. I mean, these characters, these people, they were a mess...they were—"

"Miserable?" I finish with a quick nudge to his shoulder.

He laughs. "Yeah, you think?"

"But seriously," I go on, "I get what you're saying. It's hard to maintain a tragic atmosphere while kids in the audience are throwing grapes at each other."

"Exactly."

Mrs. Leonard starts ringing her little bell again. Next scene in a few minutes.

Before I start to push myself up to a standing position, I feel his shoulders tighten beside me .

"Hey—before you go..."

I sit. I wait to hear more.

"Do you have an envelope for me?"

Oh, right. The weird message thing.

"Yeah. But how do you know it's time for my envelope?" I'm not messing this up.

"Well, my last one was number nine, so I know I only have one more...and my clue led me to you."

"Oh." I can't help myself. I have to ask. "What was your clue?"

His shoulders tense again. He clears his throat before answering. "Um, I was supposed to find the girl that will never win my heart."

What?

Now both of our shoulders are rigid.

"You know—Éponine. Falling in love with Marius."

I shake my head into the darkness and speak quickly. "Oh—right. Clever."

I stretch out my legs and remove the envelope from my pocket once again. We brush fingers as I hand it to him. And then my stomach starts dancing around again, so I hurry to push myself to stand.

"Guess we should go." I speak one last time into the darkness before opening the door to head back out to the stage. I don't turn back to see if he follows. I'm sure he would like some privacy to read his little message.

When I turn back onto the stage, the first thing I see is super shiny blonde hair. Addison is facing away from me as she tells some sort of story to Sparkles #1. Justin. Her hair swings back and forth as she talks. I really do wish I knew what kind of shampoo she—

"Hey."

I freeze.

Collin must be only a few steps behind me. I don't know if his "hey" is for me or for Addison. I don't turn around to find out.

Addison does turn around. She squeals a little as she runs over to him.

"Did you finish?" She squeaks.

He must nod or give some sort of silent gesture because the next thing I hear is her saying "Yay" and then "Happy Anniversary, honey—I can't wait."

I keep my eyes down during this exchange and try not to exist...even though I'm only a few feet away.

I'm pretty sure they're kissing now. And even though that thought makes me want to throw something, at least it means that they shouldn't notice me slipping away.

I slide my phone out of my pocket and try to look busy on it as I start downstage to the staircase.

"Oh, Alexa." All the sweetness in the world packed into two little words.

I make myself turn to look back at Addison, trying not to flinch at the sight of Collin's arms wrapped tightly around her in an embrace.

I meet her gaze. Her eyes are almost glistening as much as her hair. "Thanks so much for helping us celebrate another year together." She smiles. A big fake smile.

Collin pulls back from her a little to look at me too. And his mouth is smiling a tiny bit, but his eyes are annoyed and perhaps a little apologetic. I only hold his glance for a beat, and then I turn back to Addison.

"No problem," I say with a shrug. I then head down to sit in the empty auditorium, hoping that Mrs. Leonard doesn't decide to run a scene with the three of us next.

Chapter 6

2, 4, and 6:01

After last week's practices, Act I is just about ready to go. Full cast rehearsal today. Eric's here to pick me up. He starts talking as soon as I slide into the leathery passenger seat of his car.

"You know, my birthday always lands on long, boring, everyone's taking standardized tests-type days. Or on like a major sporting event day when everyone is talking about bad calls, scores, stupid stuff..." He sighs and continues. "You, on the other hand, get a Friday we have off from school...and the Friday of Halloween weekend...when all you have to worry about is what? Getting to rehearsal by noon and picking out a costume for tomorrow night's party?"

I smile over at him as I click my seatbelt into place. "Sorry. You wanna switch birthdays?"

He snaps his head over to me with a grin. "And what are you trying to get from such a deal? Superhag status or something?"

I groan, and he focuses his eyes back on the road as he pulls out of my driveway.

"So, I wanted to get you Collin for your birthday gift, but that hasn't worked out...yet. Maybe for Christmas." He rubs his tongue over his teeth while I roll my eyes. "But I got you a bit of high profile information instead."

"You figured out Addison's clue?" We've been trying to decipher it for the last week. I can't even begin to count the number of times we've discussed the words "Opening Night Casey's After Me (Finally!)."

"No—sorry. It's not that good. But I think you'll like it."

"Okay."

"I think I found out why Addison hates you."

For some reason, I flinch at his sentence. Even though she's mean...and not someone I'd like to have as a friend...I just don't remember having someone dislike me so much before...especially not in Drama Club.

So, of course I want to know why.

"All right. I'm listening."

"I knew you'd like your present." He smiles. "Okay—remember when you had your callback audition?"

I nod and mumble an "mmmhmm." I remember standing on the stage, knowing no one, thinking I had a shot at playing Cosette.

That seems like a decade ago now.

"Well, apparently Addison was watching you from the front row."

Hmm...I remember that too. I didn't know her name until Mrs. Leonard called her up to the stage, but I remember her perfect hair. Oh—and her talking about me being new. And—wait. She was also arguing or something with...with Collin.

"What was she saying about me?" I blurt it out, and just as abruptly, Eric turns his head to me.

"How did you know?" He must remember that he's driving, and he turns back to the road, pouting. "You're going to ruin my surprise, aren't you?"

"No—that's all I know. Honestly. And I had even forgotten until right now. I didn't think it was important. She was just talking about me being new or something."

"Yeah—she was talking to Casey, who was sitting right beside her."

I remember the other girl having plainish blonde hair...just like Casey's. It makes sense, I guess. It's funny how fuzzy faces can be when people are strangers. It was nicer back then when Casey and Addison were complete strangers to me.

I only remember two faces clearly from that day. Eric's. And Collin's. Which brings me back to my birthday present.

"Wait. What were they saying? Was Collin saying stuff too?"

"Well, yes. That is where this gets interesting. But you have to wait until I get to that part." He gives me a "be patient" look, lifting his eyebrows.

I groan and sink back in my seat to wait. And he begins. Slowly.

"Okay, so here is what I found out." He glances at me apologetically out of the corner of his eye. "She was talking about you. And it wasn't nice." He scrunches up his nose a little, and I nod for him to continue.

"I guess she somehow knew that Leonard was impressed with you during the first day of auditions."

I look over at him in surprise.

"Addison heard Leonard tell Mr. Thoms that you would make an amazing Cosette."

What? "How do you know this?"

"Sarah must've gone back into the auditorium because she lost her phone. She overheard Leonard too, and she saw Addison eavesdropping. I don't think Addison saw Sarah, though."

"Wow." Cosette was closer than I thought...

I take a moment to let that sink in a little—more for my once eight-year-old self than for anything else.

"Ready for more?" Eric brings me back to my newly turned eighteen-year-old self.

I nod.

"Okay, so during callbacks, this girl, April, was sitting like right behind Addison."

"April?"

"She's in the chorus. I'll try to point her out today." He pauses and glances over at me. "I didn't even know her until I started to hunt for this birthday information."

He pulls into a parking spot in front of the auditorium entrance to the school. Then he takes off his seatbelt and turns his body to face me. "Don't think this present just fell into my lap, Lex. I had to find out who was sitting near Addison that day, and then I had to track down this girl and try to befriend her in like two days so that she'd feel comfortable gossiping with me in time for your birthday."

He stops and licks his teeth. "And yesterday, I managed to bring up Addison with April, and soon it all came spilling out." He grabs my left hand and holds it in both of his. "Addison must've been saying all kinds of shit about you—about your voice, your outfit, and even your hair." He squeezes my hand and gives me a small sympathetic look. Like he thinks I'm upset.

But I realize that I'm not. Really, I'm just anxious to hear the rest.

I tell him that, and he moves on.

"And now, for the best part...the pièce de résistance." A dramatic pause and another lick of the teeth. "Collin overheard, and he told her what he thought." He pauses again and raises an eyebrow. "And she didn't like it."

"What did he think?" I blurt it out—I can't take Eric's slow pace anymore.

Eric smiles. "He said that he thought you were good enough to easily take any of the leading roles." Yet another pause. "And he said he thought you looked pretty."

"He did?"

Eric nods.

"Seriously? You know that for sure?"

Eric nods again with a big smile. "Yeah—I even double checked with the girls who were sitting with April. They heard it too. All of it."

I turn to look out the front window of Eric's car. I know the smile on my face must be obnoxious.

Eric squeezes my hand again. "You really do like him, don't you Lex? All teasing aside."

I nod slowly, turning back to face him again.

He lets go of me and claps his hands together. "It's about time you admitted it." He stops clapping and turns pseudo-serious. "Now admit this." Dramatic pause. "My gift was freaking awesome, wasn't it?"

I smile, nod, and give him a hug...well, as much of a hug as I can manage while sitting in a car.

As we get out of the car, he tells me that he has one more gift for me, but that I have to give him my phone for a little. I have no idea what he's doing, but I figure he can't do much damage. So I give it to him, and he promises to give it back before he leaves his part of rehearsal.

Mrs. Leonard told us yesterday that she'll be keeping some of us at rehearsal today until all trouble spots in Act I are completely polished. And I was on her "keep" list while the Thénardiers were not.

"Are you sure you want to plan on dinner after I'm done? It could be really late."

Eric holds open the main door for me as he responds. "Of course, Lex—it's your birthday. And we really need to figure out our costumes tonight...just in case we need to do some shopping tomorrow before the party. Sam is freaking out that we haven't decided by now. And normally Sarah helps us decide, but she can't even come to the party now...she has some big project due or something."

I nod to agree again to our dinner plans, and then we enter the auditorium and walk to the front where several cast members have gathered in a clump. Apparently, they are all waiting in a line to look at Mrs. Leonard's agenda for rehearsal. She has made an official scene schedule for the day, broken into mostly half hour and fifteen minute increments.

We wait for our turn to look at the list. I see Addison on the left side of the auditorium, sitting in the middle of a group of bribed boys with Sparkles #1, Justin. Casey is there too...and she is sharing one of the seats with that Michael guy who Addison was flirting with before.

Interesting.

From what I can hear, the two girls are explaining the ritual of tomorrow's Half Block party to the guys around them. I guess these boys have never been conned into doing one of Mrs. Leonard's shows before.

Addison is currently explaining her spin on a normal block party—telling how she made up the Half Block party three years ago when they had finished blocking the first half of *Footloose*. How she was inspired by the fact that the halfway blocking point hit right around the end of October—the perfect time for a costume party. Eric already explained all of this to me last week.

He also explained that the timing is off this year because the show is earlier than usual. We are much more than halfway through rehearsals. And we've already learned all of the music and some of the bigger production numbers in Act II. So the Half Block party isn't quite an accurate title this year. More like a Third Quarter Block, Eric says.

This particular Addison ritual seems to be one that Eric actually likes, though. I'm honestly kind of excited too. What student in Drama Club doesn't love a costume party? I wonder—

"Hey. Lex. Wake up—it's our turn." Eric is pulling me to look at the schedule. "Wow. I'm only here until like 2:00. Looks like the earliest you will get out is 7:00."

"Seriously, we don't have to go to dinner to—"

"Stop, Lex. We are going. Sam and I will just wait for you to call." He pulls me away so the next people can check the schedule. "Do you want me to bring you some magazines or something for your downtime? Or some binoculars to better enjoy the view?" He nods over to the bribed boys. The straight bribed boys.

I smile. "Nah—I have plenty of homework I should probably do." And I want to run lines in my little prop closet...maybe not alone for once.

We pass Addison and her bribed boy admirers as we go to sit in the auditorium. Addison is now giving the boys directions to her house for tomorrow night. As I listen to her talk and giggle and whine while she tries to convince the boys to come, another voice starts to speak—a much nicer-sounding one.

"Hey, Lexi." Collin.

"Collin, honey!" Before I can even turn to meet his eyes, much less say hello back, Addison is skipping over to greet him.

"Come help me convince all of these chorus boys that they need to come to the party." She stops to look at me before grabbing his arm and adding, "our party."

As she pulls him away, Collin catches my gaze for a brief moment. When he grins, I smile back, but I also silently pray that my cheeks aren't turning red.

He stuck up for me. And he called me pretty.

He disappears with Addison into the group of boys, and I, well, I keep thinking about him.

I continue to worry about blushing cheeks as rehearsal begins. Especially since we start with "One Day More," where all of us are present...and since we'll soon be moving on to the scenes that focus on the Cosette, Marius, and Éponine triangle...

Eric finishes his last scheduled scene work right before 2:00. He gives me back my phone before he leaves, but he refuses to tell me how to find my present on it.

"You'll know pretty soon." He says this with a smile before kissing me on the cheek and heading out with Sam.

Since I don't have anything on my schedule for about forty-five minutes, I head to my little prop closet.

I slip into the dark room. Collin's already here.

"Hey, Lexi. Don't scream—it's me."

I shut the door behind me. Behind us.

"Here—grab my hand."

We do the little sitting down dance we did before. Soon we are again sitting side by side, shoulder to shoulder. Breathing together in the quiet.

"Want to practice our lines?" He breaks our silence.

I nod...and then remember the whole darkness thing and say, "Sure."

Before we can even really get started, we are interrupted by some non-*Les Mis* music. We both look around, blindly trying to figure out where it is coming from...

And then I recognize the tune. The *Days of Our Lives* theme song.

I reach to my non-Collin side where my upside down phone sits, and, lo and behold, it's the source of the noise.

I pick it up without looking at the screen.

"Hello, Eric."

"Hey, Lex. Like your present?"

"Of course."

"I just thought it kind of would go with your other gift— all of this newly developed drama."

"Yeah."

"You sound funny. What's going on? Are you in the middle of a scene right now?"

"No. Not right now."

"Then what?" A pause. A realization. "Wait—are you with him? In your super secret closet hideaway?" I probably shouldn't have told him about meeting Collin here earlier.

"Yeah." I keep the phone plastered to my ear, hoping that Collin won't be able to hear whatever words Eric chooses next.

"You slutty little hag," Eric teases. "I should have known." Another pause. "Wow. I really nailed your birthday presents. I wasn't giving myself enough credit."

"Eric, I—" I begin.

"Go, go Lexi. We'll talk later. A lot." He laughs. "Before you try anything else, though, won't you please just ask him if he might consider turning to the other side? I just need to know that I have absolutely no chance with him before I can really be happy for—"

"I'll talk to you later, Eric."

"Yes—yes you will. Have fun, Lex."

"Bye." I put the phone back down beside me and continue to pray that Collin hasn't heard anything. I try to act naturally, but I know that my breathing is uneven and that my shoulders are more tense than they should be. So I do the only thing I can think of and separate my tense shoulder from his, moving to face him—well, I would be facing him if I could see...

"Okay...ready to rehearse?" I ask.

"Well, we only have a few more minutes. I've got to be on the stage at 2:15." He pauses. "Want to meet later, though?"

"Sure." Of course.

Before he leaves, we talk out our blocking schedules for the day and find that we seem to have a common break every two hours. So we plan to meet again at 4:00.

Since I don't have to be at the piano with Mr. Thoms until 2:45, I hang out in the darkness a little longer...and try to quiet down my somersaulting stomach.

It's 4:00. I open the door to the prop closet. Collin is once again already here.

"Hey. I finished fifteen minutes ago out there. I've already gone through two of my songs back here. You are behind."

I can hear the smile in his voice.

"Well, let's get started then." I say this as I reach down for his hand and sit back down into our shoulder to shoulder position.

In the darkness, out of the silence, he slips into Marius and begins to sing the end of "In My Life." His volume is soft, but the intensity is all there. I am so wrapped up in his emotion, his sound, and the feel of his shoulder against mine that I am somewhat startled when he gets to the point in the song when he calls out my (well, Éponine's) name. He faces me and grabs both of my shoulders, just like Mrs. Leonard has us do it. It feels different, though, when we are here alone in the dark whisper singing...without Addison only a few feet away.

The heat from his hands sends a buzz through my shoulders.

I don't want to push him away when it's my turn to sing my little aside, but it's kind of in the blocking so I do it anyway. And then I sing about wanting to belong to him...to Marius.

At the end of the song, I feel the same rush I felt when the whole cast sang "Do You Hear the People Sing?" on that first day in our group circle, the same way I feel when an overture begins for a Broadway show, the same way—

Who am I kidding? It's not the same way.

It's the same way times a hundred.

After we sit for a few moments in silence, he speaks. "More?"

"Yes."

We practice the end part of "A Heart Full of Love" in the same way—singing quietly, running our blocking, and trying to focus on the emotion of the song.

At 4:30, we both leave the closet to rehearse our scenes together with Mrs. Leonard...and Addison.

When we walk onstage at the same time, Addison looks at me with a squint. She then turns to Collin, beams, and runs up to embrace him, asking how his practicing has been going.

So she knows that he practices during his downtime...I was wondering...

Does she know where? Or that—

Now they are kissing. I've got to move.

I go to the other side of the stage and wait for Mrs. Leonard to tell us where to start. She is currently talking to her group of bribed boys, telling them to keep practicing the blocking that Addison just gave them.

So that's where Addison has been.

"Oh—you two do make such a lovely couple." Mrs. Leonard has now turned her attention to the stage—to the spot where I am trying desperately not to look.

Fortunately, we then get started on our scenes.

After we finish "A Heart Full of Love," Mrs. Leonard stops us and says, "Alexa, Collin—it's obvious that you've really been practicing. Collin—your elation is just oozing out of you. And Alexa—your distress...brilliant."

I don't look at Collin as we both murmur a thank you.

I don't really look up at all...I carefully avoid getting tangled in the glare I'm sure Addison has on her face.

Thankfully, I'm scheduled to see Mr. Thoms again next, so I quickly make my exit.

At 5:59, I check my phone. He should be here in one minute.

But he's not.

6:00.

Did she tell him he couldn't come?

Did he—

6:01.

A soft click as the door opens. He's here.

And he's all lit up. I can actually see his face.

"These are for you."

He hands me the source of his light—three pink fiber optic roses.

"Happy Birthday, Lexi."

For the first time in our dark closet, I look at him, and I am able to actually see his eyes. And the smile on his face.

"Thanks," I respond slowly, still stuck in his gaze, "but how did you—"

"Eric," he says simply before sitting down beside me. "He texted me about an hour ago. So I ran to the coffeehouse on the corner—this was the best I could do." He nods toward the roses in my hand. "Sorry."

"They are perfect." I nudge his shoulder with mine. "Just what we needed in here."

I balance the little bouquet on the prop shelf to my right and then turn to face him.

With my back to the flowers, there isn't enough light for me to see his eyes anymore. But that's okay. Our plan was to do this in the dark.

"Ready to get back to work?" I ask.

"Sure," he responds. "Why don't we start with the end of scene—"

Light pours into the room as the door slams open. No soft click this time.

"Just. As I. Thought." Addison leans against the doorframe and looks down at us.

Collin gets up quickly, ripping all of the warmth from my shoulder.

Addison isn't done.

"So, what, I'm not allowed to be in here with you while you practice…" She pauses to look at me before continuing. "Or as you pretend to be practicing…but she is?"

"We are practicing. We were." Collin spits his words out quickly, not once looking back at me. I'm clearly not meant to be part of this conversation. I'm just here. And it's about me.

"Sure. It looks like it—running lines in the dark with the soft glow of—" She pushes past him, reaches over me, and grabs the roses—my roses.

"Where did these come from?" She pushes the roses into Collin's chest.

He moves so his full back is to me. But I can still hear him.

"Stop," he whispers. "It's her birthday. I was trying to be nice since, you know, she's new and everything."

"So you really don't like her?" I can hear the pout in her voice.

"No—not like that." Still whispering. "I'm with you, remember?"

I push my head down as I hear what must be them kissing...yet again.

And then, Collin's voice. "Let's get out of here, Addie."

He pauses. "See you in a little, Lexi."

I give him a small wave without looking up to meet his eyes.

"I'll be right there, honey." Addison pushes him along and then turns back to me, still holding my roses. "I have a little birthday present for you too," she pauses with a smirk, "Lexi."

I keep my head down.

She keeps talking anyway. "You know that little blue envelope that you gave to Collin, the one that I never sealed because I just figured you'd want to read the message in it?"

Head down. Cheeks probably a little too pink.

"You are welcome, by the way. I tried to make it as easy as possible for you to break into it."

I. am. not. going. to. lift. my. head.

"Well, I hope you still remember what it said...so you can really enjoy this little gift."

Of course I remember what it said. The words haven't really stopped spinning through my brain since I read it.

"Normally, I end our little hunt with clues for Collin's final surprise. A special dinner. Tickets to a game. You know, my ultimate anniversary gift for the year."

She pauses and crouches down beside me. I don't look up. Or move at all.

"I always give him a list of information to tell him about the event. I use the same order every year—so he really never has trouble figuring it out."

I can feel her breath on my cheek. And her shoulder on mine.

"Wanna know the order?" Pause. "Of course you do." Another pause. "First, I tell him when the event will take place."

Opening night. Got it.

"Next, of course, he needs to know where to go."

Right. Casey's house.

"Then I tell him when it will happen."

After...after the show, presumably.

"And last..." A huge pause. And she somehow moves even closer to me. "Last, I tell him what he's going to get to do when he gets there."

Me...the clue said "Me (Finally!)"

Wait. What?

I can't help it. My face snaps up as I realize what she's saying. She catches my eyes with a smirk and then tosses my roses into my lap.

"Happy Birthday, Alexa."

Chapter 7

"Lovely Ladies"

Needless to say, Sam, Eric, and I didn't spend much time at dinner last night discussing costumes. We discussed Collin...and Addison...and her "gift."

Sam and Eric did more of the talking than I did. I sat there with a full plate of food and just felt kind of stupid. I still do. Stupid for hanging out with a guy who has a girlfriend. Stupid for starting to like him.

Stupid for telling Eric about it.

Now he's never going to let it go. He's even talking about it again already this morning as we comb through racks of thrift shop dresses.

"Really, Lex. You'd be much better for him than she has ever been. She is always so—"

He keeps talking, but I don't hear him anymore.

I can just hear Collin responding to Addison.

"No—not like that."

"I'm with you, remember?"

He's with her. He likes her. And I knew that. I've always known that. He's just a nice guy. A friend.

I can't believe I let myself even think about there being more to it.

"Lex, are you listening? I think I have the perfect way for you to get him. If you just tell him that there was no accident during that first rehearsal, that she—"

"Stop, Eric." I turn to look at him. "I don't want to do any of that. Seriously. Let's just work on finding our dresses."

Eric turns back to the racks of gowns, mumbling, "Oddly self-righteous for a hag."

Laughing, I swat him on the arm.

And then I spot the display dress hanging on the wall.

Purple. Sparkly. Perfect for Eric.

"Look." I point it out to him, and he holds his palm over his chest, covering the little sign language "I love you" symbol on his shirt.

He walks over slowly to look up at the dress.

"This. Is. It. Lex, this is it."

He runs back to pick me up and spin me in the air. He barely has me back on the floor before he runs to the cashier for help.

"That dress." He points up to it. "I must have it." A dramatic pause. "At any price."

The not so Eric-loving clerk looks at him dryly. "It's five dollars."

He gives her a dazzling smile. "I'll take it. Hold the gift receipt."

Without another glance at him, or at me for that matter, the clerk gets a stepstool from behind the register, places it against the wall, and pulls the dress down unceremoniously.

Eric runs over to rescue it. "Careful. Careful with that." He hugs the dress to himself and then dances it over to the register.

He doesn't let go of it as he pulls five ones out of his pocket to pay. He refuses the cashier's offer to put the dress in a bag, and we walk out the door of the little shop.

"I'm pretty sure I'll win the costume contest tonight now." Eric folds the dress over his left arm and then links his right arm with mine. "Really—like anyone is going to do better than this." He pauses. "Except maybe you and Sam."

If the costume awards are based on how many pounds of makeup are worn, I'm pretty sure I'm going to win.

As Eric applied my makeup earlier, he tried to explain why I had to wear so much more than him. Something about males as drag queens needing to only wear enough to make them appear female...and females as drag queens having to first be made up to look like men and then made up again to look like men dressing as women...

"It's very scientific," he closed off his explanation as he put finishing touches on my face and then moved on to complete the same process for Sam.

And now I'm here on Addison's doorstep—a girl dressed as a guy pretending to be a woman—wearing the yellow gown I wore when I went to the prom back home last year. Eric okayed the dress, saying that he could make it work if he added some big pieces of jewelry (which he did). I think he liked the fact that Sam also picked a yellow dress to wear—I overheard him mumbling something about a pair of matching drag hags...

He did make it clear to both of us that his dress would outshine both of our outfits.

And he was right. He's glowing. Long blonde wig. Purple shimmery dress. Strappy purple sandals. Violet eye shadow. Clip-on earrings. He's perfect.

And I'm so glad that he's escorting me (and Sam) tonight. As long as I don't have to spend any time alone with Addison...or Collin...or, even worse, both of them together, I should be fine.

That's what I keep repeating in my head, anyway. Perhaps I—

The door starts to open, and Addison appears. And then Collin does too. I look everywhere but into his eyes.

Addison is dressed in a soft, white sweater and a big pink poodle skirt. Collin's wearing tight jeans and a black leather jacket. No question about who they are supposed to—

"We're Danny and Sandy, the roles that got away," Addison exclaims, grabbing Collin's hand and pouting as she flings her head onto his leathery shoulder. "We just don't get to spend enough years in high school for us to be able to do all of the good shows."

"Didn't you do *Grease* last year in Ohio?" Eric looks over at me and then continues talking before I can answer. "And didn't you play—"

"Yep. We did *Grease* last year. One of my favorites." I keep talking so Eric can't. "What are some of your other favorites, Addison?"

She gives me a big, over-the-top smile and motions for us to come in as she starts talking about *Miss Saigon*, *Phantom*, *Cinderella*, and—

"Sandy," Eric whispers to me. "You played Sandy. Why don't you want the little princess diva queen to know?"

I look at him with big, "don't talk about this right now," eyes and whisper back, "There is no reason to give her something else to somehow hold against me. I do like playing Éponine, and I'd rather Addison not find a reason to make Mrs. Leonard take the role from me."

Just as Eric whispers back, "I don't think that could hap—" we pass Mrs. Leonard, who is standing and talking to an impeccably dressed middle-aged man, presumably—

"This is my dad." Addison cuts off her discussion of her favorite Broadway musicals in order to make introductions. Her dad turns from Mrs. Leonard and greets us with an amused look.

"Interesting costumes," he says with a laugh. Sam says a thank you for the three of us, and then we all smile and say our hellos...not really knowing what else to say.

I think it would be kind of awkward to thank him for funding our entire production right now—especially since Mrs. Leonard doesn't really like to talk about it. Hopefully the cast sends him a card or a gift or something at the end of the show.

Addison moves on, dragging Collin by the hand and leading us through a stainless steel-covered kitchen and some sort of formal living room with old fashioned settees, antique-looking lamps, and a smattering of crystal. When she finally drops us off in the family room, where other cast members are sitting, laughing, and eating, I turn to Eric.

"You didn't tell me that Mrs. Leonard comes to the Half Block."

He looks back at me somewhat pensively. "She never has before." He raises his eyebrows, giving me an even better glimpse of his layers of purple eye shadow. "This is probably the most expensive show we've ever done, though. Maybe she feels she owes it to him to show up and offer some extra gratitude." He pauses and licks his teeth. "Or maybe she needs more money."

Interesting.

We find an empty leather couch and sit. Sam and I take the sides, and Eric sits in the middle. I wait until all of us have crossed our legs in an ultimate ladylike manner before I ask my next question.

"If Mrs. Leonard is really hurting for money, don't you think she'd do whatever might become necessary to keep Addison's father in her pocket? Even if that might someday mean taking my part away?"

Eric looks at me, truly thinking this out, it seems. "Okay, Lex. I'll admit it. It's probably not a bad idea for you to be careful around Addison..."

Sam is nodding vigorously beside him, her fake gold hoop earrings bouncing up and down with her.

Eric continues. "But you still have to enjoy yourself. This is your senior show. For most of us, it's probably our last show...unless we dabble in community theatre projects when we're in our thirties and bored or something..." He stops and shakes his head, shaking himself out of his digression. "Just try to have some fun, Lex. Don't let Addison ruin it all for you."

He pauses again and pulls my chin so we are face to face, almost nose to nose. "But you're going to have to pretty much stay away from Collin. No more dark quiet closet time for the two of you."

I move my head away. "I know, Eric. Remember, I already said that last night...and this morn—"

"Hey, guys."

Speaking of Collin...

He stands in front of us, hands in his jean pockets. I (stupidly) let myself look up, and all of a sudden, his eyes are burning into mine. Showing concern? Apologizing for yesterday?

More like making me do something that I'm not supposed to be doing.

I force my eyes down to my lap.

He clears his throat. "Do you guys want some drinks?"

I don't look back up.

Eric responds right away. "Oh, we'll go get them in a minute, Collin. Thanks for thinking of us."

"Oh...okay. Great. Well, have fun." I can see his sneakered-feet out of the corner of my eye as he turns and walks away.

"Wow," Eric exhales in a whisper. "He *really* wants to be in your storyline."

I raise my head to roll my eyes. Eric catches my gaze. And he looks serious. Well, as serious as he can look with a face covered in purple sparkles.

"I've never seen him look at Addison like that. Never. In four years."

I look back down at my lap, away from the surging honesty in Eric's eyes.

And even though my stomach has started to skip and my head has gotten a little fuzzy, I try to ignore it. No point having these feelings...or any hope about Collin. And Eric knows that.

"Sorry," he whispers and reaches over to squeeze my hand. "Maybe he'll get it together and break it off with her on his own."

"And lose his part too?" Sam says my thoughts for me. "I'm pretty sure he's started to really like doing these shows. He's all—"

She continues, but I shake my head, trying to brush off the conversation and the defeated feeling in my stomach.

I think Eric is pretty aware of the fact that I don't want to talk about it anymore; he changes the subject in record time—even for him.

"Look—they're bringing the costume prizes out." Addison walks out with Casey (who is dressed as some sort of Greek goddess), and they are carrying two trophies each.

"They are judging already?" I spit out my first question. Then my second. "And they use real trophies for this?"

"Of course they use real trophies. Her dad buys new ones each year." He looks at me in question. "Why did you think I wanted to win?"

I smile. "For the honor and glory, I guess."

He tilts his pretty face with a grin. "Well, that too, but what I really want is a trophy. My brother is always bringing home ribbons and stuff from his various sporting events." He pauses. "Seeing as how I don't even know the names of these events, much less how to play in any of them, I think this is my only chance."

"Okay." I grab his hand Miss America and runner up-style and close my eyes. "You've got this."

"Not now, Lex."

I open my eyes at the sound of the "DUH" tone in his voice.

"The trophies are going to be on display all evening. Winners won't be announced until the end of the party."

"And that's only after the costume parade and the depositing of ballots," Sam chimes in.

Eric continues to explain. "It's a night full of rituals, Lexi. High pageantry."

As if on cue, Addison claps her hands and looks around to get the attention of everyone in the room. Most of the partygoers calm down pretty quickly to wait for her announcement.

While Addison stands, arms crossed, waiting for complete silence from the rest of the people, Eric nudges me in the side in an "I want to roll my eyes with you right now, but we'd probably get caught" kind of way. Before I can nudge him back in agreement, Addison begins.

"I would just like to welcome everyone to the last Half Block party, our last Half Block." She nods over to Collin to make sure everyone knows how to interpret the word "our."

Collin is looking at me, though.

I snap my face right back in Addison's direction. Eric nudges me again, this one a slow, intensity-building, "He's looking at you again" nudge.

I push his elbow away in an "I know—leave it alone" type response.

Addison is now announcing the schedule for the evening, so Eric sits up to listen, dancing a little in his seat when she says that the costume parade will begin in less than an hour.

Apparently, we each get to vote for our favorites in the main categories: funniest, most authentic, and...best couple costumes.

I squint my eyes in puzzlement and look over at Eric. I didn't know there were categories. And now I'm not quite sure which one he's hoping to win.

He slides his eyes over to mine and, I guess, reads my mind before whispering, "Authentic. Obviously."

Soon, Addison finishes her presentation, holding up her poodle skirt in a little curtsy before telling us to carry on with our partying.

Sam gets up to grab us all some sodas (three Sprites— Eric refuses to let any colored drinks get near his dress before the judging). We then spend the next half hour just people watching...watching Mrs. Leonard join Mr. Fiero and Miss Price (who are standing rather close and dressed as Romeo and Juliet) in the left corner of the room...watching a large circle of people sitting on the floor and playing some sort of chanting game or something...watching Casey flirt with a group of bribed boys who actually came to the party, just not in costume...watching Casey hold hands with that Michael guy...

And that's really all that I'm watching.

Eric and Sam, however, are tracking Collin's movements and occasionally giving me unsolicited updates.

Collin has apparently been sitting at a table with the Sparkles duo and some of the not Casey-occupied bribed boys for about a half hour now. Addison, I guess, occasionally goes up to him to rub his shoulders or whisper something in his ear.

And he's looked over at me exactly four times. So I've been told...

Pretty thorough updates, I must say. Even though it would probably be much better for me not to be hearing them at all.

Especially the last part.

We continue to watch the activity around us. Groups change, people move around and mingle, but we stay on the couch.

"I wonder what Collin—" Eric starts.

"Hey—I'm going to run to the bathroom to, um, check my makeup before the big costume show," I interrupt him and sidestep another Collin conversation.

"Your makeup looks just awesome," Eric exclaims as I stand.

"Well, I just want to make sure—don't want to embarrass myself in my first parade." I smile and turn away, knowing quite well that Eric isn't buying the idea that I care about my makeup.

Fortunately, Addison has posted neon green signs to direct people to the bathroom, so I don't have to stop and ask anyone. I manage to follow the signs while still walking quite far away from Collin's table...or the table where Collin was sitting earlier. I don't know if he's still there...and I'm not looking that way now. I'm not.

I move out of the party room and into a new hallway which is lined with pictures of Addison throughout the years. Another neon sign with an arrow also hangs on the wall, so I must still be going in the right direction.

And there it is, a small powder room with a wide open door. And a few steps away is another open door, this one leading outside to, I guess, the backyard. Since I really have no reason to go into the little powder room, I veer to the right and head outside.

And it's beautiful out here. An intricate stone patio, twinkly hanging lights, a massive pool, and lots of indoor-looking outdoor furniture.

I walk around a little, enjoying the air and the luxurious silence.

I clearly don't pay enough attention to where I'm walking, though. I almost run my legs into a low lounge recliner.

The only thing that stops me from collision is the sight of the two people entwined on that very piece of furniture. Two people making out...and all that I can make out of them is a long, somewhat curly tonight, blonde ponytail and a guy's tight dark jeans.

Addison and Collin.

I think I would have preferred to get a large black and blue welt on my legs.

Before I can plan a quiet escape, Addison moves her face from Collin's to look at—

Wait.

It's not Collin. But it is Addison, and she's staring right at me now. Without moving her eyes, she waves her hand to dismiss...Michael, and he quickly scampers back toward the house. In no hurry, she sits up, placing her black and white saddle shoes on the ground. I've never seen Sandra Dee look so venomous.

When she begins to talk, she slowly forms each word as if trying to make sure she is being crystal clear.

She is.

"I'm sure you have all sorts of ideas running through your frizzy little head right now. But before you think about running to tell Collin...or my father..." Her eyes flicker to the ground by her feet where a glass bottle of...well, something that I assume involves alcohol...sits. This is honestly the first time that I'm seeing it.

I don't tell her that, though. Her eyes are back on mine, and she clearly has more to say.

She crosses one leg over the other and pushes out both of her arms to lean back on the palms of her hands.

"Let's just start with the part that will be easiest to explain." A little smirk settles onto her face. "If you go running to my father..."

I don't interrupt her to tell her that I would never dream of doing that.

"I'll just tell him that you brought it." She makes this weird, kind of painful looking, scrunched up face and says, "Daddy, I didn't even know what it was. I can't believe someone would bring that to our house. Your house."

She releases her fake, I don't know, innocent, or sad, or maybe scared, face and continues. "Needless to say, he'd get Mrs. Leonard to kick you out of the show right away...he has no tolerance for anyone when it comes to drinking...and he allows absolutely nothing like that in his house."

Wow. I just stare at her mouth, watching each perfectly formed word breathe out of her.

"And as for Collin..." Now she leans completely back, resting her head against the back of the chair and propping up her feet. "If you tell him...if he somehow finds out about this, you won't be able to just play the martyr, step aside, and give up the show so you can protect Collin...or have Collin." She pauses and presses her lips together in another smirk. "If he finds out, you won't be the only one losing a part; everyone will. Well, everyone that matters to you."

I move my gaze up to her eyes in surprise.

"I'll have my father convince Mrs. Leonard that she has to cut people from the show...convince her that otherwise he'll tear up his checks, pull the bank roll. He'd be so upset to hear that someone made up a story about his little girl that caused Collin to break up with me."

Wow. Again.

"If you haven't noticed, no costumes or set pieces have even arrived yet. It'd be so easy to just shut it all down...unless, of course, you have a spare twenty to thirty thousand tucked into your pathetic little costume." She pauses. "But it will never get to that point. Mrs. Leonard won't let that happen. She'll just have to do some recasting..."

My head is pounding...I'm starting to feel a little nauseous.

Maybe I do need to head to the little powder room after all.

As I try to come up with a way to just leave without her somehow deciding to use that alone as a reason to take me out of the show, Casey accidentally manages to save me.

"Addie!" She is yelling from the back door, you know, the one I stupidly came out of only minutes ago. "Costume Parade. Three minutes!"

Thank you, Casey.

Addison stands up, picks up the bottle and shoves it into a nearby bush, and then begins to walk away. She looks back at me after she's walked only a few steps.

She looks me up and down in a swift glance. "Good luck with the costume competition. Lex." Another smirk, and she is gone.

As much as I want to sit down and take some time to process everything...or better yet, to just leave the party and go home, I can't. Eric would be devastated if I missed the competition and, hopefully, his acceptance speech at the end of the night. Sam and I have already promised to take pictures on our phones from different artistic angles—for his Facebook page, I think.

I make myself move toward the door, my yellow stiletto heels (Eric insisted) feeling much heavier than they did when I first came outside...

Eric jumps up with a "There you are!" as soon as I enter the party room. He takes my hand and leads me to the end of the line that's forming.

"Here is your ballot slip. These are supposed to be filled out during the parade so we are all ready for the submission process right after." He hands me a slip of paper, a pen, and...a copy of *Dangerous Liaisons*.

I hold the book up to him in question.

"To write over—since we have to stand in line as we watch. We were supposed to pick books from Addison's shelf. I liked this one for you."

I roll my eyes and put the ballot on top of the book, balancing and scribbling Eric's name quickly for Most Authentic.

Eric smiles over at me with a tilt of his head. "Thanks, Lex."

The parade begins, and each person in line takes a turn to stand on the little makeshift stage Addison just made out of a coffee table.

Faces and costumes go by, all blending into one another. When Casey steps up to the stage, I can't help but wonder how she would feel about Addison's little affair with Michael...not that I would tell her about it...just like I won't tell Collin...even though he deserves to know.

Speaking of Collin...

"Here's the happy couple now," Eric whispers to me.

Addison pulls Collin up onto the coffee table with her and—and she's changed clothes. She's now dancing around in the tight black leather outfit that Sandy wears at the end of *Grease*. She's trying to get Collin to mimic some of the memorable dance moves from the movie, but he's not really giving in. He looks uncomfortable yet again.

Before I know it, he catches my eyes with his. He looks miserable.

I force my eyes away, only to see Addison now looking at me—watching me watching him. She narrows her eyes a little and then pulls Collin in to kiss her.

"GROSS," Eric whispers emphatically.

I just lower my eyes and my whole head as I try to release all of the tension that's building in my stomach.

I don't lift my face until I hear Addison jump off of the table. I assume that she takes Collin to have a seat with the other people who have already presented and those who didn't wear costumes tonight...which would include Michael...but I don't look over at them to find out.

I continue to keep my eyes away from the seated audience as Eric leads Sam and me to the coffee table. Sam and I decided earlier that we would just stand below Eric on the floor, framing him to give him the spotlight...and we do just that. We stand and smile, I try not to look directly out into the audience, and Eric poses...some sort of Madonna "Vogue" position.

When our turn is over, we head back to our original couch seats. My ballot is still empty except where I've voted for Eric. I try to think about the other costumes, but I have a hard time thinking of anyone but Sandy and Danny.

And I'm not putting those names down for Best Couple.

"Ballot submissions will begin in two minutes." Speaking of Sandy...Addison stands again on the coffee table, now holding a big decorated box.

Eric looks over and sees the blank spots on my paper. He quickly whispers some suggestions: the two teachers as Romeo and Juliet for Best Couple and Sparkles #1, um Justin, who apparently is dressed as a tampon, for Funniest.

Works for me. I scribble down the names, fold my paper, and sink back into the couch.

The submission process begins moments later, and we again get up to stand in a line. This line goes much faster than the last, though. Each person walks up to Addison, who is now standing (alone) by the trophy table, and slips a ballot into the box.

When we reach the front of the line, I lower my eyes yet again, put my ballot in the slot, and wait for Eric and Sam to do the same...well, almost the same. Eric kisses his ballot and makes the sign of the cross before submitting his votes.

"Are you Catholic?" I ask as we walk back to our couch.

"No, but Madonna used to be," he (sort of) explains his little prayerful gesture as he daintily sits back in the middle of Sam and me.

"Where is Collin?" He changes the subject with no warning, making my stomach start to jitter again.

I just shrug. I know no more than he does. Well, about Collin's current whereabouts...

We sit on the couch and wait. Another stretch of people watching, but not Collin watching, passes, and soon Addison is up on the coffee table again, excitedly rubbing her hands together.

"We have the results," she yells out eagerly, and the room quiets down once again. "I know that Collin and I traditionally present these awards together, but he's not feeling well, so I left him resting in my room."

Do not think about what they were doing in her room. Do not think about what they were doing in her room.

"So Casey has so kindly offered to help me tonight." She nods over to Casey, who picks up one of the trophies.

Eric grabs my hand. Probably Sam's too.

"And now..." Addison pauses to smile. "For Most Authentic costume, please give a round of applause for...Justin the Tampon. The very realistic-looking tampon."

Eric's bare shoulder slumps a little against mine, and he lets go of my hand. I reach over and take his hand back, squeezing hard and telling him that it's not over yet.

But really, it is.

Funniest costume ends up going to a girl who plays one of the people working in the factory with Fantine. I'm not even quite sure what she's dressed as, but she's wearing gum wrappers, various brands of toothpaste tubes, and...dental floss, maybe? Making some statement about dental hygiene, I guess. I don't really find the costume that humorous, but lots of people laugh when she accepts the award, so I must be missing something.

I'd ask Eric, but now is probably not a good time to try to talk to him. Especially about something award-related.

"Now...I'd like to wait another half hour or so to announce the couple award—just to give Collin some time to rest." Addison flashes a smile and then jumps off of the coffee table to talk to Casey.

"So they won?" I ask as I roll my eyes at Eric.

He doesn't even turn to me. "They win every year. Another tradition."

"Wait. Why did you have me vote for Romeo and Juliet then?"

Still not looking my way, still staring sadly at the trophy table, he answers my question with one of his own. "Even if you had known that Addison and Collin were definitely going to win, would you have been able to write their names on your ballot?"

Good point.

"And in the case that Addison ever actually looks at the ballots, I'd like to think it would royally piss her off to see another couple with votes."

"Wait. Do you think she looks at the ballots for the other categories, though?" I ask, starting to wonder if there was any point in filling out the ballot form at all.

Eric actually looks over at me as he speaks this time. "Never can tell...but it's probably important to note that she's recently been all buddy buddy with Justin. The tampon." He pauses and then squints his eyes a little in a slow realization. "Wait—and I also think she was the one who kept bitching about Bradley's breath last year..." He looks forward again to think about it and thus misses the confusion on my face.

"I bet she does just pick all of the winners—it makes sense," Eric murmurs, not really even upset but merely resigned to the facts.

I put that information together and formulate an answer to the question still bouncing around in my head. "So that girl in the hygiene or whatever costume was meant to make fun of that Bradley guy?"

"Yep."

This makes me worry for a moment about the status of my breath. I did brush my teeth before I left for the party, but that was a long time ago. I really don't want anyone dressing up to make fun of—

All of a sudden, there is a loud scream coming from outside. Addison rushes to the door, and Casey follows quickly after her.

"Oh my God." I hear Addison's exclamation seconds later. "It's Mrs. Leonard."

Eric, Sam, and I get up now to head toward the door. We beat many of the other cast members out, and we soon see Mrs. Leonard sprawled out at the bottom of the porch steps. Her legs are bent in a way that, well, legs shouldn't bend, and some blood is seeping out through a hole in her pants.

Eric and I push past Addison and Casey, who are still on the doorstep, and run down the stairs to Mrs. Leonard. Sam pulls out her cell phone and dials 911 after she reminds us not to move her and potentially hurt her more.

We listen to Sam (her mom is a nurse, after all), and we just sit by Mrs. Leonard, letting her know that she'll be at the hospital soon.

As we sit there, a crowd of cast members appears at the door. Some come down to join us in keeping Mrs. Leonard company, while others, at least two others, start to loudly whisper about this situation reminding them of "The Fall of Éponine."

I ignore it. I ignore them, trying to focus on getting Mrs. Leonard to stay awake. I haven't gotten the chance to ask Sam if this is important in a case where there are really no outward signs that she hit her head...but it's the only thing I can think of to do right now that might be helpful.

I don't turn around when I hear a familiar voice asking what happened...what he can do. I listen as he runs down the steps, apparently feeling better after his rest in Addison's room, but I don't look.

When he comes up right behind me, leaning over and trying to converse with Mrs. Leonard, every inch of me tenses. But I still don't turn around.

And when he moves closer to Mrs. Leonard and accidentally brushes his leg against my back, I shiver a little, and everything gets a bit fuzzy, but I do not turn my head.

It's a good thing, too. Seconds later, Addison runs down the steps and stands in the space between him and me. She offers a few words of comfort to Mrs. Leonard before asking Collin how he is feeling. I try to disappear, closing my eyes and keeping them shut until I hear the ambulance approaching.

And I do feel a lot of relief for Mrs. Leonard when I hear those loud sirens. But I must also confess that I feel some relief for myself as we are all forced to stand up and get out of the way, which gives Eric, Sam, and me the perfect reason to leave this wretched party.

Chapter 8

"Master of the House"

Unfortunately, now things are even worse—something that I didn't really think was possible.

After talking to Eric and Sam about catching Addison with Michael, about her threats, about trying not to ruin the show for us, I vowed to keep my mouth shut and to stay away from Collin.

Isn't that bad enough?

Apparently, it's not. I just got to school, expecting to be told, kind of hoping to be told in light of my recent resolution, that practice will be canceled for the next few days—until Mrs. Leonard comes back. Instead, I just heard the announcement that rehearsal is on—and that Addison is in charge.

Needless to say, my day drags on. I spend my classes just dreading going to the auditorium after school.

Eric, wearing a black shirt with the words "Go Team" written in gold across the middle, stops to pick me up at my locker so we can walk to practice together.

"Maybe we'll just do a run-through of Act I," he says as we move away from my locker. "Then she'll be so busy playing Cosette that she won't have time to turn the entire show into the movie."

I just nod, half listening. I'm not that worried about what we'll be doing onstage...Mrs. Leonard can fix things when she gets back if Addison starts trying to change our blocking.

I'm worried about what I'll be doing when I'm off of the stage...trying to avoid Collin, and Addison, and Collin and Addison together...and Casey...and the prop closet...

At least Eric will be at the entire rehearsal today—I guess I can just glue myself to him backstage and hope not to get myself into any sticky situations.

But then there will be the times when Eric (and Sam) will be on the stage and I will not...

Eric keeps telling me that I should try to branch out a little and make more friends in Drama Club...but every time I think about it, I can't help but remember all of the "LIKES" that the picture of my fall got on Instagram. I don't really know how to separate the people who "LIKE" that picture (even if they didn't declare it online) from those who might like me.

But do I really want to know? What if Collin—

We are here—in the back of the auditorium. Students are gathering at the front in a clumpy circle around Addison. Just like we usually do around Mrs. Leonard when she has an announcement.

Eric and I make our way down to stand at the back of the group. More cast members show up and join the clump. Collin's dark head is in the crowd near the front of the group. I try to avoid looking in his general existing area, but I don't do a great job.

Soon, Addison clears her throat and begins her speech. "I know we are all very upset about Mrs. Leonard having to be away from us. I got an update from my father this afternoon, and she is apparently going to be kept in the hospital for another night so that doctors can monitor how her injured leg might complicate some of the troubles she's had with her hip or something." She laughs and rolls her eyes a little. "A bunch of doctor gibberish, really. But it sounds like she'll be back, on crutches or in a wheelchair, maybe in a couple days."

She continues. "In the meantime, here's the plan. She's going to have Mr. Thoms do a music-only rehearsal tomorrow, and you will see that schedule soon. For today, though, she wants us to run Act I so we don't get too far behind." She smiles proudly. "So she put me in charge of making sure this happens." Another smile. Then she looks over to Mr. Thoms. "Now, if you'll be ready, Mr. Thoms, we will plan on starting in about two minutes."

Mr. Thoms nods back at her from the piano.

Eric nudges me. "Lucky man. Now he gets to be bossed around by a high and mighty eighteen-year-old too," he whispers.

"Okay...PLACES," Addison yells, raising her arms as though she is conducting us to our spots for the opening scene.

I, however, am not in the opening scene anymore, so I sit down in the audience with Eric to watch.

I really do try not to notice what Collin does, since he isn't in this scene either, but I cannot stop my eyes from seeing him walk backstage. To the left. To our closet, I'm sure.

I look away, back at Eric, before Addison somehow catches me noticing Collin's movements.

The opening music begins—only Mr. Thoms still. The pit will arrive little by little over the next week.

And the first scene looks good. It really does. The chained bribed boys and girls pretending to be men move with fluidity as they cross the stage together. And even though a part of me still resents not being in the scene, I'm glad it looks good—a solid start to our show.

Addison sings along and marches in place to the music, but she doesn't join the chain gang today. She instead watches from below the stage, holding a clipboard and taking notes throughout.

She reads some of the notes aloud and makes some comments at the end of the song, but I cannot hear what she is saying from my spot in the auditorium.

Eric is more upset about this than I am. He has tucked his feet up under him to try to arch forward in his seat. Eventually, he slumps back, giving up. "I guess we'll have to get the info from Sam later." He pouts. "I want to know how many times she referred to the movie."

Before I can comment, Addison rings Mrs. Leonard's bell and calls places for the next song. Eric and I remain in our seats and start our whole audience member process again; he stretches to hear Addison's comments (when he's not making comments of his own), and I try not to think about not being in the prop closet.

And then the bell rings, and we do it all again.

We break from this routine when our first scene comes up—the young Thénardier family portion of the show.

Somehow, I get through my part without getting any notes (good or bad) from Addison. Truthfully, she pretty much ignores me—she doesn't even look my way when we are both on the stage together.

She does some of her parts up on the stage with us, and she occasionally sits down to watch the scene from below, still saying her lines when appropriate.

When it's time for "Master of the House," I get a short break...without Eric and Sam, though, obviously. I do consider going back out to sit in the audience with Sarah, but then I see Casey out there talking in the middle of a large group of people and, incidentally, sitting almost right on top of Michael.

So I decide to just wait in the rather small wing off stage right.

Not a lot of room here. No closets to slip into. But that's okay since there are also no other people back here right now.

I stand behind the traveler curtain so I can still kind of see what is going on onstage. Eric is just getting into his vulgar audition movements when I hear...and feel...someone come up behind me.

His cologne is already making me a little dizzy; he must be pretty close.

He is. I can feel his breath on my neck as he speaks.

"Hey. What happened to you today? I've been rehearsing all alone in the dark."

Do not turn around, Lexi. Do not let—

"Lex?" He whispers. "What's wrong?"

Time to see how far my acting skills can get me backstage.

I flip my head toward him quickly with a small, closed-mouth smile before turning back to look at the stage. "I'm fine."

"You just hit me in the nose with your ponytail," he laughs, talking again to the back of my head. "And you didn't even notice." More serious now. "You aren't fine."

I don't move, staring ahead and half-seeing Eric and Sam prance around the stage.

Half-seeing. Nervous...shaky...blurry...seeing.

He whispers now. "What did she say to you?"

Still not moving. Still not really seeing.

And then his hand is on my shoulder as he gently pulls me to face him.

Eyes dimmed with concern. Mouth in a straight, serious line.

"Well?"

"What? I don't know what—" Words and phrases start to splutter out of me. I try to catch them before they rush past my mind's filter...but I struggle to keep up since his hand on my shoulder is taking up most of my brain space.

"She didn't say anything *today*."

LEXI! No emphasis should have been put on the word "today." In fact, the word never should have attached itself to the end of that sentence.

"Today?" He asks, confusion wrinkling up his eyes.

Great. Fix this, Lexi. So you can keep your part...and he can keep his...so we can do the show.

"Oh, I um, just felt bad when she came in while we were rehearsing the other day." I move my eyes down as I shake my head a little. "I just, she, um, didn't seem to want me to, um, rehearse with you in there, so well, I—"

"So you decided to assault my nose with your ponytail?" I look up and meet his now smiling eyes.

"Seriously, don't worry about that, Lexi. I explained it all to her. And besides, we, um weren't, well—"

I swear his cheeks are blushing a little.

He finishes his sentence. "We weren't doing anything wrong."

"No—of course—"

"Time for your scenes, Épo—"

Addison. I turn around to face her as Collin moves his hand from my shoulder.

She squints her eyes at me for a beat and then looks over at Collin with a similar expression.

"Your scenes too, Collin. Come on." She turns around, blonde hair waving frantically, and I, well, follow. I don't turn back to look at Collin. I only assume he's following as well.

And we run through the Éponine, Marius, and Cosette scenes, thankfully starting with the ones where Jean Valjean and the Thénardiers are also involved.

I don't look at Addison—my blocking fortunately doesn't call for it.

I do have to look at him, though. As though I am in love with him.

As though Éponine is in love with Marius, that is.

And the scenes go smoothly, just as we've practiced them. The emotion is there. The intensity is there. We don't miss any notes or mess up any lyrics. Addison doesn't give any of us notes when we break for a new selection of scenes.

Before we are due in places for "One Day More," the finale of Act I, I meet up with Eric and Sam. I fill them in on

Collin's hand on my shoulder, Addison's squinty eyes, Collin's blushing...

"He really likes you, Lex," Eric whispers before stopping to rub his tongue over his teeth. "I think he wants to do things with you in that closet."

Sam laughs, and I punch Eric on the shoulder.

"Now you're the one blushing, Lexi," Eric continues to whisper, making his eyes all big and raising his eyebrows. "Maybe after this whole show is over, the two of you—"

"PLACES IN ONE MINUTE," Addison yells from the front of the auditorium, sitting below the stage and ready to watch the upcoming scene. Guess she's not going to do her blocking onstage for this one.

Eric links arms with me on one side and Sam on the other, and then we all head up to the stage together.

When Eric drops me off at my place, he gives me a quick kiss on the cheek, reminds me that this is the last scene for today, and promises to take me out for some "super fattening" ice cream after rehearsal.

And then Mr. Thoms plays the famous opening notes of "One Day More," and we begin. Pretty much everyone sings at some point during the song, and the music and the voices keep getting louder and stronger and more and more intense.

It sounds amazing. It feels amazing.

When we get to my part, I wrap my arms around my waist, just like Mrs. Leonard wants me to do it. I hug myself, close my eyes, and sing with all of the desperation and misery Éponine is feeling at this moment. The emotion feels raw, as real as it did when I practiced in that little dark closet.

We all eventually build up to the layers of lyrics that make up the end of the song.

When the last note ends, the stage is silent for a moment, but then it gets crazy. Several cast members are clapping. Some are cheering. Others are dancing around.

Addison doesn't stop us right away. She leans over the piano for a minute to talk to Mr. Thoms, and then Mr. Thoms gets Valjean and they go off together, I think to the practice room. Once they exit the stage, Addison quiets us down and says out loud what most of us are thinking, hoping. "This is the most difficult show most of us have ever done, but we're doing it. We're rocking it. We're going to blow the audience away."

Another cheer escapes from the stage. It stops, though, when Addison holds up her hand, her palm, to squelch it.

"The audience will love it if..." She pauses. "If..." She looks around. "If we can all work together to fix a major area of concern."

While confused glances start spreading around the stage, Addison's eyes land on me. They are even more squinty than before—but only for a moment. She soon flashes an enormous, yet obviously fake, smile to me and to the others standing on the stage.

And then she begins to speak.

"You all know that Alexa is new this year to our school, to our Drama Club."

Lots of eyes begin turning my way.

Addison continues to smile. "I think we all need to understand that maybe her old school didn't expect the same caliber of performance as we do here. And we need to take her inexperience not as a problem, but as an opportunity for us to help, as an opportunity to use our talents to help another."

Oh. My. God.

I try to make my throat swallow, but I'm finding it impossible...so I concentrate instead on trying to stop the moisture that is building in the corners of my eyes.

She isn't done, though.

"In this scene, Alexa, Éponine is tormented, devastated even, because she essentially has lost something she never even had. Marius."

During her pause, I feel Eric move to my side. When he squeezes my hand, I clench my eyes shut to try to discourage any more buildup of liquid.

"I," Addison pauses and smiles, looking around again, "no, *we*, need to see that you have lost, and that you know you have lost any chance with Marius."

"Addi—" Marius himself tries to cut her off.

"Oh—I'll take further suggestions in a minute, sweetie." She flashes him her smile. "But right now I have an idea for Alexa, something that I do when I'm acting."

I barely even notice the various throat clearings and whispers that follow this statement. It doesn't matter what the other cast members think about her. Or her acting. Or this, whatever it is that she is doing right now.

Addison continues. "I like to pick something memorable, something poignant to focus on to help me visualize a character's emotions."

Again, I ignore the quiet comments behind me. So does Eric. He just continues to squeeze my hand as Addison keeps talking.

"You, Alexa, for example, could visualize the part where you have to deliver that message, the letter from Marius. This is when you essentially realize that your only purpose is to help these two, Marius and Cosette, of course, recognize their love for each other." A pause and then she looks right at me.

"Try to internalize the grief Éponine must feel at that moment as she delivers a letter that means her true love will never love her back, never be hers." Another pause and then a hint of the squinty eyes comes back, even though her smile is still stapled to her mouth. "Try to imagine what message that letter holds." She raises her eyebrows. "How those words just slice into you."

"Addison—stop." Eric.

"Oh, Eric, does this mean you are willing to help her?" She doesn't wait for a response. "Oh, thank you. I'll write that down for Mrs. Leonard so that she knows we are working toward a fix, or at least an improvement. I don't want to give her too many things to have to worry about when she gets back."

Before Eric can speak again, Addison turns to the whole group and keeps talking.

"Now, everyone, thanks for a great rehearsal. Remember to check tomorrow's schedule to see when you are to be here for music practice. Mr. Thoms left a copy with me before he went to rehearse with Mr. Fiero." She holds up a schedule and then places it on the edge of the stage. "Mrs. Leonard intends to be back on Wednesday, but if she can't make it, I'll be here to help you with your blocking for scenes in the second act."

Another gigantic toothy smile. "Now go home and get some rest, and—"

And she looks pointedly at me.

"And let's practice, practice, practice."

Chapter 9

"Castle on a Cloud"

I don't know how I got off the stage two days ago after Addison's "helpful" comments. And I'm not sure how I managed to walk past Collin without meeting his eyes. And honestly, I have absolutely no idea how I later managed to only cry a little as I sat and ate ice cream with Eric and Sam.

At least I know how I got through yesterday's rehearsal. I owe it all to Éponine since she dies and makes me unnecessary for much of Act II. And, well, I guess I owe a little to Mr. Thoms, who only had time to run parts of Act II and so chose certain songs, mainly solos. I was only scheduled for one song, my song.

And, believe it or not, I was first on the schedule. So I sang "On My Own" on my own in the auditorium. It was just Mr. Thoms, the piano, and me.

And then I managed to leave, still on my own, before the next scheduled song began. As I went to my car, I did pass Sarah, who must've been scheduled to sing my song after me, but that was it. She tried to tell me how bad she felt about the day before, but I told her not to worry about it. She is obviously stressed enough already with her schoolwork and understudying.

After we talked, she still looked concerned, but she let it go and went in the school, leaving me alone again.

So, all in all, I was very lucky yesterday.

Today is a different story.

Today, Mrs. Leonard is still not back. So Addison is in charge again.

I've spent most of the day trying not to think about rehearsal, but really then only thinking about rehearsal instead of statistics, French paintings, and the dissection of frogs.

And now the school day is over, the bell has rung, and it's time to stop thinking about it. It's time to go in.

Eric pulls open the auditorium door and heads in first.

"Oh, this is ridiculous." He stops right inside the doorway. I push him over a little so I can see what is so bad.

First I just see crates and boxes and panels and power drills...everything needed to build the set. But then I see it.

Addison, Casey, and the Sparkles duo are already working on a piece in the center of the stage. An enormous princess-looking castle. With clouds underneath of it.

Now Eric is giggling. "Well, we already were sure she knew nothing about acting. We just didn't know that her dramatic interpretation might be even worse."

"Leonard's gonna die when she sees this." Sam comes in behind us, staring at the fairytale palace in front of us.

"Will she though?" Eric asks. "She let Addison help order the scenery this year...and Addison did say something about them having some creative differences..."

"Well, it's pretty clear that Addison won the battle of creativity, if that's what we're calling this."

"Her dad's money won the battle," Eric mutters. "It wins every battle." He pauses, shakes his head, and holds out his arms like two teapot handles. "All right, my hags. Let's do this."

Giving him my own version of squinty eyes, I refuse his arm. He just pushes it out further. "Miss Alexa Grace. May I have the honor of escorting you?"

Sighing, I take his arm, and Sam does the same.

Eric starts skipping quickly to the front of the auditorium, pulling us with him, before he says, "Best hags a guy could ask for."

I wait until we stop moving to hit him.

And then I have other problems to focus on...

Addison turns around as we arrive. Before she can say anything to me, though, someone calls out her name from stage right.

Well, not just someone calls out her name. Collin does.

I don't look over his way to verify that, but I know that voice. There's no question.

Addison skips over to him, and Eric, Sam, and I take seats in the auditorium, waiting for everyone else to arrive.

Cast members trickle in over the next ten minutes, some just finishing up calls on their cell phones and some coming in with little snacks from the coffeehouse on the corner. Once everyone settles (Even Casey and the others from the stage come down to sit. I try not to notice as Collin sits a few rows behind me), Addison begins to speak from the stage.

"As you can see, our set has arrived, and Mrs. Leonard has asked that we use today's rehearsal to start putting things together." She pauses to smile. "Not the bigger pieces, of course. I don't think she wants us to try to follow the seven hundred pages of instructions for putting together the barricade or Javert's bridge. Or for the turntable."

A few cast members laugh.

"I believe some shop teachers will be coming in to take care of all that." She looks around with a smile. "So what *can* we take care of today? The accessories to the main set. For example..."

She stands back and holds her arms out to her castle cloud scenery. "A few of us had a study hall last period, so we started to work on this." She pauses and points to Casey and the Sparkles duo in the audience. "Well, they worked. I just read the directions to them." She clasps her hands in front of her chest and squeals a little. "But it's my castle. On a cloud. You know, for my first song."

Eric nudges his elbow into my side so hard that I'll probably have a black and blue mark later, but I refuse to look at him. He'll make me laugh, and then Addison will despise me even more.

I do hear whispers around me...cast members wondering why there is an actual castle on top of a cloud as part of the set...discussing how it will disrupt the rest of the drab, but completely appropriate, scenery...trying to figure out why the castle is bright pink...

I don't turn around. I don't look at Eric. I just wait for Addison to say more.

And seconds later, seemingly oblivious to the scattered commentary in the audience, she continues to talk, now giving instructions for the day.

She will be finishing up her castle direction reading with Casey and the Sparkles duo. The rest of us are assigned to certain set pieces. She starts to read a list of people who will work on each piece, and Eric leans over to whisper to me.

"Hey—as much as I hate scraping up my hands to work with tools, and as absolutely stupid as that castle is, this is better than Leonard letting her block the unfinished parts of Act II. At least now the second half probably won't be an *exact* replica of the movie..."

I give him a small smile and then continue to listen for my name. The list goes on and on—different rolling wagons to be constructed, pieces of furniture to be gathered and assembled.

Somehow, mercifully, I am assigned to a group with Eric, Sam, and a couple of bribed boys (not Michael). Thank God. We are supposed to build a double-sided wagon. One side will have some pub-type scenery for "Drink With Me" and "Empty Chairs at Empty Tables," and the other side will have some background images for Fantine's deathbed scene.

We head up to the stage to gather tools as soon as Addison is done with her list of assignments. As I grab a power drill and several screws, I am overly aware of the fact that Collin is doing the same thing only a few spaces away. I can feel his eyes on me, but I concentrate on the task at hand, carefully counting the screws I put into a container (even though I have no idea how many I need...or how many I really have as I keep losing count).

"Lexi." Everything is in his voice. Sorrow. Pleading. Concern.

But I can't do this.

Fortunately (I think), I don't have to right now.

"Alexa—I need you to come over here to talk with me for a moment." Miss Price, the journalism teacher. Fantine.

I turn my head back to face her, deliberately skipping over Collin's eyes as I move. I see him out of the corner of my eye, though. And his face has all of the emotions I heard in his voice.

"Sure. I'll be right there." I give Miss Price a small smile, gather my drill and container of I don't know how many screws, and move over to meet her at the front of the stage.

She tilts her head to have me follow her off the stage, back into the audience, and down the aisle of seats. Away from everyone else.

She stops and faces me once we reach about the sixth row back. Before she talks, she does a sweeping glance of the stage and auditorium, making sure no one is paying attention. And I guess no one is, because she starts to whisper.

"I know I wasn't at the end of rehearsal on Monday, but Mr. Fiero heard some rumors about what happened." She pauses to give me a sympathetic look. "What's going on?"

When seconds pass and I don't come up with an answer, she continues.

"With Addison. Why was she so mean to you?"

I just shrug and disentangle myself from the questions in her eyes.

"Mr. Fiero was told that she went on and on...and in front of everyone. He's concerned. I'm concerned." She pauses for a beat. "With being new to the school, it's easy to become the victim of bull—"

"I'm not being bullied, Miss Price," I cut her off before she finishes her sentence.

Her eyes are still full of questions. Questions I cannot answer if I'd like to keep my part. If I'd like all of us to be able to play our parts.

"Really." I say it with a smile.

She's not convinced. "Mr. Fiero heard that she kept talking about a message in some strange way. Did she threaten you in a note or an email or something? What was that about?"

I try not to think about the words "Opening Night Casey's After Me (FINALLY!)," but I can't help it.

"Alexa?"

"Oh, um...I don't know. I guess it had something to do with the message I deliver between Marius and Cosette in the second act or something."

"That's it?" She's not buying it...

I smile and nod my head. "Yep."

"Well...I think I'll say something to Mrs. Leonard so—"

"No. No point in doing that. She has real things to worry about." I smile again. "The rest of the Act II blocking, tickets, costumes, all of this scenery that somehow needs to go together..."

"Well, I'll talk to Jack, uh, Mr. Fiero, and we'll see."

Please don't tell Mrs. Leonard. Please don't tell Mrs. Leonard.

I don't plead out loud. I just smile again and pray that this is a situation where less is indeed more.

She smiles back. "Okay, back to work then, I guess." She doesn't really look prepared for set building, though, with her light pink dress and matching pumps.

I turn and head back toward the stage.

"Alexa." I only get to take a few steps before Miss Price has me turn around again.

She catches my eyes with a much brighter smile than before.

"That wasn't the only thing that Mr. Fiero talked to me about." An even bigger smile. "He also said that you make the best Éponine he's ever seen."

I smile back at her. And it's for real this time.

"Thanks, Miss Price."

I head back up to find Eric and Sam and the scenery we are somehow supposed to get together.

M iss Price is not the only one terribly dressed for set building; Eric's perfectly white *Ain't Misbehavin'* t-shirt is, well, no longer perfectly white. With the passing of every half hour that we work, it gets dirtier and dirtier, and Eric gets more and more irritated.

"Unfreakingbelievable," he mutters as he examines a new black mark on the side of his shirt. "Let's get it right this time—I don't know how much more my poor shirt can take."

"Okay, lift on three," Sam yells over all of the noise around us.

She counts, and we try for the third time to get the back panel properly attached to the wagon. The first time, it was upside down. The second time, it was crooked and it looked really bad. We have to get it right this time—there aren't that many more stupid mistakes we can make with this.

When the panel is placed, Eric, Brendan, Cam (Bribed Boy #1 and Bribed Boy #2), and I each hold on firmly to the sides as Sam uses the drill to secure it in place with a bunch of screws.

"This is stupid." Cam speaks up. "This is supposed to be the background in the pub, but there is no hint of wine, beer, or even glasses."

"Maybe on the other panels," suggests Brendan, looking around the stage for the coordinating wagons.

"There won't be any pictures like that," Eric starts in a matter-of-fact voice. "Addison's mother died of alcohol poisoning. Her dad would never pay for anything that seems to support any sort of drinking." He pauses. "Besides, this is a school—why add alcohol when it's not necessary?" He asks this in a regularly-volumed voice before whispering "DUMBASSES" in my direction.

I can't return the amused expression on his face right now, though.

"Her mother died from drinking too much?" I ask, still surprised by this information.

Now Eric looks surprised. "Yeah. I thought you knew."

I shake my head at double speed. No, I definitely did not know.

Eric looks around in various directions before whispering, "It was really ugly. And everyone knew about it because it was freshman year, right before the show. We were doing *Footloose*, and we were in our final weeks." He looks around again. "Addison only missed a rehearsal or two and was back in her Ariel costume the day after her mom's funeral." He pauses. "I think her dad thought it was a good distraction for her, so he supported her coming back...but he was really upset then about the themes in the show. Teens partying, drinking, dying."

He shrugs. "It's not like anything could be done, though—we couldn't switch shows or anything. So he just made Leonard promise to avoid such themes in the future." He nods his head and snaps his arm Vanna White-style toward the alcohol-less bar on the panel in front of us.

"So this is what we're left with." He shrugs again. "I don't really blame her dad though. And it doesn't really change much for us."

Wow.

I know my parents are really busy with their firm and that I don't see them very much, but I can't imagine if one of them was gone...

My thoughts, and our conversation, are interrupted as Sam starts drilling again. Soon, she directs us all to work together to stand the correctly finished wagon on its wheels.

We admire our work for a moment, and then Brendan and Cam go off to socialize with the group putting together the banquet tables for the wedding scene.

Eric plops down on the floor, I guess giving up on the idea of avoiding any more stains on his shirt, and reaches out both arms for Sam and me to join him. So we do.

I, once again, cannot get Addison off of my mind. And I realize that I've not told Sam and Eric everything about the night of the Half Block.

Eric looks over at me, tilting his head to the side and lifting his eyebrows. "What is it, Lex?"

"I, well, I guess I was so caught up in everything about, um, Collin, after Addison's party that I didn't even remember the rest of it." I pause, and before I can start again, Sam jumps in.

"What was Addison drinking?" She asks it in a dramatically bored tone of voice.

I look up at her in surprise.

Eric pushes his lips together and blinks his eyes slowly. "Oh my naïve ha—"

"Don't say it." I roll my eyes with a smile before starting to ask the question running around in my head. "How did you know?"

Now it's Sam's turn to roll her eyes. "Everyone knows. She's been doing it since we met her."

"Wait—even after her Mom—" I start.

"After, before, during," Sam interrupts with a shrug. "People have even said that she spiked her own drinks at the luncheon following the funeral."

Wow.

"And her dad has no idea?"

Eric shakes his head as Sam continues to talk. "Rumor has it that some girl from the cast of *The Sound of Music* smelled alcohol on her at school one day. She turned her in to the guidance office or the principal or something, but nothing happened." Sam pauses and raises her eyebrows. "Oh, except that girl was kicked out of the show for some reason or another only days later."

Sam continues. "I think Addison told Leonard that it was actually the other way around—that Addison smelled alcohol on the girl...and that it was just too much for her, you know...with her mother and everything. So Leonard made the girl drop the show."

"So no one has told on her since, obviously," Eric chimes back in.

My mind skips over to its next question. "Wait. Everyone knows though? *Collin* knows?"

Eric leans up to pat the hair on the top of my head. "Oh, honey, Collin isn't part of 'everybody.'" He licks his teeth. "He's too hot to be jumbled into some big category."

"So he doesn't know?" I cut into his little Collin-adoring moment.

"Not about the drinking. Not about the cheating. Not about the fact that she's a complete bitch."

Sam nods as Eric speaks.

"How can he be that—" I start.

"Naïve?" Eric finishes for me. "I don't think he is—I just think she's that good at manipulating men." He stops, shakes his head, and clarifies. "Straight men." He goes on. "Collin, her father, that Michael guy...Justin too." He pauses to think. "And I know that this should throw a curve in my straight men hypothesis, but Justin isn't out yet. I don't even think he knows that he's just as gay as me." He flashes me a smile. "If that's even possible."

Before I can ask my next question, Eric answers it.

"I know it's odd that she's that good at this when she looks like a dead mouse as she's trying to act on the stage. Fortunately, I have a theory for this as well."

I look over and wait for his explanation.

"I don't think she's acting when she's lying and manipulating. She's just being herself. So if she didn't always get her way and play the soft, sweet, romantic female leads, she might actually play a good Carlotta...or Sharpay...or even an ugly stepsister. She wouldn't need any acting skills to play any of them—she'd be all set just merging their lines and her own personality." He pauses in thought for a moment and then continues.

"I think that she did better with Ariel in *Footloose* than with any of her other roles since Ariel is kind of a bad girl in the beginning of the show. She did okay with that...then, of course, she sucked the life right out of the show when Ariel was supposed to get all romantic and sympathetic..."

He pauses and stops philosophizing for a moment, looking behind me. "The sands are about to start busting out of your hourglass, Lexi."

Well, I don't need to turn around to see why he's referencing his soap again.

I can see it in his face.

And I can smell Collin's cologne.

"Lexi."

I frantically search Eric's eyes, hoping to see in them a way to get out of this situation. Instead, I see him put his tongue back on his teeth. And I realize I should probably turn around before he starts drooling or something.

So I move my legs, my arms, my body, around with my head—and get swept right up into the look on Collin's face.

"I wanted to come talk to you earlier, but my group was having trouble finishing up the judge's stand over there."

Yes. I saw. I know what you were working on. And where.

I nod my head a little. "It looks good." I explain. "The judge's stand. It looks finished."

"It is." A pause. "Your wagon looks good too. I saw that you had to, um, rework it a few times."

I know that too. I know that you saw me. Sam and Eric had a live feed of Collin updates going for most of our building session.

He's just looking at me, waiting for a response.

And then, "Hey, Lex—we're gonna go grab some sodas" comes from behind me. Eric. "I'll get you some Mountain Dew."

I turn around at his voice, and he gives me a look that pretty much says, "Get it together, Lex."

I try to make a face back to ask if I should really be left alone here, but either I don't do a very good job or else Eric just ignores my expression.

I watch him and Sam as they get up and head toward the hallway.

"Lexi. I need to talk to you. Alone."

My body sinks further into the floor as my back and limbs turn into, well, nothing—nothing more than baggage that I have to try to hold up.

"Lexi." I hear him...I feel him moving around me now, crouching down in front of me and meeting my eyes with his.

"Did you hear me? I need—"

"I can't, Collin."

His eyes flip from imploring to questioning in a blink.

"What? Why can't...I don't understand what you mean."

With some crazy invisible strength I didn't even know I had until now, I rip my eyes away, stand up, and head off stage left. Walking and thinking and wondering and hoping...hoping that Sam and Eric will be back soon. Hoping that rehearsal is almost over. Hoping that he isn't following me.

Hoping that he is.

"Lexi."

And he is.

He grabs my hand, and I, well, get all dizzy and shivery. We move together to the back corner, where the big fluffy pink castle is now standing.

He still has my hand, now held in between both of his.

"We can't do this here. Can I call you?"

"What? I mean, no. I told you, I can't do this."

"Please, Lexi." He squeezes my hand between his, almost squeezing my resolve right out of me.

Almost. Then I remember what a good Marius he makes. That he should be able to continue to make.

I shake my head and pull my hand from his grip.

"Collin, I can't. Addison wouldn't—"

"Lexi, it's *about* Addi—" He tries to interrupt, fire in his eyes.

But then we both hear the footsteps coming toward us. And Addison is here, steps away, her arms crossed over her blue, cashmere-looking sweater.

She stomps toward us. "What is going—"

"Hey, Lex—here's your Mountain Dew."

Thank you, Eric.

"You ready to head out?"

You too, Sam.

Without another glance at Addison or Collin, I turn and take Eric's arm, letting him lead me away.

He doesn't talk right away, not until we reach the hallway beyond the stage.

"Well, that looked...interesting," he begins.

"Why did you leave me alone with him? You know I can't—"

"Because you like him, Lex. And...from the way he looks at you, I'm pretty sure he's gonna stay on the dark side." He pauses to smile. "The straight side," he whispers, as if using obscene language. "That means I'm never gonna get a chance at him. So you should."

"But you know I can't."

He reaches over to squeeze my hand, the one holding onto his arm. "I know we Drama Club students don't like to talk about after the show...but there always is after the show for you guys." He smiles. "Addison won't be able to touch you then."

He moves his hand from mine and brings his tongue to his teeth.

"Now—let's talk about your little rendezvous. I noticed that the two of you were standing in front of the big poofy castle. Was that symbolic?"

"Oh—yeah," Sam joins in from the other side of Eric, speaking loudly now that we have made it out to the parking lot. "Like you are in each other's hopes and dreams—in that perfect place you imagine for yourselves."

I pretend to gag.

Sam laughs. "It's so sickeningly poetic. Almost as disgusting as the castle scenery itself."

As we both laugh now, Eric interrupts. "I don't know what's so funny. I'd love to have Collin in my cloud castle...he's much better than all of that other shit Cosette wishes for."

I shake my head, give them both hugs, and head to my car, promising to call both of them after dinner to fill them in about my little meeting with Collin.

Chapter 10

"Come to Me"/"Drink With Me"

Mrs. Leonard is back today, so we are getting to work on the rest of Act II. Well, almost getting to work. The costumes arrived this morning, so Mrs. Leonard has given us about an hour to unpack, organize, and try on.

Since the costumes are rentals, some of us will need alterations. Fortunately, my Act I outfit fits well...and I wear a trench coat for most of Act II, so I'm good to go.

Sarah isn't so lucky. Addison is about her size, so she fits into Cosette's costumes pretty well. But if something were to happen to me (like, I don't know, if I get kicked out of the show or something), she would have trouble. All of my costumes would be way too long on her. I guess Mrs. Leonard would have to arrange for last minute alterations or something.

Eric and Sam both have to get alterations. They complain a little and both worry about how long it will take to get their costumes back. I don't really blame them; the alterations box that Mrs. Leonard put on the stage just keeps getting fuller and fuller.

"I just hope that Addison's dad is paying for these to be taken to a place where there is a quick turnaround time," Eric pouts as he places his costume pieces in the box.

"I doubt it," Sam laments as she parts with her costume, "since I heard that Addison's costumes won't be needing any fixes...why would there be a need for a rush?"

We head down to sit in the auditorium. Our hour is almost up, so Mrs. Leonard should be speaking soon.

We try first to sit in the left section of seats, but we keep moving as we see Casey kissing...well, the back of his head definitely looks like Michael's...

Needless to say, we walk the whole way over to the right side of the auditorium to find seats.

When Miss Price comes out on the stage minutes later, she drops her costumes in the box and heads down the path we just took. But she stops on the left side of the auditorium.

"HEY," she yells. Casey and...yes, Michael, stop kissing to look at her. "I thought I said on the first day that I didn't want to see any making out."

"She's just jealous," Eric whispers. "She needs to find a man. Or maybe a wom—"

Mrs. Leonard's bell begins to ring. Cast members slowly trickle onto the stage and then out into the audience. At least a third of them stop by the alteration box before exiting the stage.

Collin is one of them. I don't know how many pieces he has to have altered, though, because I have to turn away when his eyes start burning into mine.

A couple moments later, after Addison loudly yells his name to get him to come sit by her in the center auditorium seats, I feel it's probably safe to look back up toward the stage.

Mrs. Leonard, who is in a wheelchair—she will be for a little while because of her hip complications—rolls herself center stage and begins to speak.

"To start," she looks around, "I want to thank you, my kind souls, for the hospital gifts—you didn't need to do anything, though." She looks over at our little group of four (Sarah has joined us). "Eric, Sam, Alexa, and Sarah—I loved the balloons. I brought them home, and my dog has been chasing them around the house." She turns next to some of the girls in the chorus who must've sent flowers and then to Zach (half of the Sparkles duo), who must've gone in to see her. Then she thanks Collin, just Collin, for the baked goods he must've dropped off at her house.

"Oh, Lex—I wish you could see Addison's face right now," Eric whispers...and then he continues, singing his words with vibrato. "She's PISSED." He pauses for a second and discreetly, well, discreetly for Eric, looks over at Addison again. "And, better yet, Collin seems to be ignoring her little tantrum."

As Mrs. Leonard moves on to thank Mr. Fiero and Miss Price for their visit, I remind my head to keep looking forward—there is no way that Addison seeing me looking at her can help this situation...or my situation...

I just smile at Eric without moving my head, thanking him for his verbal surveillance monitoring.

Soon, Mrs. Leonard announces her plans for today's rehearsal. It sounds like a pretty intense day for Marius, Enjolras (Sparkles #1, who has spent a LOT of extra time practicing his vocals with Mr. Thoms...and he's getting there...), the bribed boys, and the girls playing boys—those involved in the revolution.

I also have a few scenes today since Éponine pretends to be a boy to join those at the barricade. As Eric puts it, I am a girl pretending to be another girl who is acting like a boy. It's almost as confusing as my Half Block party costume, but like the opposite of it, I think.

I am called almost immediately for a scene with Collin and the other boys...without the Thénardiers or Cosette. I say goodbye to Sam and Eric, who are called to a practice room to go over their music with Mr. Thoms' assistant.

Mrs. Leonard begins blocking, and everything seems to be almost back to normal.

I write down my blocking carefully, making sure that Sarah will easily be able to copy the directions later.

When Marius and Éponine are not singing to each other, I try to avoid looking anywhere close to Collin's direction—especially since Addison is sitting out in the audience, loudly talking to Justin and some bribed boys...

However, it isn't long before Marius and Éponine do have to again sing to each other...and also look at each other. And since I'm already pretty anxious about Mrs. Leonard reading Addison's notes about my acting, I'm not playing any games right now.

When it's my turn to sing, when Marius sees Éponine beneath her disguise, I boldly raise my eyes right up to his face. I see a little surprise behind his deep brown eyes for a second, only a second—so Mrs. Leonard probably doesn't notice the little break in character. His face then fills with desperation, Marius' desperation, as he gives Éponine a letter...the letter for Cosette.

I, of course, can't help but think of the letter I delivered to him in that blue envelope...and its disturbing content...and the fact that opening night is quickly approaching.

I feel my cheeks heat up a little, but I just go with it, pouring all of that extra emotion into Éponine as she sadly agrees to help Marius.

When he hands me the letter, a cream-colored envelope, his thumb brushes over my hand and his eyes grab mine with more intensity than usual.

I become a scattered mess of shaky and fluttery, but I don't look away until his raised eyebrows and the tilt of his head lead me to look down at our hands, at the letter.

And then I see it. Not the letter. The letters. Beneath the plain cream envelope for Cosette is a folded sheet of white notebook paper.

I look back up, and his eyes are wide, serious, pleading...begging me to read his note. His thumb caresses my hand one more time in the brief moment before our blocking parts us. And then we go our separate ways—him to stage left and me offstage to get ready to give Cosette's letter to Valjean.

And to open my own letter.

But before I can do that, Addison shows up beside me.

I clutch my letters in my hand, hoping she doesn't see that I'm holding more than the cream-colored prop for the show.

I don't look over as she begins speaking.

"You looked a little flustered up there, Lex," she begins in a slow, malicious tone, "and I'm sure most people were impressed because it actually worked for Éponine."

I don't move my head, but I clutch the letters more tightly against my non-Addison side.

"You are welcome," she continues. "I'm sure my blue envelope message has been keeping your little mind busy...especially as we get closer and closer to opening night." A mean pause. "I'm just glad you can use your frustration to help you play Éponine. If only—"

Mrs. Leonard's bell rings. Time to move again. Time to deliver my letter to Valjean.

Still not turning to acknowledge Addison, I walk back out on the stage, managing to slip Collin's note into the back pocket of my jeans as I move.

I get through the scene rather quickly, and soon Mrs. Leonard gives us a short break. I go down to the audience, pulling Collin's note out of my pocket as I sit down beside Eric and Sam.

Lexi—please stop avoiding me. I have to talk to you.

Meet me when you can. You know where.

"What's that?" Eric. I hand him the note. Seems easier than having him drag information out of me.

He reads it, hands it to Sam, and then turns to me with his tongue already resting on his teeth. "What are you doing sitting here when he is clearly sitting alone...in the dark...waiting for you?"

"Eric," I start, with the same exasperated look I've been giving him for the last few weeks now.

"I know, I know." He pouts a little and puts his hand over his heart (where, interestingly enough, there is a tiny picture of a little red heart—I'm pretty sure he planned this little movement to go with his shirt today. He was probably just waiting for an excuse to do it). "But he's just so adorable...and the thought of those passionate brown eyes getting all sad makes me want to grab him and—"

"Eric." Sam. "Save your Collin fantasies for later." She turns to me. "You should go see him now—while it's safe."

Huh? "How is it safe?"

Sam looks around before whispering, "Addison is having a little, um, party in the girls' dressing room right now—she's been trying to get people to join her there for the last hour."

"She's drinking here?" I ask, too loudly.

"Shh..." Sam scrunches up her eyebrows to shut me up. "If she gets caught, I'm sure she'll somehow manage to get one of us in trouble for it."

"Sorry," I whisper.

"Don't be sorry," Eric joins the conversation. "Just go while you can. Find out what he needs to say, and then get back here to fill us in as soon as you can." He pouts again. "Nothing interesting has happened yet today. I need to hear something to keep myself going." He flings his head on Sam's shoulder as though a lack of gossip might just kill him.

A second later, I stand up to follow Eric's directions. Not because I'm trying to save or entertain him, though...

No...because I have to know what Collin wants to tell me. And also because the thought of leaving him sitting alone in that closet waiting and waiting for me makes my—

"Lexi—hurry. Go now, before it's too late." Eric pushes me to move. As I walk away, I hear him whispering to Sam. "Shh...*DAYS* is about to start."

When I make it backstage, I almost run right into Casey and Michael, who are kissing.

"Oh, um, sorry, I—"

"GUYS—COME ON. You can make out later," Addison interrupts me, yelling in from the stage left hallway.

As Casey and Michael go to follow her, Addison catches my eye with a smirk, and then she turns to go off to her little party—too distracted by her own plans to even worry about mine.

I wait a few moments...until I can't hear her voice anymore...and then I head back to the little prop closet.

I slip inside quickly, and then we step right back into our old routine. Collin says hello and reaches out to help me sit. I take his hand. And I get a little dizzy. Then I sit down beside him.

And he keeps my hand, like he did that first time. I don't think it's an accident this time, though.

He rests both of our hands on his knees and then begins to rub his thumb back and forth over my fingers, just like he did on the stage.

And we sit there shoulder to shoulder, breathing together in silence.

Fortunately, I have a pretty hard time focusing on any one of the thoughts running through my head—thoughts about the fact that I shouldn't be here, worries that someone could walk in at any moment (specifically a blonde someone), nagging reminders that Collin has a girlfriend...a girlfriend who wouldn't appreciate the fact that I'm holding his hand right now...

I just let these thoughts jumble together in my not unpleasantly dazed mind.

I don't know how much time passes before I finally hear him breathe in to speak.

"I'm not with Addison anymore."

What?

I wait for more words.

"I haven't been with her for a long time—since, um, right after callbacks when she got really mad at me for, uh, something I said."

"She broke up with you for that?" For defending me? For saying I was—

"For that—wait, you know?" He moves a little without dropping my hand. Then I hear three clicks, and my pink roses, my birthday gifts, are now shining from the shelf where I left them many days ago.

Now he's caught my eyes.

"Um, yes." I look down a little. "I heard something about her being mad about what you said about, um—"

"About you," he whispers.

I nod my head, not brave enough to meet his eyes again yet.

"But Lexi," he continues quietly, once again tracing patterns on my hand with his thumb, "she didn't break up with me. I broke it off with her."

"You did?" In my surprise, I look back up at him, at his slightly flushed cheeks and wide, emphatic eyes.

"Of course. She was being so mean—so awful. So different than I'd ever seen her."

"She wasn't always like, um, how she is now?"

"No...well, maybe. I guess I just might not have seen it." He leans forward in thought. I remember Eric saying that she has done stuff in the past, but nothing anything like what she's done this year.

"She just...this year...the rude comments with Casey the first day in the circle when she was so mad at me for sitting by you...and then her tripping you and making it look like your fault...it was horrible."

"You knew that was all her? Even back then?"

"Yeah. I knew that she and Casey were the ones whispering that day in the circle—they were sitting right beside me. And then it only made sense that they tripped you."

"What? Why?" I look over at him again in surprise.

He doesn't look back at me, though. And his cheeks are even more flushed than they were before.

"Because she wanted to put you down in front of me." He continues to look forward. "She was so angry that I defended you...your acting...your looks. She got really jealous...thinking that I maybe...liked you. And she just couldn't stand it."

Maybe...liked me. Maybe, not for sure. And *liked*...not necessarily *like*...

But he does still have my hand.

Now I'm looking forward, straight ahead, too. We are back in our shoulder to shoulder position.

"After I broke up with her, she really lost it."

"When did you break up with her?"

"After that first rehearsal when they tripped you."

"Oh."

"It had to stop. I wanted her to stop doing stuff to you to get to me." A pause. "But I made it even worse." Another pause. His thumb traces some more circles on my hand, and then he continues. "Now she's doing more stuff, worse stuff—like that day she gave you those acting notes in front of everyone. She knew that would infuriate me."

"She's doing all of that stuff to me to make *you* upset?"

He looks over with a small smile. "Kind of. But I know that she's more than happy to be hurting you as well. She's so jealous of you."

I look over at him, scrunching my eyebrows in doubt. "Sure."

"She is—really. Jealous of your voice, your acting, your..."

He looks away.

"Your hold on me."

My shoulders freeze as I stop breathing. His don't move either.

I have so much to say...so many things I need to ask him and tell him, but I'm afraid that my voice will be all shaky and awkward if I open my mouth now.

So I wait. We wait. Shoulders together. *Not* breathing together.

When Mrs. Leonard's bell rings in a warning, I realize that I have to know one thing before he leaves.

"But if you broke up with her, why are you still with her? Throwing a party with her, kissing her, meeting her at Casey's house on opening night?" I spit it all out in a rush before I lose my nerve.

He looks over at me, his shoulders moving up and down again and his face flushed.

"You know about that? The note—what it said?"

I nod slowly.

He also nods his head slowly, but in thought. "That makes sense then—I couldn't figure that one out."

"Wait. What?"

He looks over and talks quickly, knowing that Mrs. Leonard's "GET BACK ONSTAGE NOW" bell will be coming any second.

"I had, um, have, to pretend I'm still dating her...I'll explain that later. But I've gone through the motions—the party, the, um, kissing," he blinks away from me for a second, "and the scavenger hunt...so no one would know that we aren't together. But I couldn't figure out why she'd bother writing that last clue for her hunt—especially when all of the other blue envelopes I got that day had blank pieces of paper inside." He pauses. "She didn't even seal that envelope that you gave me—she wanted you to read it."

Now it's my turn to look away. "I shouldn't have read your message. Sorry."

"Lexi—stop it." He squeezes my hand until I look back at him. "I don't care that you read it. I'm sure she orchestrated everything to make you so curious that you had to read it." He looks at me questioningly. "But wait—how did you know what it meant?"

"Addison told me."

"Of course she did. It all makes se—" He stops himself and looks at me with huge eyes. "That isn't going to happen, Lexi." Even bigger eyes now as he shakes his head. "That was never going to happen—she just wanted you to think it was, I guess."

He rolls his eyes. "Before now, when I thought the message was really just for me, I figured that maybe she thought her, um, gift would be some magical, sick way to get me to come back to her. I couldn't think of—"

And there is Mrs. Leonard's bell. Time to get moving. But neither of us do.

"Meet me here later," he says in a whisper. It isn't a question.

I just nod and then listen as he tells me how we're going to get out of here. He's going out first, and he'll distract Addison so I can leave in another couple minutes.

"But what if she suspects something when you—" I start.

"She's not going to notice. She's drunk."

And yet again, I look at him in surprise.

"Yeah—I know that too," he says with a smile before squeezing my hand, putting it on my lap, and getting up to put our plan into action.

I sit there against the wall for two minutes, thinking, questioning, hoping...

And then I get up, turn off my roses, and sneak out of the closet and back onto the stage.

A later with Collin doesn't come. When we all get back out to the stage, Mrs. Leonard tells us that she wants to run a couple of later Act II scenes with the revolution men (and women playing men). She tells the rest of us to go home a half hour early.

That means that Sam, Eric, and I are all excused. Addison would be too, but she is staying to help Mrs. Leonard, I guess.

Right now, she's hanging all over Collin. When she starts kissing his cheek, I get up and move to leave the stage, but I don't get very far.

Collin's eyes lock with mine. They are apologetic...and reassuring...and heated...all at once.

My legs stop moving, frozen in place. Just like my eyes.

Just as Addison starts to turn my way, Eric notices my predicament.

"Hey, Lex." Eric grabs me as he speaks. "Let's pretend we are in *The Wizard of Oz*." He spins me around, right out of Collin's glance. Then he skips Sam and me down the stairs and out of the auditorium, singing the entire time about scary bears, big tigers, and roaring lions...and also about monkeys, cheetahs, and fish.

He stops as soon as the auditorium door closes behind us, facing me with an expectant look.

"All right, Lex. Spill it all over me." He pouts. "You've already made us wait like forever."

We walk toward the parking lot, and I start, not even sure of where to start. I just let the information fall out as I remember different things Collin said...different things he did.

When I pause for a moment as we reach his car, Eric exclaims, "He held your hand the entire time?"

Before I can answer, he grabs my hand and smells it.

"Yep—smells like male. A fresh, yet husky scent. Would be delicious if it wasn't so...heterosexual."

Sam laughs and nudges him. "You do know you'll never be able to change guys over at your whim, right?"

Eric puts his tongue on his teeth. "Yes...but only imagine if I could." He smiles. "Think what you girls would be left with."

Sam hits him and then spins her cloud of red hair back around to face me again. "Okay...so he knows about her manipulating, her drinking, her—"

"Absolute bitchiness," Eric interrupts her.

"Yes." Sam agrees. "But he's still sort of dating her?"

"Well, something like that. Pretending to, he said." I try to recall the exact words he used, but it's all fuzzy.

"I'm sure she's threatening him just like she's threatening you, Lexi," Eric hypothesizes. "She's probably telling him that she'll get him kicked out. And I think he'd be pretty upset if he lost his part...and upset that the show would be all ruined with no Marius and no understudy."

I nod. I figured that. "But why does she even care? I mean, seriously, if she's messing around with Michael, what does it even matter?"

"Oh, Lexi...you still don't get it." Eric pushes my head on his shoulder and pets my hair. "She wants to have it all—the popularity, the main role in the show, control of the production, the adoring and loving boyfriend. The status," he ends simply.

I lift my head, and my face must still look confused.

"Think about it," he starts again. "How would it look if you, the person who Leonard even thought should've gotten to play Cosette, were able to steal her boyfriend of, like forever?" He pauses. "She would look weak...not in control...all of a sudden not the most desirable thing in the world—in the singing world *and* in the relationship world." He raises his eyebrows and bites his lip. "A serious loss in status."

But there could have been another way. She could have—

"But why didn't she just break up with him?" I verbalize my thoughts.

"Well, because she's dumb," Eric tosses back. "Had she spent less time with all of her threatening, she could've put a much more impressive plan into action." He takes in a big, dramatic breath. "If I had been the one blocking her miserable life, I would've had her break up with him right away, citing a different reason than jealousy over you, of course. Then she could've played her little games on both of you—tripping you up, making you both look stupid in front of Leonard, and eventually getting both of you kicked out of the show."

I scrunch up my eyes in question.

"Calm down, hag. I didn't say that this is what I would've *wanted* to happen...or that it is a decent human being thing to do...I'm just saying that it would've been a smarter move for Addison. Much better than what she's doing now."

"Okay...and you know what she's doing now how exactly?"

"Well, I've known her for years, and I've seen her manipulations—small and rather innocent as they used to be before you came into the picture."

"Face it, Lex," Sam joins in. "With the information you've just given us, it's pretty obvious. Remember—she can't act. She's a freaking wide open, pages scattered all over the place, book."

I smile at her less than conventional metaphor.

"And now she's really screwed it all up," Eric takes over again. "She has different threats, different pieces of blackmail going on all over the place. Plus, she's drinking on top of it. I'm surprised it hasn't all fallen apart yet."

"But she's not dumb, Eric," I contradict his earlier statement. "She has us—she knows that we don't want to lose the show. For ourselves or for others." I look up at him and over to Sam for emphasis.

"Oh, I'm not saying that she doesn't have you, Lex. I'm just making the point that she's getting sloppy. Her plan is sloppy. Everyone can see how talented you are, and her attempts to make you look like you don't know what you're doing just make her look like a jealous bitch."

"But—" I start to speak.

"I'm not finished," he cuts back in, holding up his left pointer finger. "Her attempts to keep Collin are even worse. Everyone can see the annoyance on his face when he looks at her...and then, of course, there's how he looks at you..."

Eric sighs and continues. "I've spent a lot of time focusing on that perfect face of his throughout the years. A lot. I've never seen it look the way it does when you're around. Not when he's looking at me...unfortunately. Definitely not when he's looking at Addison."

Sam nods in agreement.

"And everyone can see it," Eric continues. "So when she parades herself around with him in front of you, she just once again looks like a big old jealous bitch. A super bitch, if you will."

I just shake my head, taking it all in. "So now what? What do I do when he wants to talk to me again? Should I tell him what I know about Addison?"

Eric holds up one hand to silence me and then throws his arms and head over the hood of his car. It only takes a second before he springs back up, stands up straight, and dusts off his shirt.

"I have to think about it, Lex. But I need time. I feel like I just completed one of those ridiculous geometry proof problems right now." He licks his teeth. "Actually, I feel better than I do when I finish my math homework. I think I actually got this one right. No—I know I did."

He smiles. "I've solved Addison."

I sigh. "You might have figured out what she's doing...but the real problem is that she's still doing it."

He smiles and kisses my cheek and then Sam's before opening his car door. "Give me time." He slides in, closes the door, and rolls down the window.

"Ye hags must have faith."

He drives off, window still down, before I can slap him.

Chapter 11

"Turning"

E ric sent me two texts before school this morning. In the first, he told me to wear a coat today.

Apparently, it's getting cold outside.

In the second, he gave me non-weather-related advice. He thinks I should go talk to Collin when he asks to talk to me today—he says he doesn't think I'll be able to say no anyway, so he doesn't see a point in debating it.

Eric was right about the coat. It's freezing today.

I'm pretty sure he's right about Collin too.

As we are about to enter the auditorium for rehearsal, Eric stops and blocks the door for a moment.

"Lex—I'll do my best to keep Addison occupied today. I'll go all Javert on her—you know, crossing enemy lines and everything..."

Just as I shake my head and start to tell him that he shouldn't do that, he puts a finger over my lips to stop me.

"Come on, Lex—it'll be fun to mess with her a little.

I'll just keep asking her how to make each of my movements more like Sacha Baron Cohen's in the movie version. She won't catch on. Promise." He pauses. "Besides, I'd like to think that you'd do the same for me if I wanted to meet some gorgeous guy in a closet."

I smile and pretend to bite his finger so he'll move it and let me talk. "Oh, I would. Let me know when you find him."

He sighs and moves out of the way so I can open the door. "Any day now, Lexi. Any day."

We start to walk into the auditorium, but we both stop in the doorway, shocked by the view in front of us.

Up on the stage, Mrs. Leonard (in her wheelchair), Mr. Fiero, and a couple of chorus girls are busy painting over the fluffy pink cloud castle. The pink is almost gone, and the entire castle is transforming into a dull gray color.

Addison is standing right below the stage with her arms crossed heavily in front of her.

"Oh—my job today is going to be more fun than I thought." Eric jumps up and down, and then he runs down ahead of me to talk to Addison.

I walk slowly down to the right side of the auditorium, far away from Eric, who has already gotten Addison to demonstrate some movements from the movie.

I sit with Sarah, who is looking over her lines.

"I guess it's pretty impossible to understudy for two parts in a huge show like this."

She smiles over at me. "I'm getting there. I just keep accidentally switching some of Cosette and Éponine's lines in the songs where they both sing."

"Makes sense." It really does...with them both being hopelessly stuck on singing about Marius.

I offer to help her run some lines, and we sing through a scene before Eric shows up.

I wait until Sarah leaves to buy some water, and then I ask Eric about Addison.

"Well?" I ask with a smile. "Did she toss you aside, seeing through your little game?"

"Oh, no—she was flattered that I asked her for help. I could tell. At first, I thought she was just humoring me to try to get me to change teams."

I snap my head over to look at him in surprise.

"Oh—not those teams, Lex. Please. I'm all set." He pauses and whispers, "I mean from Team Alexa to Team Addison."

"Ah. But, wait, she didn't try to do that?"

"Well...not yet. It might be in her longterm plans, though."

I raise my eyebrows in mock concern.

"You've got nothing to worry about, Lex. She would never be good hag material. Too much lying...and manipulating...and whining."

I put my hand over my forehead and sigh out some fake relief. "Thank goodness—I'm so glad my position is safe."

He smiles. "Always."

"Okay. So if she's not applying for my spot in your life, what was she doing talking to you so easily?"

"Well," he starts, "we have been on generally okay terms in the past...pretty much because I usually just ignore her shenanigans and stay on her good side. And even though she pretty much hates you—" He pauses. "Sorry."

I shrug. No need to sugarcoat it.

"Well, even though I'm sure she absolutely despises the fact that I'm with you, um, all of the time, she's never really outwardly turned on me. So it's really not like she needs to act any differently around me...and I think she is so pissed today that she'd vent to almost anyone. Well, except you, of course."

"Wait." I sit up in my chair. "Why is she so mad? Does she know I talked to Collin?"

"Calm down. Calm down." He pets my head until I'm again slouched back against my seat. "She doesn't know anything about that. She's all upset about her castle." He starts to whisper again. "Apparently, Leonard HATES the castle and didn't understand why Addison wanted to order it in the first place. I guess in the end Leonard gave in because, well, we all know why, but she must not have realized how pink it was...hence today's paint job."

"So you tried to sympathize with her castle situation, and she took the time to give you help you didn't need with your dance moves. Got it. Nice work, Javert." I lower my voice and look around a little. "But Collin isn't even here yet."

He whispers back. "Well, I thought it would be good to start my distraction operation before he arrived...you know, to throw her off what I'm trying to do here."

I smile and raise my hand to give him a soldier salute. "Gotcha. Good plan."

"I know—it's ingenious." He pauses. "But let's go back to that Collin not being here yet statement. How do you know he isn't here? What if he's already in that little closet waiting for you?"

I roll my eyes over to him. "Eric—you know I haven't been able to think of anything else for the last ten minutes."

He bites his lower lip. "I know. Me too. But I couldn't think of an inconspicuous way to get Addison far enough from the stage for you to be able to slip back there." He pauses. "Don't worry—you'll get to talk to him today. I'll make it happen."

"Thanks, Eric." I pause. "I'll be careful—I won't let you lose your part."

"Eh—I won't lose my part. If Addison tries to pull anything with me, I'll handle Leonard. She can't afford to get rid of a male who can match a pitch."

That's true.

"But still, I'll be careful. For Sam and Sarah too."

He smiles. "I know you will, Lex. Now...just be ready to be amazed by my powers of distraction today."

"Oh, I'm ready." I smile.

Moments later, Mrs. Leonard rings her bell. She is ready to start her announcements for the day. Cast members who have been slowly filtering into the auditorium begin to grab seats. Mr. Fiero and the chorus girls on the stage put away their paintbrushes and come down to sit.

Sam runs in from the back, saying something about having just finished an art project. She plops into the seat on the other side of Eric.

And then Collin shows up...entering from the left side of the stage.

He *was* in the closet.

As he walks, his eyes search the auditorium, not stopping until they rest on me.

And he was waiting for me.

I give him a tiny shrug and point my head over to Addison, who is now sitting with Justin in the front row by the stage. Collin follows my gaze and then turns back to give me a small nod and a slight smile before he looks away again.

"Collliiinnnn—over here." I can actually see the tension build in Collin's shoulders as he turns to follow Addison's voice, her directions. I stop looking at him then—not wanting her to see me looking at him...not wanting to see him with her.

"Gross," Eric mutters beside me, grabbing my hand and slumping back in his seat.

Mrs. Leonard, still on the stage in her wheelchair, begins to run through the day's schedule. And it's busy. Really busy. Music rehearsals in certain practice rooms, costume alteration appointments (already!) in classrooms, and scene work sessions on the stage.

Since Mrs. Leonard is still stuck in her wheelchair, Miss Price is now going to be helping with blocking and choreography for some of the scenes, so she might also be calling different groups throughout the practice.

Eric leans over to whisper in my ear. "Miss Price better watch her back. Addison is probably PISSED that she wasn't asked to do that."

I nod slightly. He's right. She can't be happy about it.

But I have other things to worry about right now...like how Collin and I are going to even get a second to talk amidst this crazy schedule.

Mrs. Leonard continues. She reads off our first assignment locations and says that she will post where we each will need to be for the rest of rehearsal. She is also going to post the schedule for tomorrow (Saturday), which will be similar except for the fact that we will have more hours to rehearse.

For now, I'm due in Practice Room I to run "On My Own" with Mr. Thoms' assistant. Eric and Sam are both scheduled for costume fittings in a little bit. And Collin is due onstage with a large group of boys and girls pretending to be boys.

As I stand to go, Eric looks up to me. "You'll get to talk to him today, Lex. Stop freaking out. I'll take care of it somehow."

I just smile and head in the direction of Practice Room I. On my way through the auditorium, I see him. Collin. Coming right toward me. Addison is beside him holding his hand, but she is leaning over and whispering animatedly to Justin, who is on her other side.

When we are only a few feet apart, Collin looks right at me, but he doesn't slow or stop his pace, Addison's pace. Addison doesn't notice; she keeps talking.

At the moment that we pass, Collin's arm brushes against mine ever so slightly, starting a whirlwind of flutters in my limbs, my head.

I somehow convince my legs to keep moving. I don't get very far before my phone starts buzzing in my pocket. I pull it out as I continue on my way to the practice room.

Eric.

I saw that little brush of skin...even if Addison didn't...

At the end of his message, he has added a little smiley face with its tongue sticking out. I guess there isn't an emoticon where the smiley face puts its tongue on its teeth.

I turn back to look at Eric. He's still sitting with Sam in the same place in the auditorium. I guess they are just killing time before they have to go for their fittings.

I roll my eyes and give him a brief smile before I exit the auditorium to practice.

After running some of my music, I head to the spot in the hallway where Mrs. Leonard (or probably Addison) has hung one of today's schedules. Just as I get to it, my phone buzzes again.

Eric again.

More drama is afoot, Lex. Sam heard Casey tell another girl that she thinks Addison is messing around with Michael.

Casey is all fired up.

Just keeping you in the loop.

P.S. How was that for a vocab sentence?

I smile. His attempts to use the word "afoot" in yesterday's vocab homework were ridiculous. His text sentence at least makes sense.

I start to type back.

Oh, wow. Is she going to say something to Addison? What if Addison thinks I told her?

P.S. I'm impressed with your vocabulary usage. Perhaps now we need not worry that a failing vocabulary grade is afoot. However, we do still need to work on the word "artifice."

While I wait for his response, I turn back to the schedule. I do have a short break for now, but Collin currently has a music rehearsal for "Drink With Me." And then we're both supposed to be on the stage to run the letter scene that we blocked yesterday.

Before my mind is totally lost in thinking about yesterday...and my letter...and his words...his hand, my phone buzzes again.

I don't think you need to worry about this one, Lex.

Casey doesn't even know that you know, so there's no way that she'll mention your name—if she even talks to Addison about it at all.

And it buzzes again.

Now...any luck with Collin?

I've been stuck in this costume room for so long that I feel completely out of touch.

And they are still only working on my first outfit!

I sit in the hallway, lean against the wall, and write him back.

You've been in there for a half hour. Tops. Calm down.
And, no—I haven't seen him yet.
Busy schedules today.

He writes back immediately. I hope he isn't driving the costume people crazy, answering texts instead of holding still.

Hmm...let me think of what artifice I can use to arrange your little talk.

I reply, smiling.

Not bad, not bad. You seriously might pass the test next week.

He buzzes back.

Don't give me too much credit. I used the dictionary on my phone.

During my break, I run lines with Sarah for a little, look over yesterday's blocking a little, and think about my upcoming scenes more than a little.

When Mrs. Leonard rings her bell, I head slowly up to the stage, passing Zach, who was just running Javert's suicide scene. Soon, bribed boys and girl boys start filtering in around me to stand in their spots by what will be the barricade (right now, we're just using chairs and random theatre boxes).

Mrs. Leonard wheels herself off to the left side of the stage, saying that she's going to go through the hallway, down the ramp, and around to the seating area in the auditorium so she can watch.

And then Collin arrives...but once again, Addison is on his arm. When he looks at me, he quickly rolls his eyes up to the ceiling and then over to Addison.

I start to smile but look away when I see her head turning toward me.

As soon as she sees me, she snuggles in closer to Collin, resting her head on his shoulder and then standing up on her tiptoes to kiss him on the cheek.

I try not to watch—because she wants me to watch...and also because it's making my stomach all crampy—but I can't seem to rip my eyes away.

And I guess I'm kind of glad I don't look away because soon she pulls Collin into a hug—one where she gets his arms, but I get his eyes.

He stares right at me...right into me, shaking his head slowly in annoyance, in apology.

So here we are. Addison embracing him. Him lazily holding his arms up around her. His eyes clinging to mine. My feet fused to the floor.

I do take a second to realize how ridiculous the three of us must look.

But I cannot move.

I don't move—not until Addison pulls back from her hug and breaks the moment. She wishes Collin luck with the scene and then flips her shiny head of hair around, gives me an even shinier smile, and finally goes to walk down the stage steps and into the audience seats.

As I head to my starting place, I see her plop down in the front row. I'm guessing there will be absolutely no chance that I'll get to talk to Collin during our scene work today.

Unless Eric manages to get out of the costume room so he can work some miracles...

Eventually, Mrs. Leonard comes wheeling in from the back of the auditorium, a little out of breath from her trip through the hallway on the side of the stage, down the ramp, and around to the back of the auditorium.

"Wow. That took longer than I thought it would," she says as she parks herself in front of the stage. "Now, make it worth my time, my little stars. Make this good." She smiles and then nods for Mr. Thoms to begin the opening for Act II.

And I hope we are making it worth her while.

It feels good. It sounds good. No one is missing any cues, and the blocking seems to be going smoothly. Even my blocking with Collin runs smoothly.

To a viewer in the audience, I would assume that we just look like the fiercely intense Marius and the passionate, yet rejected, Éponine. I doubt from, say, even the first row, that it's obvious that Collin holds my eyes a couple seconds longer than the blocking calls for...or that his grip on my arm is much stronger than necessary.

Hopefully, that viewer, that blonde viewer, in the audience also doesn't notice that Éponine is trembling slightly more than usual, that her stomach is pounding so hard that she can barely hear the lines being sung around her...

From what I can tell, Addison hasn't noticed anything. But she's watching closely. VERY closely.

So I'm rather torn when it's almost time for Collin to hand me the letter from Marius; I want there to be a letter for me as well, but it's a little too risky for him to give me a note right now.

I panic a little as he pulls out that cream-colored envelope...panic that there will be another hidden underneath...panic that there won't be...

He gives me the letter, staring at me through his Marius eyes and brushing my fingers oh so slightly—as though by accident.

I hurry off stage right, my hand still tingling, unable to tell if I'm holding more than a prop.

I'm not, I realize as I get to the side of the stage and look. There's no letter for me...just the cream—

My phone buzzes in my pocket. Maybe Eric has come up with a way to get Addison out of the auditorium.

I have a couple minutes while the bribed boys are switching up our makeshift scenery, so I pull out my phone to check the text.

It's not from Eric, though. It's from a new number.

Lexi—it's Collin. Eric gave me your number. I hope that's okay.

We need to talk, but she's EVERYWHERE today.

I look up, out toward the stage, and *he* is looking my way from the left wing. I can't make out the exact look in his eyes from here, but his mouth is smiling.

Mine is too.

I only have a couple seconds before I have to go out to give the letter to Valjean, so I type quickly.

I've noticed. What's that about? Does she know something?

I look out to the stage, and the boys are still fiddling around with the pretend barricade. Mrs. Leonard is yelling about this having to be a faster change once we have the real scenery.

I look off stage left, and Collin is just putting his phone in his pocket, smiling over at me once more.

And now my pocket is buzzing again. I still seem to have time, so I check it.

No—I don't think that she does.

I think that Casey suspects something, or knows something, about Addison fooling around with Michael—so Addie's being extra clingy with me, I guess.

I flip my head up and look over at him. I know my mouth is hanging open a little.

You know about Addison and Michael?

I hit SEND, and then it's time for my scene with Valjean.

My phone buzzes three times during the scene, but it's on silent, so there's no way that Mr. Fiero, or Mrs. Leonard, or Addison can hear it over all of the piano and drums and singing.

I have another moment on stage right before "On My Own" is set to begin, so I pull out my phone yet again.

Three texts. The first one is from Eric.

Did he text you?

I write back quickly.

Yes. You are awesome.

Then I open my second text. From Collin.

Well, I overheard Casey whispering something about it to Justin earlier today.

Then Justin talked to Addie, and Addie got all flustered and clingy.

So I guess I just figured that something was really going on with them.

My third text is also from Collin.

Wait—do *you* know something about Addison and Michael?

I bite my lip, wishing that Eric could be beside me right now to help me answer that question.

My phone buzzes again as I stand there. Well, Eric is kind of here, I guess.

I open his message.

I know I'm awesome. What is he saying?

I peek out and see that pieces of scenery are STILL being moved on the stage as Mrs. Leonard yells a stream of directions.

He wants me to tell him what I know about Addison and Michael.

Eric buzzes back almost immediately.

Tell him.

Another buzz.

He won't tell her. He likes you too much.

There is another smiley face with its tongue hanging out at the end of his message.

Scenery still moving. Quick reply.

Okay. Thanks, Eric. What would I do without you?

Another buzz.

**You'll never have to find out.
#HagsgettheVIPtreatment.**

And another buzz.

**By the way, I'm FINALLY done with my costumes. I
have a break now.**

**On my way to the auditorium to watch you do your
song.**

I send back a smiley face and then put my phone back in my pocket.

My intro begins seconds later, so I step onto the stage and throw myself into Éponine.

I end the song all by myself on the stage, kneeling on the floor, hugging my arms around my stomach. Anguish on my face.

I hear Eric whistling as Mrs. Leonard says, "Thank you, Alexa. That was most definitely worth my trip down here to watch."

Then I look over to the left side of the stage, where Collin is smiling and silently clapping his hands for me.

Needless to say, Éponine's grief vanishes pretty quickly from my face.

I get up, and Mrs. Leonard rings her bell again. Time to move on.

I am scheduled next to run some finale music with Valjean and Fantine while Javert and the soldiers work on the next scene on the stage. As I head back to Practice Room I, I see Collin once again. He still stands behind the curtain in the left wing.

His eyes grip mine as I get closer, but I don't stop; Addison would definitely notice.

I just keep walking, keeping my eyes on his. When I pass, he brushes my arm with his again and then rubs the back of his hand against mine.

And there is nothing but him and me and a buzzing in my head. Our fingers interlace and clench together for a moment, a second only, and then they separate.

I move past him without (hopefully) drawing any attention to us.

I try to regulate my breathing as I turn out into the hallway, but then Eric jumps out and grabs me, taking away my breath altogether.

"You were awesome up there, Lex. I think you made my makeup run."

I pull back a little in his arms to look up at him. "You aren't wearing any makeup."

He smiles. "I know—but if I was, it would've been running."

I smile. "Thanks, I think."

He loosens his arms a little so we can walk side by side, his arm slung over my shoulder.

"I hope you had a little moment with him on your way out here. I managed to get Addison's eyes off of the two of you, but I had to pretend to care as she told me her sob Casey story."

I smile up at him in thanks as we stop in front of Practice Room I.

"Did you tell Collin about Michael?"

"Not yet." I shrug. "No time yet."

He cracks open the practice room door, sees that it's empty inside, and then starts to push me forward.

"Well, get in there—you should have a second before the others arrive."

I open the door further, slipping my phone out of my pocket simultaneously. Eric pushes me in.

"Go ahead. Text him. And then write me."

He gives me a final push and then shuts the door behind me before heading to his next session.

Okay. I sit on the floor, lean against the wall, and tell Collin everything I'm supposed to be keeping from him.

I do know about Addison and Michael. I saw them together at the Half Block. And then Addison saw me and said that she'd get me...and Eric and Sam...and I guess you, kicked out of the show if I told you. I'm sorry I have to tell you this and that I didn't say anything sooner. But her threats seemed pretty real. And she's been so mean ever since...

Even though I can't stop thinking about nightmare scenarios where Addison sees this message on Collin's phone or just somehow finds out about this, I hit the SEND button.

No going back now.

No time for more messaging either.

Mr. Fiero and Miss Price have just arrived, so I'm sure we'll be starting soon.

I wait until my music session is over, until I get back out into the hallway, to check the three messages that have made my pocket buzz during the last twenty minutes or so.

They are all from Collin.

Message number one.

You don't need to be sorry about anything. I'm sorry she threatened you.

She's doing the same thing to me...if I don't pretend to be dating her, she's not only going to try to get me kicked out...but you too.

I won't let that happen. Don't worry.

Message number two.

And don't be sorry about Michael. I don't care what she does or has done with him.

It keeps her away from me.

One more message.

I want to talk more, but I probably won't be able to text you tonight. I have to go—now, actually. Mrs. Leonard just told us to leave a few minutes early to get ready. I have to take Addison to this memorial service for her mother. Her dad has one every year, and he obviously thinks we're still together—so I have to go.

But I wish I could be with you.

My hand, my arm, my stomach—they all shake a little as I get up the nerve to write back. But I manage to do it.

Me too.

Chapter 12

"Empty Chairs at Empty Tables"

Today begins just like yesterday—with two texts from Eric. The first one comes right at 7:00, just as I'm getting out of bed.

Ready to die today?

The second one comes moments later.

Wear a scarf. Really cold. Chance of snow. Or freezing rain.

Fortunately, I understand both of these messages. I hit reply as I walk toward the bathroom to brush my teeth.

Getting ready now. 8:00 call time. When are you coming in?

I finish with my teeth, wash my face, and put in my contacts before my phone buzzes again.

Not until 11:00. You'll already be dead and gone.

I roll my eyes at the phone.

Eponine will be dead. I will be home trying to finish my paper for French class.

I start to get dressed, but soon my phone goes off again.

You'll be home so early. I'll expect regular Channel 12 updates.

I roll my eyes again.

Eric—I am not sitting and watching local programming all day just to hope for a glimpse of your hot weatherman substitute.

Dressed. Hair up in ponytail.
Another buzz.

You don't know what you're missing, Lex.

He'll be so excited about the storm.

It's gotta be a pretty big break for a sub. He'll be all fast talking and hair tossing.

I know his tongue is on his teeth right now.

I might check him out while I'm writing my paper.

I liked it better when you were obsessed with the shopping channel guy, though.

I'd rather watch new clothing and gadgets than weather maps.

I add a smiley face before I send the text.

Breakfast time.

Another buzz.

Sorry, Lex. Gotta follow my heart and all of that cliché stuff.

Besides, the shopping channel guy got all stuffy after he switched to selling jewelry and started selling out all of the time.

The arrogance just wasn't attractive.

Another buzz.

Now he's sent me a picture of the substitute weather guy. Not a great picture—clearly a picture of the TV taken from his phone.

I write back.

He is pretty hot. And humble-looking, I guess.

Buzz.

Oh I know, Lex.

Another buzz.

He's no Collin, though.

Speaking of Collin...I hit reply.

Hey—I've gotta run. Don't want to be late. Talk later.

He replies right away.

Have fun, my sweet Eponine.

There are only two other cars in the parking lot when I arrive at school.

Only Collin and I are scheduled for the first block of rehearsal today. That means that the only people here will be Mrs. Leonard, Collin, me...and Addison, I'm sure.

I walk into the auditorium and see right away that I'm correct. Mrs. Leonard is in her wheelchair at the front. Addison is right beside her, sitting in the first row of seats.

Collin is by himself. He's sitting on the edge of the stage with his arms leaning back on his palms and his legs dangling.

Dark jeans today. Gray hoodie. The start of a smile on his mouth as I approach the front of the auditorium.

I give him a tiny smile too and then turn away quickly—before Addison catches me.

As I put my coat (and scarf—thanks, Eric and hot weatherman) down in a seat, I am reminded of the text that came late last night when I was already in bed.

Interesting night. Casey and Michael came too. Lots of mean looks...but no catfights.

Thank God the memorial service didn't give them much opportunity to talk.

Have happy dreams. See you tomorrow.

I feel a smile creeping back up on my face, but I manage to squelch it before I look over toward Mrs. Leonard...and Addison...for instructions.

Mrs. Leonard is ready to start.

"All right, Alexa. Why don't you jump up on the stage? I want to get this blocked and ready to go before it gets all noisy in here."

As I start toward the stage left staircase, I hear Mrs. Leonard explain to Addison that it's a good idea to block intimate scenes like this in a quiet environment...that this part is such a quiet, yet intense, scene that it would be completely broken if other cast members and scenery builders were milling about.

I don't hear any response from Addison. And I don't know if she is looking at me, so when I arrive on the stage, I sit a safe few feet away from Collin. And I don't look over at him.

"Oh, you two are going to have to get much closer for this scene." Mrs. Leonard wheels herself right up to the edge of the stage as she talks.

Addison doesn't say anything. But I can see the fire in her eyes.

"This part," Mrs. Leonard goes on, "I feel, is the most powerful love scene in the whole show."

I don't look at Addison. Or Collin.

"Cosette and Marius are in love, yes, but they don't have a scene as tragically passionate as this one." She puts a finger on her bottom lip in thought. "I think that sense of tragedy...that sense of passion...is what makes this scene so memorable, so compelling for the audience."

She looks over at me. "Alexa—you, Éponine, have lived this life of misery, and in this moment you are clinging to Marius, clinging to the one chance you have for a moment of happiness, a precious moment in his arms before you give in to death."

She takes her finger from her lips and balls her hand into a fist, clenching it for emphasis. "I have to see all of that, feel all of that, from a seat in the audience—the initial pain of being shot, the euphoria of being in his arms, the effort you use to cling to him, and then, finally, the contented way you slip into death."

I nod and take some mental notes as she turns her focus to Collin.

"And from you, I need anguish and an...an overwhelming want, no, need, to hold her, to comfort her. To be with her."

I see Collin nod out of the corner of my eye. I also notice that Addison is angrily flipping through pages in her script...actually not looking at us for a second.

I sneak a glance at Collin...and see that he is doing the same thing—looking at me. His lips are slightly parted, and his face is somewhat flushed.

I cannot breathe. Or think.

"Okay." Mrs. Leonard claps her hands, forcing our faces back to her. Addison's head also lifts back up at the sound. "Here's what I need you to do."

She begins to read through her blocking for the scene. I take down notes in my script for Sarah and for me in case I forget anything later.

I don't look over at Collin. I look only at Mrs. Leonard, my pencil, and my script as I write down where I'm shot, when I fall down, how he'll hold me, the way she wants our faces to be positioned only inches apart...

When she finishes reading us our blocking, she gives us a minute to look over it all before we put it on its feet. Since we already have these lines memorized, we will be working without our scripts—so we'll "have our arms free," as she puts it.

I read over the notes I've taken. Well, I try. Everything looks a little blurry right now.

And soon it's time. Mrs. Leonard claps and tells us to get into our starting places.

I stand up and head toward stage right just as Collin starts to move to the left side of the stage. Our eyes come together for just a blink as we cross paths.

He's still pretty flushed.

I'm sure I am too.

Somehow, I move past him to my spot on the right side of the stage. From there, I look out into the almost empty audience and see Addison.

Her face is red too. REALLY red. She catches my eye for one brief, scathing look and then turns away sweetly, asking Mrs. Leonard how she can help with the scene.

Mrs. Leonard tells her to just watch with her for the first run-through. And then she tells us to begin. No singing—just movement since we aren't running it with Mr. Thoms yet.

"Just get wrapped into the feel of it," she says.

Okay. Here we go.

I pretend to be shot, falling backward and holding my wound. He rushes over behind me and guides me down to the floor. As we fall down together, he begins to move his arms to hold me, to pull me closer and—

"Stop." Mrs. Leonard.

He pulls his arms back. We both stand up.

"You've got to fall so you end up closer to him—so the top half of you is resting on his lap...but with your faces out so you aren't hidden from the audience."

She nods for us to return to our places. "Try it again. Keep up the emotion—I love it."

I go over to stage right, and he returns to stage left. I get shot again, and I hold myself in shock, in agony.

When I feel him approach, I begin my fall. He moves right behind me and pulls me into him, my back pressed firmly against his chest and his breath on my neck.

We fall down together, just like that, and I end up sprawled out over his lap, our faces so close togeth—

"Stop. But don't move."

We both freeze, looking out. Heads close together, his chin right beside my forehead.

"That is almost perfect, but I'm missing some of your face, Éponine." She looks at us pensively. "Collin, if you could just move your arm over. No, not like that. If you just—"

"Mrs. Leonard?" Someone is behind me...well, behind us, on the stage.

"Oh—Jim." Mrs. Leonard looks away from us for a second. "You are here already. Excellent. I'll show you the small pieces I'd like you to work on while I'm still using the stage for rehearsal. Then after 2:00, the stage is all yours, and you can do the barricade and the bigger flats."

"Sounds good." Jim starts to talk about his crew, and his tools, and some other stuff, but I'm not really hearing much of it.

I'm hearing Collin as he breathes beside me. And I hear the fuzzy noise in my ears that started as soon as he pulled me against him. And—

"Okay, Jim, I'll be right there. I'll meet you in the hallway to show you where everything is."

Jim heads out to the hallway, and Mrs. Leonard looks back at us.

"You two—don't move. I'll be right up to fix your arm, Collin. And we'll have this. We're so close."

We just continue to stare out as she flips her chair around and heads back the auditorium aisle.

And then she pauses after wheeling only a couple feet. "Addison—why don't you help me? If I do this myself, it's going to take forever. And we just don't have that much time anymore."

Addison looks up at us. Angry, vicious eyes. I move my own eyes down to avoid her glare.

This isn't my fault. It isn't anyone's fault.

And she knows that there is no logical reason she can give to say no to Mrs. Leonard.

I watch the bottom half of her with my lowered eyes as she gets up, walks over to the aisle, and begins to push Mrs. Leonard back toward the exit doors.

Everything is silent...everything stands still as Addison slowly pushes her out of the auditorium.

I keep my eyes lowered. I don't know if she looks back.

I do know that Collin's grip on me has tightened...and that my skin under his arms is prickling with heat.

As each second passes, I can feel both of our heartbeats getting faster and faster.

And then the auditorium door slams shut.

I move my eyes up, and I look out into a sea of completely empty seats.

"Lexi," he whispers, and his face gets even closer. He leans his chin down, rubbing his face against my hair. And then his lips are pressing a kiss on my forehead as his arms tighten even more around me.

Time stops. For I don't know how long.

I can hear myself breathing. Unevenly. Without—

"Lexi." Another whisper.

Slowly, I push up my eyes, my head, my lips, and we are just a few breaths away from—

The stage left hallway door is opening. The fast click of heels approaching can only belong to one person.

In just a slight adjustment of our heads, we are back to our blocking position. Almost. Collin hasn't loosened his grip around me.

I brace myself for her looks, her words. But surprisingly, she gives us neither. She is behind us, upstage, though.

"Over there is the castle for my scene." She is talking to someone. A member of the crew? "Mrs. Leonard thought this dim color would be the best choice for it, but I'm sort of afraid that it won't, you know, pop out to the audience. Is there some sort of shiny coat—"

Another sound from that stage left door. Wheels rolling.

"Addie, did you show Austin the tape we put down for the barricade?"

"I was just getting to that." Her heels click around a little as she, I guess, points out the small pieces of glow in the dark tape that mark where the barricade is supposed to be placed.

As she does that, Mrs. Leonard's wheels come closer to us.

"Okay." She shows up right in front of us, reaching out and grabbing Collin's arm. "Let's try here." She puts his hand further down on my arm and then pushes his chin to tilt it closer to my head.

"Perfect." She pulls her hands back to her lap and smiles. "This is where I'd like you to begin the song."

I can feel his head nod as I murmur in understanding.

"Okay. Let's try it again. Back to starting positions."

As we disentangle ourselves from each other, I pray that my face is not quite as red as it feels...and that I can convince my feet to walk over to my starting place.

It works. Well, I make it over to the right side of the stage, moving without meeting Collin's eyes...and without looking at Addison, who is still with us on the stage.

I can still feel the heat on my face, though.

Mrs. Leonard says "GO" and we start again, me getting shot and him holding me.

And we do it again.

And again.

Our scattered breaths and his tight hold on me just become part of our blocking.

Addison eventually watches us from below, and Mr. Thoms and part of the pit show up, so we add in the song.

Collin sings, looking right into my eyes with a piercing gaze. I sing back to him, falling further into his arms and breathing in short gasps (which is actually called for in Mrs. Leonard's blocking at this point).

At the end of the song, he lets out a cry as I pretend to die, resting my head on his lap...his hand in my hair.

And Mrs. Leonard claps. And claps. And she tells us that this scene will steal the show.

Then she is ready to move on...now to some Act II scenes with Marius and Cosette.

I slowly lift my head, my body, from the warmth of Collin's lap. He squeezes his arms one last time around me before releasing me.

My eyes dart back out to the audience to see if Addison noticed that extra second of embrace. I can't tell, though. She just looks angry in general.

Now no longer touching Collin at all, I make my way off the stage, careful not to look in his direction.

I am done for the day...I'm done with Act II blocking in general. Well, I do walk on as a ghost for some lines in the finale, but Mrs. Leonard doesn't want me to stick around for that—she plans to just add me (and Miss Price) in when we start our run-throughs next week.

So I head out, stopping to pick up my coat and scarf in the auditorium on my way to the back doors.

I try to think of an excuse to turn around, to see him, to be able to say goodbye, but I can't. I know Addison is going to see me if I try...and she's already mad.

So I push through the doors and leave the auditorium.

I haven't quite reached the main doors of the building when my phone buzzes in my back pocket.

I slip it out as I continue to walk toward the doors.

I couldn't think of a way to get to say goodbye to you.

I wanted to, though.

Smiling, I walk through an exit door and out of the building...warm all over even as it begins to snow outside.

Chapter 13

"A Little Fall of Rain"

What started out as a little bit of snow has turned into a mess of wind, freezing rain, and ice. It's now Monday, and the storm hasn't let up for the last two days. We don't have school today, and they've already called us off for tomorrow.

With only a week and a half until opening night, I'm pretty sure Mrs. Leonard is freaking out. The email she sent us early this morning was pretty calm, though.

My Stars,

I've gotten special permission to run a modified rehearsal schedule today. I am allowed to bring essential cast members in to run scenes that still need work before we begin our run-throughs (hopefully) on Wednesday. I would like to see Valjean, Cosette, Javert, Marius, and the revolution students at 8:00. If any of you listed above cannot make it (if your neighborhood roads are too bad or if your parents don't want you to come in), please just give me a call.

As for the rest of you, you have today and tomorrow off. Your scenes already seem to have that flow we need for starting dress and tech rehearsals. We will start these rehearsals on Wednesday, and it looks like your first little audience will still be coming that day.

No need to panic. We will get through this, I know. The set was finished yesterday, and costume alterations have been completed. We just need to put all of the pieces together, and we will on Wednesday.

Get your beauty sleep, take some Vitamin C, and rest those lovely voices.

Love,

Mrs. Leonard

"I can't believe those little sixth graders are still coming on Wednesday. Seriously, I know that Addison's father already arranged for the rights or royalties or whatever...but I really thought Leonard would have canceled at least Wednesday's dress rehearsal performance." Eric closes my laptop and leans back in his spot on my living room couch.

"Did you really think I'd lie about what Mrs. Leonard wrote in her email?" I roll my eyes at him from across the room in my dad's recliner chair.

"Well, I just thought you read it wrong or maybe too fast before you called me this morning."

I shake my head. "Nope. They really are coming. Our first audience...and our first whole run-through on the same day."

Eric flings his head against the back of the couch. "This storm blows—it's gonna ruin our show." He sighs. "It's almost worse than Addison...if that's even possible."

He sighs again and rolls his head over to the television. "Hello, gorgeous. You are the only bright side of this whole day." He puts his tongue on his top teeth and stares at the weatherman, his substitute weatherman, who has been popping on and off the screen all morning.

"I'm so glad I could be off school to share his big day with him." He looks over at me. "How many substitute weathermen get to cover such a big storm?"

I shrug my shoulders. I don't know. I've honestly watched more weather reports today than I've ever seen in my entire life.

"Thanks for watching with me, Lex." He smiles for a beat and then stops as a new thought occurs to him. "I guess we'll have to figure out a way to switch back and forth when *DAYS* comes on."

"I'm sure we'll be able to work it out." I smile at his television predicament and then slip my phone out of my pocket. Even though I haven't heard it buzz recently.

"Did he write?"

"Not this morning yet, no." I try not to be too disappointed. He is at rehearsal, after all.

"Why don't you send him one first today?" His eyes start to gleam. "I can write it if you want."

"No," I reply quickly, putting my phone back into my fuzzy pajama pant pocket before he can reach over and grab it out of my hands. "He might be on the stage. And he might have forgotten to put his phone on silent. And—"

"And you are nervous about making a move on your own." Eric props his slippered feet up on the coffee table and raises his eyebrows at me. "He likes you, Lex. You have nothing to worry about."

I look away from his bossy eyes. "But, technically, he's still sort of with Addison."

"Yeah—but only because he's protecting you from getting kicked out of the show," Eric flings back.

A pause. A breath. "But he'd probably do that for anyone...so it doesn't necessarily mean anything...and he's never come right out and said that he likes me..."

A pillow flies at me from the other side of the room, knocking my glasses into my face.

"HEY," I yell and throw the pillow back at Eric. "You're lucky I have been too lazy to put my contacts in yet. Are you trying to blind me or something?"

"You are already blind. Somehow, you are missing all of the heated looks Collin's sending your way." Tongue back on teeth again. "If he looked at me like that, I wouldn't be able to look away. Ever."

"I know how he looks at me." And how he manages to brush up against me casually when we pass each other. And how his heart beats in an erratic rhythm when we are really close. And how he almost kissed me on Saturday...

"All right." Eric slides over on the couch so he's closer to my chair. "Show me his texts from the weekend." He reaches his hand out for my phone.

When I hesitate, he blinks his eyes and tilts his head a little toward me. "I promise I won't send him any messages...even though I should. You two are never gonna get this thing moving."

I slap the phone into his hand. "We can't get anything moving, remember? Not if we'd like to be in the show."

"But the show is almost over...and at this rate, it's gonna take until graduation for you to even go out on a date."

He thumbs through my phone, trying to find Collin's messages from yesterday. "Now, shhh...let me read. I deserve some entertainment after I risked my life biking on the ice to keep you company today."

I move over to the couch to sit beside him. "Yeah—the news is always clogged up with stories about hospitalized ice storm bike riders."

He looks up from my phone with an over-the-top offended look. "Do you want me to go?"

I put my head on his shoulder. "No. I'd be so bored." I would be bored. My parents still went in to work today, even though a lot of businesses are closed. When they woke me up to say goodbye this morning, they said something about trying to build a client list and needing to be available.

And I understand. It's just really boring being alone in the house.

Eric smiles. "Okay...I guess I'll stay then. Your neighbors will just have to miss out on another glimpse of me pedaling in my pajamas this morning." He strikes a little pose in his purple and white striped pajama set.

"They'll have to deal." I smile, and we both turn back to look at my phone and Collin's messages from the last two days.

Eric scrolls up to the one he sent right after I was leaving rehearsal on Saturday.

"Wait—where are the ones from before this?" He looks down at me.

I raise my head off of his shoulder. "I deleted them."

When he scrunches up his eyes in confusion, I continue. "Those messages were proof that I told Collin about Michael and everything. I couldn't stop worrying that I'd leave my phone somewhere and Addison would somehow find it and see what I did and then get us kicked out of the show. Even if I lock my phone, there are ways to get around—"

"Stop. Stop." He shakes his head to stop my stream of concerns. "It was probably smart." He pushes his lips together and then out in some sort of thought. "Especially with phone collection coming up—I forgot about that."

"Wait—what?"

"Oh, our phones interfere with the microphone system or something, so Leonard makes us put them all in a box from tech week on...just to make sure that no one is tempted to use them backstage. She makes a big old obnoxious announcement to the audience before the curtain opens too...basically nicely, but not that nicely, telling them not to ruin all of the work we've done just to send a message or update a status on Facebook or something."

Oh. "I guess I'd better delete the other messages too, then." I reach over for the phone.

He swats my hand away. "Wait. I get to see them first."

He starts to scroll down from that Saturday message, and we both just lean back on the couch to read.

I read silently. Eric reads every word aloud dramatically...he even reads when the messages were sent. He thinks it makes it more theatrical.

Saturday 2:00 P.M.

Whole show is blocked now. Just finished the finale. Mrs. Leonard sang your part.

Saturday 2:01 P.M.

Wish you could've stayed...

Saturday 2:02 P.M.

Me too. Addison would have freaked out, though.

Saturday 2:04 P.M.

She's already freaking out. She asked if I kissed you.

Saturday 2:10 P.M.

Oh. What did you tell her?

Eric puts the phone down and laughs. "It took you six entire minutes to respond to his message?"

I swat him on the shoulder. "Shut up. I didn't know what to say."

He shakes his head with a little smirk and then picks up the phone to continue reading.

Saturday 2:12 P.M.

I told her the truth. Well...the truth about what happened.

Not about what I wanted to happen.

Eric pushes the phone down on his lap again and then starts fanning himself with his hand.

"Holy Madonna and Gaga, Lex. You think he hasn't told you that he likes you?" He pauses. "I'm pretty sure that was his oh so hot way of doing it right there."

Before I can open my mouth to respond, he grabs my chin and pulls me to face him. "And now you're blushing, Lex. So innocent for a hag."

I scrunch up my apparently flushed face in a grimace. He goes back to my phone.

Saturday 2:13 P.M.

But she still seems really suspicious. And clingy.

Saturday 2:14 P.M.

Hey—it looks like she is finishing up her conversation with Mrs. Leonard right now. Gotta run.

I'll text you later tonight—after another party with Addie.

Saturday 2:15 P.M.

Okay. Talk later ☺

Saturday 10:00 P.M.

STILL at the party. Casey and Michael are here too.

Saturday 10:33 P.M.

Sorry. Just got this. Was taking a shower.

Saturday 10:33 P.M.
Are Casey and Addison talking again?

Saturday 10:35 P.M.
Sort of. You can tell that Casey's still mad, though.

And she keeps making out with Michael in front of us.

It's rather disturbing.

Saturday 10:36 P.M.
Ew. That does sound disturbing. How is Addison taking it?

Saturday 10:37 P.M.
Oh, fine, I think. But I've caught her and Michael giving each other looks a couple times. I'm pretty sure stuff is still going on there.

Saturday 10:37 P.M.
Wow.

Saturday 10:40 P.M.
It's ridiculous.

Hey—Addison is waving me over to her. She wants to dance or something.

Gotta run. Talk tomorrow?

Saturday 10:41 P.M.
Sure. Goodnight.

Saturday 10:41 P.M.
Night, Lex.

"Night, Lex." Eric looks over at me and bats his eyes.

"Shut up." I push his face away, back toward the phone.

Sunday 11:00 A.M.
Back at school. Scenery is up. It looks awesome!

Sunday 11:03 A.M.
Can't wait to see it. But with this storm, I wonder if we'll even be going in tomorrow.

Sunday 12:13 P.M.
Sorry. Addie came out and was ready to do pictures. We just finished.

She's changing out of her costume now.

Sunday 12:13 P.M.
Mrs. Leonard is all worried about tomorrow's forecast. She thinks school will be canceled.

Sunday 12:14 P.M.

That means no rehearsal, right?

Sunday 12:15 P.M.

I guess so.

Sunday 12:15 P.M.

But what will we do? We have those sixth graders coming in on Wednesday already.

Sunday 12:16 P.M.

Maybe the sixth grade performance will get pushed back. I don't know.

This hasn't happened before.

Sunday 12:16 P.M.

Gotta run. I hear Addison coming back. Talk Later ☺

Sunday 12:17 P.M.

Later ☺

Sunday 4:05 P.M.

"Hold on." This time, I am the one who pushes the phone down. "What was with Addison and the pictures? What were they doing?"

Eric rolls his eyes. "Oh, just another ritual. Addison gets in her different costumes and has pictures taken in front of the various set pieces. She makes Collin do it too. Then she makes a scrapbook or something. It's ridiculous."

"And Mrs. Leonard helps with this?"

"Well, not really. They usually do it on a day when Leonard is already in there organizing costumes or props or something. Collin takes most of the pictures. I guess Leonard only takes the ones of the two of them together."

He shrugs. "They've done it every year, so I'm sure Leonard is just used to it by now."

I shake my head a little. "I just can't believe that she is making Collin do all of this when they aren't really even together anymore."

"She's determined, Lex. She's trying to maintain this image where everything is perfect and she has it all—a leading role, the guy, the father with all of the money and power..." He pauses. "But seriously, she's not doing a good job. People are starting to see through her with the Michael stuff, all of the drinking, the crap she's been doing to you..."

"Why is she slipping this much though if she really wants people to believe she has it all together?"

He sighs. "I don't know, Lex. Maybe she's just so delusional that she doesn't think people will figure it all out."

"Maybe. But it seems strange. Like she's really losing it or something."

Eric snaps his face over to me. "Don't tell me you're starting to feel bad for her."

I shake my head. "No...but it's just odd, I guess."

I pull the phone back up from his lap. "Let's keep reading so I can delete these messages."

Sunday 4:05 P.M.

Just got the call. No school tomorrow. Mrs. Leonard's gonna flip.

Sunday 4:06 P.M.

We're never going to be ready for Wednesday. Those kids are going to laugh at us.

Sunday 4:07 P.M.

Seriously—some of the scenes really need work. Yesterday, two of the guys bumped into each other and spilled water everywhere during "Drink With Me." It was a mess.

Sunday 4:08 P.M.

The sixth graders would have found that hilarious, I'm sure.

Sunday 4:09 P.M.

Yeah...but at least they're young.

They won't really be going around and giving us bad press.

Sunday 4:10 P.M.

By the time the eighth graders see it next Monday, we should have everything together.

Sunday 4:10 P.M.

I hope so.

Sunday 4:10 P.M.

Hey—gotta go get ready. Early dinner with my parents tonight.

Sunday 4:11 P.M.

Have fun!

"You had dinner at 4:30 or something? What are you? 85?"

I swat him for like the tenth time today. "Hey—my parents had a late meeting with a new client. I'll take what time I can get with them."

Eric starts to scroll down my phone once again.

Sunday 10:00 P.M.

Just heard from Addison. Sounds like Mrs. Leonard has a rehearsal idea up her sleeve.

I'm pretty sure there will be an early and LONG practice in the morning, so I'm gonna go get some sleep.

Maybe I'll see you tomorrow! Goodnight.

Sunday 10:01 P.M.

Goodnight, Collin.

Eric tilts his head over to me in a pout.

"What?"

"I'm so sad that there is no more to read. And that you don't get to see him at rehearsal today."

Me too.

And about the fact that he hasn't sent me a message yet today.

Eric hands me back my phone and then leans back on the couch. "Now what? I need more entertainment."

We decide to watch *Singin' in the Rain*. We have to pause the DVD and turn back to Channel 12 every fifteen minutes to see if there is a weather update, though. And then, if there is a weather update, we of course keep the movie paused to watch it.

When it's time for *DAYS*, we stop the movie and then flip between Channel 12 and Eric's "story" for the next hour. I try to focus on the characters...and on the weather guy...but I spend most of my time looking at my phone and wondering why it still isn't buzzing.

After *DAYS*, we make some sandwiches and go back to our *Singin' in the Rain* and Channel 12 routine.

I realize that I must've fallen asleep on the couch when I'm all of a sudden startled by a buzz at my side.

A text. Finally.

I grab the phone to open my message.

WAKE UP!

From Eric.

I look at the other side of the couch, and he is silently laughing at me. I grab the pillow under my head, getting ready to throw it, and he yells, covering his face with his hands.

"Wait, Lex. I wasn't being mean. Really." He smiles and claps his hands a little. "Your phone buzzed right before I sent you that message, and you didn't hear it or feel it. So I just sent one to try to wake you up."

Oh. I put the pillow back under my head.

And then I sit straight up on the couch.

"Wait—there was another buzz?"

Now he's laughing out loud. "Yep." He raises his eyebrows. "I thought you might want to check it out."

I pull my phone back up to my face and see that I do have another message.

And from Collin.

As I push the button to open the message, Eric slides over beside me on the couch.

Hello, Alexa. This is Addison.

Oh my God.

Eric moves even closer to me, our faces both locked on the phone. We both read silently.

Imagine my surprise when I collected phones this morning and found your name in Collin's contact list. As if that wasn't upsetting enough, I then saw that he sent you a text yesterday to give you a heads-up for rehearsal.

Maybe I'll see you tomorrow!

I'm not quite sure why he has your number, but I'm even less sure of why you would even respond to a message from a guy with a girlfriend. Especially when *I* am that girlfriend. I suggest that you no longer communicate with him at all when you aren't in the middle of a scene. No text messages, no little visits to the prop closet, no anything. Unless you don't really care about getting to be in the show. Or about Eric, and Sam, and Sarah. I think you do care, though. So you'd better start making some careful decisions. I'll be watching.

Oh—sorry if you pathetically thought this was going to be from Collin.

He won't be writing to you anymore.

I drop the phone onto my lap, no longer wanting to be anywhere close to her poisonous message. I turn my head over to Eric and see that his mouth is hanging just as far open as mine is. Neither of us is going to say anything...cause, really, what is there to say? Even if—

My phone buzzes again. We both reach for it, but I get to it first.

One message. From Collin.

Or so it says.

Lexi?

I drop the phone once more, knowing that I can't write anything back.

Seconds later, it buzzes yet again.

Eric and I repeat our blocking from before, except this time he gets to the phone first and pushes the button to open the message.

Lexi—are you there?

I snatch the phone from Eric's hands and reach out to put it on the coffee table, far away from my dangerous fingers. When I lean back on the couch, Eric grabs my hand and sits with me in silence...both of us staring straight ahead at the phone in front of us.

When it buzzes, vibrating against the wooden table, it makes both of us jump. Eric looks over at me, squeezes my hand, and then reaches forward to grab the phone with his other hand.

And a second later, the text is open in front of us.

Good girl, Alexa.

Just testing to make sure you understand my rules.

You passed. This time.

Now, delete Collin's number from your phone.

The snow is finally slowing down. And it's Tuesday. It looks like we'll actually go to school tomorrow. I hope so. Mrs. Leonard emailed us again early this morning. She called the same people as yesterday for rehearsal today. And she does plan on having our promo performance for the sixth graders tomorrow.

Eric is going to come over again today to keep me company. We'll watch *DAYS* and the weather and just lay (Mr. Fiero would have said "lie") around.

We won't be reading any texts, though. Collin is no longer even listed in my phone.

Eric and I decided it would be best...easiest...safest...to listen to Addison for now, especially with phone collection coming up tomorrow. We deleted Collin's number before Eric biked home last night.

I was so relieved that Collin must've gotten rid of our earlier texts...so grateful that Addison didn't just figure the whole thing out...that I didn't freak out that much when I hit the DELETE button.

I freaked out much later, when I was already in bed for the night and left with nothing but thoughts about him...thoughts about what she probably said to him...thoughts about what he might have said to her...thoughts about what might happen when I see him again...

I'm freaking out again tonight, sleepless in my bed.
I watch the minutes and hours tick by on my alarm clock...watch it getting closer and closer to tomorrow.

Eric did offer to try to distract Addison during our run-through tomorrow to give me a chance to see Collin. I told him not to...I don't need to give Addison any new reasons to be suspicious.

But what's going to happen when I see Collin tomorrow? How am I going to walk away if he wants to talk?

How am I going to handle it if he doesn't?

Chapter 14

"Stars" and "Little People"

It's noon. Time to get ready for our first promo performance.

"It's *Rainbow Tour* time," Eric squeals excitedly as we head with Sam to the auditorium.

"I still don't get why you call it that every year," Sam starts, and then Eric joins her as they both say, "We don't even go anywhere" in ridiculously annoying voices. Then they both start laughing as I stare and wait for them to explain this little moment to me.

Sam stops laughing first and starts to enlighten me. "Addison says that to Eric every single year—always like she's coming up with a brand new thought, a brand new sentence. Listen—you'll hear her say it to him today."

"Well, that's only if she decides to talk to me today," Eric stops laughing and joins in the conversation as we reach the back auditorium doors. "I kind of doubt she'll be talking to anyone who associates with my girl, here." He pulls his hand from the auditorium door so he can put his arm around me.

"Now, Lex, for the million dollar *Double* Hag *Jeopardy* question, do you know what I mean by the *Rainbow Tour*?"

I smile over at him as he looks at me expectantly and also somewhat nervously...like he thinks I won't win the game show.

No need to worry. I'll win.

He holds his hand (the one not around my shoulder) up to my mouth as a fist microphone.

"Well, *Alex*, I might not be able to put my answer in question format, but I'll wager everything on this one." I lean down to speak directly into his microphone.

"This whole approaching week where we do part of our show for students of younger grades is called the *Rainbow Tour* because we're taking time out of our busy schedules, in our case out of our school schedules since we have to miss a few math and science classes—"

I pause for a moment as Eric interrupts to say "Thank God...and Leonard...and Cher."

I give him a look and then continue. "We miss these to promote ourselves, to promote our show, and to thus ensure a higher success rate, measured by greater ticket sales."

I lower my voice and slow down dramatically. "This is much like what Eva Peron did in *Evita* when she took the time to tour different countries in order to further herself and further her husband's success in Argentina. And Eva Peron's experience was called the *Rainbow Tour*."

Eric drops his fake microphone and picks me up for a spinning hug.

Sam claps beside us, yelling, "*Alex*, we have a winner!"

Eventually, Eric puts me down and opens the auditorium door, but we are still all laughing as we walk in.

But not for long...

Addison and Collin are again kneeling on the stage, just like they were when this whole thing started. This time, however, they are in their wedding attire.

And they are just about to kiss.

"Sorry, Lexi," Eric whispers over to me and grabs my hand. "I forgot that this would be coming today. I usually try not to pay attention to their schedule of rituals."

I glue my eyes to the floor and trust Eric to guide me down the auditorium aisle.

He nudges me. "Hey—at least this is the last one they do onstage."

"That we know of," Sam blurts out on the other side of him.

I feel Eric move his body to now nudge her.

"Sorry, Lex," Sam says, probably looking over at me but I really can't tell. "Just giving full disclosure."

"Thanks, Sam." Head still down. Watching my feet getting closer and closer to the stage.

"Couldn't they have done this over the weekend...or in the middle of the night...or at least at some point when the rest of us aren't around?" Sarah comes over to us and whispers her questions as we reach the front part of the auditorium.

I look up at Eric in a quick warning. Sarah doesn't know everything about Collin yet...only bits and pieces that she's overheard.

He gives me an exaggerated offended look, offended that I might think he'd forget who knows what gossip, and then turns to Sarah.

"Sarah, you know the routines have specific times and places. The end scene costumed extravaganza," he waves his hand in the direction of the stage, "*always* happens on opening day of the *Rainbow Tour*."

Sarah laughs and adopts the annoying voice I heard both Eric and Sam use earlier. "I still don't get why you call it the *Rainbow Tour*."

Sam and Eric both join in as Sarah says, "We don't even go anywhere."

I can't help myself from laughing with them.

Apparently we are too loud, though.

Addison clears her throat from her spot on the stage. I forget not to look in their direction and end up staring right into deep brown Marius eyes.

Just like all of those weeks ago when I saw him in the same position, he looks bored, uncomfortable, embarrassed...

There's more there now, though. Irritation. Concern. Anxiety. And at least a little of what was on his face the last time that I saw him...when I was in his arms, only inches away from his mouth.

Addison clears her throat again, and I tear my eyes away from Collin.

Addison speaks. "Everyone is supposed to get dressed and then report to the band room for hair and makeup. The sixth graders will be here at 12:45." She pauses and then looks right at me. "Oh, and the phone collection box is in the band room."

Eric tugs on my arm, and we move quickly up onto the left side of the stage and out into the stage left hallway. I keep my eyes down until we finally reach the girls' dressing room, where Eric drops me off. We agree to meet back up in the band room in a few minutes so he can help me with my hair and makeup.

When I open the dressing room door, multiple girls look my way, and Casey, who is in the center of a large group, stops talking mid-sentence.

Before I even know how to react to this, Casey says, "Oh, it's you. Shut the door, please."

I do as I'm told and then pretend not to hear the conversation going on around me...rumors that Addison is meeting Michael secretly on school nights after practice...questions about the status of her relationship with Collin...comments about her stupid cloud castle...

I dress quickly and leave the room, again closing the door behind me. When I meet up with Eric in the band room, I fill him in, shocked that so many people were talking about Addison behind her back.

"Let me guess," Eric whispers with a roll of his eyes as he tries to find a tube of foundation to match my face, "you feel bad for her."

"Well..." I don't know how to finish my thought.

Eric puts his hands on my cheeks so I can't look away from him. "There should be no 'well' or any question about this. Have you forgotten all about your little first rehearsal trip, or about the acting notes she gave you in front of everyone? And what about this week's text message?"

"Of course I haven't forgotten." I pry his hands off of my cheeks. "But still...you yourself said that she's been slipping...that she's not on top of her mean game anymore. Something's wrong."

"You are unbelievable." Eric shakes his head and goes back to his foundation matching.

I shake my head. "I'm not saying she isn't awful or that the very thought of her doesn't make me feel like sticking something in my eye. I'm just saying that something really must be wrong if even Casey is complaining this much about her and if so many people are noticing her little slipups."

"Okay, Lex." Satisfied with the latest tube he picked up, he begins to apply foundation to my face. "But that is not for you to worry about. What you need to worry about involves getting to see Collin without getting caught."

"I don't know if that is going to happen. She's not going to let him out of her sight."

Eric motions for me to close my eyes. "Something will work out." He rubs foundation over my eyelids. "I'm sure he'll find a way to talk to you."

I just shrug, trying not to move my face too much.

I don't know that he will try to talk to me. I don't know what Addison said to him...or what he's thinking...

Eric asks me to open my eyes so he can do my bottom liner, and soon he has me shut them again so he can work with my eye shadow.

He starts going on about layers and blends of colors for Éponine, saying that he talked to Mrs. Leonard about how to redo some of my makeup when I switch from the young Éponine to the older one. He then spends a few minutes detailing the changes he'll make.

And then, all of a sudden, he stops.

"Don't open your eyes, Lex, but—"

I start to interrupt. "I won't until you're finis—"

"SHHH," he whispers close to my face. I can feel his breath on my nose. "They just walked in together. And he looked at you. Right at you, Lex."

I use every bit of control I can come up with to keep my eyes shut.

"I wish you could've seen the look on his face, Lex." He leans even closer to me, his breath now even warmer on my face. "Like I said before, I'm pretty sure he'll find a way to talk to you today." He pauses. "I'm positive."

I feel a brush of eye shadow sweep over my eyelid. And then another. And another. He wasn't kidding about blending colors.

Eventually, all of the brushing and blending moves to my other eye, and then I hear Eric open his mouth to start whispering again.

"Lexi."

Only it's not Eric's voice. And it's not Eric's cologne I'm breathing in.

"Don't open your eyes. Eric will kill me if I mess up your makeup."

I hear Eric laughing from inches away...inches away from me...and inches away from *him*...which means that *he* is only inches away from m—

"Addison just left for a second to get a brush or something, so I don't have much time." He pauses. "I need to talk to you, though. Soon. I will figure something out." Another pause. And a squeeze of my hands in my lap. "You look beautiful. Those sixth graders are going to love you today."

And just like that, his hand is gone, his voice is gone, and my stomach is fluttering all around.

"Told you." Another whisper. Eric again.

"What did you do?" I whisper back.

"Nothing. I swear. As soon as she left the room, he was over here. And I'm pretty sure he came because he wanted to talk to you. Not because he was trying to find an excuse to sit so close to me." He pauses and sighs. "Unfortunately."

I smile, trying to use just my mouth, not my eyes. I don't want to get into trouble for messing up my makeup either.

Moments later, Eric tells me that he is done with my eye shadow...that it's time for me to be able to see again.

Before I open my eyes, I ask him where they are...where I should try not to look. Apparently, they are a few rows behind us. And Addison is putting on Collin's eye makeup right now, sitting almost in his lap.

I definitely don't want to see that.

So I look straight ahead as Eric finishes with my cheeks, lips, and hair. And I continue to look forward as Sam and Sarah join us. Eric does his own makeup and then works on both Sam and Sarah while we all try to help Sarah run her Cosette and Éponine lines. She really has both parts down.

"You are freaking amazing," Eric tells Sarah as he applies blush to Sam's cheeks. "I didn't have all of my own lines down until last week." He pauses. "It blows that you don't even get to perform these roles. You don't even get any credit for doing all of this work."

"Well," Sarah says gently beside me, "it'll be in the program." A pause. "And hopefully it makes Mrs. Leonard think about giving me a lead next year."

"You better get a lead next year," Eric exclaims. "And we'll be there in the front row to obnoxiously cheer you on."

Sarah laughs. "I guess we'll see."

Eric isn't done with the conversation. "You have to beat Casey out for the lead—don't let her become the new Addison."

"Maybe we'll do another show where there will be more than one female lead," Sarah responds. "Like *Guys and Dolls* or something."

We spend the next ten minutes or so trying to come up with shows that have two female leads.

Eventually, Mr. Croft, the sound guy, comes in to help us with our microphones. And then Mrs. Leonard shows up to talk to us. We all cheer when we see that her wheelchair is gone. She quiets us down, saying that she isn't much faster on the crutches she's now using.

She reminds us that we're all responsible for the schoolwork we will miss on these performance days. She then encourages us to keep trying to sell tickets. And finally she tells us that it's time to get into places.

After that, there is a lot of hugging, a lot of excitement. Even though this is really only a dress rehearsal performance and even though it's for such a young audience, everyone is pretty pumped.

An audience is an audience.

And we get to be in costumes. And the set is up. And the whole pit is here.

It *is* pretty exciting.

But I don't get to think about that for very long. Because soon I'm walking out of the band room. And Addison is standing at the door with a big box marked PHONE COLLECTION.

She looks me right in the eye as I place my phone in the box. Her text message, her warning, flashes through my mind.

I move past her as quickly as I can, and I head to my place (which isn't actually on the stage since I was kicked out of this first scene).

I try not to look for Collin as I walk across the stage to the right wing. Well...I try not to make it look like I'm looking for him.

I don't see him, though.

And before I know it, the house lights are off and the music is beginning.

The bribed boys and a bunch of girls dressed as men are in place for the opening song. And one of them, one of those dark shapes on the stage, is Addison. It's too dark to know which one, which means that it's also too dark for her to be able to see me.

I take a bit of comfort from that thought as I stand in the wing, listen to the pit play, and wait for the curtain to open.

When it finally does open, the stage comes to life. Dejected men in dark, drab prison outfits move across the stage in their chain gang.

They look good. Their movements are together, and the sheer number of people chained in a row on the stage creates the pure misery that surrounds this show.

A little, only a little—because it was a long time ago now—of the anger from getting kicked out of this scene comes back as I stand there and watch.

But then I think of all that has happened since that day, since my fall, and my mind takes on a whole new train of—

And then I see him. Collin. Across the stage, right behind the curtain on the left wing.

He raises his hand in a little open-fingered wave. I am just about to wave back when I feel a tap on my shoulder.

I turn around, and it's Miss Price in her Fantine dress and wig.

"Hello, Alexa."

"Hi," I reply, hoping that Collin can see that she stopped me...that I didn't just turn away from him.

"I'm just following up on that little conversation we had recently." She pauses. "About Addison, remember?"

I look around to make sure no one is listening. "Yes, I remember," I whisper back.

Miss Price looks me straight in the eyes. "Is she still harassing you?"

"No, um, she wasn't...she's not harassing me."

"Why does she keep staring at you then? She's even done it a couple of times in the last few minutes—from the stage."

She has? Wow. Maybe I should be grateful that Miss Price stopped me before I could wave back to Collin.

"What's that about?" Miss Price is still staring at me.

"Um, I'm not sure exactly. But it's fine. Nothing to worry about."

"Well, I'm worried about it. And so is Mr. Fiero."

"Well, um, I guess I can let you know if she says anything to me."

She smiles a little, feeling that we are making progress here, I guess. "Wonderful. Now, if you want me to say something to Mrs. Leon—"

"Please don't." Now I smile as reassuringly as I can. "There's really nothing to tell her anyway."

She raises her eyebrows, back to a serious face. "Okay...for now...but you let me know if anything changes."

"Sure. No problem."

Fortunately, she has to get on the stage for her opening scenes.

I watch from that same spot, trying to keep my eyes on the new scenery and the costumes and the characters on the stage...trying not to look over into the left wing.

When another tap hits my shoulder, I am surprised since Miss Price is currently on the stage with Mr. Fiero.

I turn around and see Addison, who is now dressed like the young, filthy Cosette.

Our eyes meet, but she says nothing. Just glares. I don't even know why she's over here. Her next entrance is from the other side.

But soon, I get it.

"Oh, Collin. There you are." She rushes to the back part of the wing, where Collin has just appeared.

I try not to let my head, my eyes, focus on him, but I don't succeed. Not at all.

I catch his frustrated eyes for a split second before she moves in and starts kissing him. Now, at least, I succeed in moving my eyes away.

I can still hear her, though.

"How did you know to find me over here, honey? Did you see me walk around?" She says it in a firm, "you'd better answer this correctly," tone.

He mumbles a yes-type sound, and she says something about him being so sweet.

She says it even though she knows that he is lying. Even though she knows that he wouldn't have been looking for her, considering they haven't really been dating for weeks...

She asks him to walk her back around behind the dark stage, saying she's afraid that she'll trip in her dress.

She never says why she is over here in the first place, but she doesn't need to. All three of us know what she is doing. And she is succeeding. Collin and I don't even get a second together.

Soon, they are gone, and I continue to watch the action on the stage until it is my turn to go on as the young, sitting because I'm too tall to actually be playing a child, Éponine.

Eric and Sam play the ever-loving parents to me. They run their fingers through my hair and lean down to give me hugs every chance they get.

After our scene, Eric grabs me in the hall and asks if I heard the kids in the crowd gushing about the cloud castle.

I did.

Based on the noises from the audience, I would say that the castle is definitely a hit with the sixth graders, who are probably finding some of the themes and lyrics above their heads.

I'm guessing that will be the case for Eric's upcoming "Master of the House" rendition. Actually, I hope so.

At least the kids got permission slips signed for this...

The show continues and I watch again from the sidelines, this time from the left wing...from the spot where Collin was standing not so long ago.

Eventually, I head back to the dressing room to transform into the older Éponine. Once I have changed, Eric finds me and reworks my hair and makeup a little—some different shades of color, a new hairstyle, and some dirt looking stuff on my cheeks.

As Eric paints my face, he complains about some of the missed lighting cues and sound mistakes. Apparently, his microphone went in and out a little during his song. And Sam's did too. I tell him that I didn't notice anything like that from the side of the stage, but it's really hard to notice sound issues unless you're in the audience or the one wearing the microphone, I guess.

I try to comfort him, reminding him that these types of things are supposed to happen during tech week. He's pretty upset, though, since there is still an audience out there.

I don't blame him. I would be upset too.

He does ask me if I've talked to Collin, but, of course, I haven't. I haven't even seen him since he left to walk Addison to the other side of the stage, and that was many scenes ago.

I'll be seeing him soon, though. Onstage. Our scenes are going to start in just a couple short minutes.

Eric brushes some powder over my face and tells me that I'm ready to go. Then we walk together back to the left wing of the stage.

And then I see him. Collin. Waiting only a few steps away from us.

But there are arms wrapped possessively around his waist...so I don't go anywhere near him.

When the lights dim, I find my place on the stage. I can't help but notice a ringleted head of fake hair now standing in that spot just behind the left wing curtain.

Addison in Cosette's wig.

She's going to be watching us even while we're on the stage...giving us no opportunity for an unblocked look at each other...no chance for anything really but for Éponine and Marius to talk about Cosette.

And we both stick to that, stick to our blocking. The looks we give to each other belong to Marius and Éponine.

When the three of us all sing "A Heart Full of Love," Éponine's face fills with desperation for Marius. The adoring love on Marius' face is directed at Cosette.

When we finish the song, Mrs. Leonard yells "STOP" from the audience.

From what Eric told me earlier, Mrs. Leonard does this at a designated time when the promo performance must stop—no matter how far we've gotten. It has something to do with giving the audience members enough time for a Q&A session before they have to leave to catch their busses.

Mrs. Leonard asks Mr. Croft to turn on the house lights, and she tells all cast members to have a seat on the stage. The sixth graders are then given fifteen minutes to ask whatever questions they have.

Not many kids raise their hands. Maybe ten out of like seven hundred.

Some of the questions are about the plot of *Les Misérables* itself, some are about the costumes, and others are about trying to get tickets.

Only one question stands out. A kid in the third row with red wavy hair and glasses stands up and says that she's seen this show on Broadway and also the movie version. She says that she doesn't remember there ever being an actual cloud castle. And she wants to know why we have one.

Eric starts poking me in the side, and I can hear him trying to hold back laughter. I don't look at him. I can't. I bite my lip and look down at my lap as Addison snaps something about "creative interpretations" of the show. Justin tries to help her with her answer, but the rest of the cast sits silently.

Eric leans over. "Did you notice that Leonard isn't even acknowledging this question?" He whispers, "I love that she's refusing to take any responsibility for that dumb ass cloud castle."

I keep my head down, knowing that I'll laugh if I look up.

Fortunately, the question and answer session ends after Addison's response. The kids leave, and we pick up right where we left off—right after "A Heart Full of Love."

Addison keeps up her watch—both on and off of the stage—as we finish Act I and go into Act II. Eric has started to call her MCA for Mall Cop Addison. I guess her efforts remind him of those mall security guards who keep close eyes on teenagers on Friday and Saturday nights at the mall. Sam reminds him that Addison probably has more power than those, as she calls them, "mall stalkers."

The two of them carry on this discussion as I wait to head back onto the stage for "On My Own" and my upcoming death scene. I can't concentrate on their words, though, as I start to remember what it felt like to be in Collin's arms...where I'll be again in only a few moments...

Well, more than moments now, I guess. The change of scenery takes forever. Mrs. Leonard again yells the whole way through it.

And then, finally, it's done. It's ready. I sing "On My Own" to the empty auditorium, and before I know it, I'm just about to get shot again.

And he's there just as I start to fall. He guides me to our position on the floor. Me in his arms, his chin resting on the top of my head.

When I start to sing to him, we both pull back a little to look at each other. And his eyes are sorrowful...and gentle...and loving.

For a moment, I feel a pang of jealousy...jealous of the way that Marius is looking at Éponine.

And then I realize that I have no need to be envious. As I sing, he opens his lips and mouths "Lexi" as he delicately brushes a piece of hair from my forehead. My breath catches a little, and my deathbed singing is probably a bit shakier than usual, but I get through it, raising my hand up to his warm cheek right before I exhale for the last time.

The song ends, Mrs. Leonard shouts that she "loved the emotion" today, and soon it's time for me to be carried off and away from him.

And I can't talk to him. Both of our microphones are on. I can't even look up at him. I'm sure Addison would notice.

So I do what I can do; I let my hand fall on his before some bribed boys come to pick me up, out of his arms. I squeeze his fingers ever so slightly and listen as his breathing stops for a second. Then, before I know it, I am lifted up and taken off the stage, already thinking about getting to do this scene again during tomorrow's run.

Thursday's run is much the same. Except there is no audience, and our entire rehearsal is after school.

Addison is still everywhere, Eric and Sam continue to make fun of her, and I just keep waiting for the five minutes that I get to be with Collin.

And when we get to that scene, when I settle down into his arms, he holds me even tighter than the last time, our faces closer together than ever before as he sings me to my death.

Mrs. Leonard again applauds the emotional intensity of the scene, and we again reluctantly part for another twenty-four hours.

F riday brings our faces even closer...but before we even get there, we perform Act I and the start of Act II for an auditorium full of seventh graders. We finish the scene where Éponine takes the letter from Marius, and then we have to stop for the Q&A session.

Mrs. Leonard congratulates us for speeding up scene changes and shaving about fifteen minutes off of Act I, and then she begins to take questions from our young audience. These kids have more questions than the sixth graders did, and the questions are slightly more intelligent.

One kid asks why Javert is so mean to Valjean (Sparkles #2 fields this question for his character). Another kid asks a specific question about the building of the barricade set, a question that Mrs. Leonard attempts to answer but really just dances around.

There are also questions about buying tickets, which is great because, well, that is our main purpose in even doing these promo days.

The kids' voices and comments begin to blend together until one little boy in the back mentions me in his question.

"What does Marius write in that letter that he gives to Éponine?"

I don't jump to answer because, really, Valjean reads the letter in the show and could easily answer this question. It's not Mr. Fiero's voice that speaks up, though.

It's Addison's. It sounds like she is sitting somewhere on the right side of the stage. And I'm sure that Collin is sitting beside her. I don't look, though.

"Well, the letter is a declaration, a promise of love for Cosette and Marius. For Valjean, it means a realization that Cosette is in love." She pauses. "And for Éponine, it's a painful reminder of what she can't have...what she'll never have. So it means different things to many different people."

I feel the familiar jab of Eric's elbow leaning into my side and then hear his whisper. "Just like her face means different things to different people. Personally, for example, it makes me think of wanting to scratch out my eyes."

"Shhh." I nudge him back, laughing.

And soon the Q&A session is over, so we move on to the rest of the show.

Before I am pulled out of Collin's arms, I let my hand rest on his a little longer than usual. I won't see him all weekend. I have no idea where he'll be or what he'll be doing. But I know that he'll be with her...and that she'll be watching him carefully.

My weekend almost passes without any excitement. Some family time when my parents aren't in their office, some thrift store shopping with Eric and Sam, and lots of time catching up on class work I've already missed during the *Rainbow Tour*.

Not much excitement...not until Sunday morning, when my parents find a package for me on the porch. "Lexi" is scribbled on the outside of the yellow shipping envelope. I take the package from my mother and run upstairs to open it. Inside, there is a note, just a couple of lines.

One more week, Lexi. Then no more pretending.

—Collin

Attached to the note are three fiber optic roses, much like the ones he gave me for my birthday.

I worry for a moment that this might be some sort of trick, that the package might actually be from Addison.

But the handwriting looks like Collin's. It's nothing like what I saw in that disgusting blue envelope message that Addison wrote.

And, besides that, Addison doesn't know that I know about all of the pretending.

I still call Eric for reassurance. He agrees with me; he says it has to be from Collin.

He sounds really sure. Too sure.

"How do you know that?" I ask suspiciously.

"Well," he starts slowly, teasingly, "he might have asked me for your home address on Friday during rehearsal..."

It really is from him. My face finally feels free to smile, and I turn on the roses and place them in a little cup on my dresser as I balance the phone with my ear and shoulder.

"Thanks, Eric. I owe you one."

"What I need you to do," he starts right away, "is to get the regular weatherman on Channel 12 to get sick again." He makes his voice overly pouty. "I miss him, Lex. My sub. I don't know if I'll ever see him again."

He goes on about his lost weatherman for a bit more, and then he starts to talk about the new student (I'm not the new kid anymore) who just joined our French class. Apparently, this guy, Lance, just called to ask Eric to go somewhere with him next week, but Eric can't go because of rehearsal. Eric reenacts the entire phone conversation for me, using different voices so he can play both himself and Lance. He then ends this part of our conversation, saying that he plans on setting something up with him as soon as the play is over.

Moments later, when we're on a new topic involving English homework, Eric all of a sudden exclaims, "Wait—we should double." He pauses. "For the prom. If you start seeing Collin, and things work out for me and Lance, then we can all go to the prom together."

"Eric—the prom is in May. That's like five months away."

He gets a little fake huffy. "What are you saying? Don't you think I can hold a relationship for that long?"

I laugh. "Of course I do. I'm just...I don't know."

"Nervous about Collin?"

"Well, a little, yes. Nothing has even really happened yet. With Addison lurking around so much, it's hard to believe that it ever will." I pause and smile into the phone. "And you are probably already mentally designing my prom dress."

"Aqua. Princess cut. Hair not in a ponytail for once. Strappy sandals. Long silver earr—"

"ERIC." I can't keep myself from laughing even as I yell.

Then I change the subject back to him. "Just ask the guy out, okay? Then we'll go from there."

There is silence on the phone as Eric waits to make sure that I'm finished talking.

"As I was saying, long silver earrings..."

I groan, but he keeps going.

"A tasteful, yet sparkly, wrist corsage...and the most gorgeous guy in school on your arm."

I try not to let myself get too wrapped up in his fantasy. Addison might still have something else up her sleeve. I can't get that out of my mind.

"We'll see," I reply to Eric, before quickly adding, "the outfit does sound pretty awesome."

"I know," he says.

And then we agree to get off of the phone to try to catch up on some schoolwork. We have another half day tomorrow for our last promotional performance.

"Bye, Eric."

"Night...hag."

UGH!

Chapter 15

"What Have I Done?"

The *Rainbow Tour* isn't exactly over, but it's definitely different today. Our audience this afternoon is made up of eighth graders, and these kids bring whole new challenges to the performance. Teachers, their teachers, are standing throughout the audience, closely monitoring behavior. Apparently, two kids have already been taken out by one of the junior high principals. Sarah saw it happen when she was onstage for the "Lovely Ladies" scene.

What makes this really crazy is that only certain students were even allowed to come today. Students with low grades and those with previous discipline issues (and those, I guess, who fall into both of these categories) were left behind at the school.

Sam has a younger sister in eighth grade, and she (Katie) filled her in on all of the details. Katie was eligible to come today, and I'm pretty sure she's one of the students not getting into trouble in the audience right now.

Mrs. Leonard gave us a pep talk before we started. She reminded us that "bright and shining performers" should always be grateful to have an audience, happy to have people who want to see us onstage.

And then she told us that we must ignore anything that happens amongst these "people" as we perform. If teachers are yelling, students are talking, people are throwing things, or whatever, we must just keep going.

So that is what we've been doing. And the show has been going really well. We've gotten Act I down to a reasonable length now that scene changes and lighting cues seem to be running pretty smoothly.

I also try to make my own agenda go smoothly; I attempt to avoid Addison and try not to notice that her eyes follow me everywhere...on the stage, off the stage, in the dressing room...even when I'm in the halls during the school day.

I don't try to talk to Collin. I think I do a pretty good job of pretending that my eyes don't naturally move to his when he is in the same room, that I don't have to physically push down my head to stop myself from looking for him backstage...

And when we are on the stage as Marius and Éponine, our glances are intense and our moves are passionate, but Addison can't really fault us for that. It's in our blocking.

What's not in my blocking is the heat on my face...and the quickening of my heartbeat...but I can't be called out on either of these. The lights could be making my face red...and, really, who can hear my heartbeat?

When I talk to Eric about this in between acts, he brings up that Poe story..."The Tell-Tale Heart"...where the insane guy says he hears a heart beating. Then Eric starts to compare Addison to that guy. As I listen to his ridiculous comparisons, I check my makeup and adjust the belt on my, well, Éponine's, trench coat.

And soon, Mrs. Leonard calls us for a quick Act II pep talk. We gather around her in the band room. I stand between Sam and Eric and try not to notice Addison as she clings to

Collin on the other side of the room. I do notice, though, and I accidentally meet Collin's waiting eyes for a split second before I snap my head back to look at Mrs. Leonard.

Before Mrs. Leonard talks, Addison gives a quick reminder about the party at Casey's house on opening night. At first I think that this is the first time I'm hearing about this. But then I remember the note in that blue envelope. I look over at Eric and whisper that I don't want to go (even though what Addison wanted to happen at that party shouldn't be happening). Eric says that we can do something else that night. He also whispers that he's surprised that Casey is still even having the party now that she and Addison aren't exactly on the best terms.

Soon, Mrs. Leonard takes over. She asks us again to focus and to just ignore any distractions from the audience. She also reminds us to keep going if there are any other technical mishaps as we go into Act II.

Apparently, there was an odd flashing of the lights during Fantine's "I Dreamed a Dream" scene. And then something must've fallen loudly backstage during Javert's solo. From what Mrs. Leonard says, Miss Price and Zach (Sparkles #2) handled themselves perfectly, without missing a beat. That, she says, is exactly what she expects any one of us to do when and if there are small glitches on show nights. She then leads us in a round of applause for Miss Price and Zach.

And soon she calls places for Act II.

I start to leave immediately, walking out of the band room with Sam and Eric and leaving the cuddling Addison and Collin behind.

I don't check to see if his eyes are still waiting for mine. It's too risky. Besides, I know I'll have those eyes...and his voice...and his arms...all to myself after a few scenes.

I head to my place, and we begin the second act. Marius gives Éponine his letter, and she delivers it to Valjean.

During "On My Own," I don't flinch at all when the sound system makes a screeching noise. I just keep singing. I can tell that my microphone is going in and out a little, but I keep forcing Éponine's misery, and not my irritation, to shine through on my face.

When I sing my last note, the eighth graders break out into applause. Not because they could hear me, I'm sure. So it must be that they feel at least a little bad for me. Guess they aren't as terrible as everyone has been saying...

When the scene changes, Mrs. Leonard hobbles across the stage and meets me in the right wing to check the battery on my microphone. The battery, however, must not be the issue, so she next checks the placement of the microphone on my trench coat. Everything seems to be clear there too.

And there isn't time for any more checking. I have to get back out on the stage for my death scene.

Mrs. Leonard whispers to "hope for the best" as I walk out, but I can tell almost immediately that our hopes aren't going to be good enough. My microphone starts making weird popping sounds as soon as I get on the stage.

I just keep moving, though, moving to get shot, and then moving to fall into Collin's arms. Finally.

When it's time, he pulls my back firmly against his chest and cradles my upper body tightly in his arms. Our heads are somehow even closer than they've been before, and he leans down so that his chin is closer to my cheek than it is to the top of my head.

And I don't even care that my microphone starts acting up again when I begin to sing. The audience disappears, and I sing to only him.

When he starts his lines, the microphone situation gets even worse. Both of us pop and squeal and screech until Mr. Croft must just turn both of us off. We keep singing, though. There is no way that the audience can hear us over the orchestra pit, but we don't stop.

When it's time for me to look up at him, I turn my head...and his face is so close to mine. One breath away. My lips keep singing Éponine's words, but I am lost, fuzzy, shaking. He has stopped breathing, and his eyes are serious, heated.

In the interlude before we sing together, he parts his lips and whispers to me.

"I want to kiss you."

I catch my breath and don't start my next line on time. Neither does he.

It doesn't matter. No one can hear us anyway.

Time stops for a moment.

It starts right back up again, though, when I see Addison out of the corner of my eye. Offstage. Watching intently.

I open my lips to mouth my words, and soon he does the same, his breath blowing across my lips.

Reluctantly, I pull back from his face to fall into his arms and die.

And then Mrs. Leonard yells "STOP" from the side of the stage as she slowly moves out on her crutches and calls for all cast members to sit for the question and answer session.

Addison is out on the stage beside us before I can even start to get up. Her eyes are full of fire.

I jump out of Collin's arms as quickly as I can and then start to head over to Eric. I don't turn around. I don't look at Collin.

I do hear Addison's angry words, though. "*That* didn't look like your blocking."

I can't hear Collin's response. I'm too far away by the time he starts to talk, and there is no way that I'm slowing down or turning back. I can barely focus on walking as it is—my head is spinning and my breathing is still all uneven.

When I get to Eric, he is fanning himself and looking at me with his tongue on his teeth.

"Wow, Lex," he says. "Hottest scene I've ever seen in *Les Mis*."

I feel more heat creep up into my cheeks as I sit down beside him. I don't say anything, and he just laughs and grabs my hand.

Then he leans over to whisper. "I'm pretty sure you'll be together at prom...and graduation...and—"

I nudge him as Mrs. Leonard begins to take questions. Several eighth graders have their hands up. Some of them wave around and start to make noises to try to get Mrs. Leonard's attention. The walkway teachers are right on top of these kids, moving closer to shush them.

Mrs. Leonard picks a quiet girl in the front row to ask the first question.

The girl asks not about the show but about how to join Drama Club when she is in ninth grade next year. Mrs. Leonard gives her a quick rundown of the audition process.

Eric leans over during this. "I wonder if there will even be any money to do a show next year."

He has a point. If Addison won't be here, why would her father fund the show?

That makes me sad for the underclassmen in the show, especially Sarah. I also feel kind of bad for the girl in the front row with the first question. She seems so excited.

The next questions are about different aspects of the play. The scenery. The costumes. Questions just like the ones the sixth and seventh graders asked.

Mrs. Leonard answers most of them, and I, well, I zone out a little, thinking about Collin...replaying his words in my head over and over.

I want to kiss you. I want to kiss you. I want to—

I don't realize that I've looked over at him until I'm trapped in his eyes. I blink away quickly—before Addison turns my way.

I didn't mean to look at him, but I wasn't thinking. Or maybe I was thinking too much. About him. I think that's it.

Thankfully, Addison wasn't looking. But he was. And his face was still pretty flushed. I wonder if—

"I have a question." A loud male eighth grader voice. A really loud voice. He's in like the tenth row. Two of the surrounding teachers scold him and remind him that he's supposed to raise his hand and wait for Mrs. Leonard to call on him.

Mrs. Leonard politely says that it's okay, and she tells him to ask his question.

The kid looks over in Addison and Collin's direction. And then he starts in his blaring voice again. "So what's the deal with Marius? Who does he end up with? He says he wants to be with that curly-haired girl, but he was just all over the one in the trench coat." He looks over at me.

I freeze. Even Eric freezes beside me, unsure of what to do with this.

Before anyone talks, the girl beside him, also loud, speaks up. "You are so dumb. That girl in the trench coat just died."

Multiple kids around the room start to laugh. The teachers start fluttering about, trying to calm down the commotion.

"Oh." The loud kid again. "I couldn't hear anything. I just thought they were about to kiss or something and then she passed out...because of him or the bullet or whatever."

Mrs. Leonard steps in again, somehow maintaining her polite hostess voice. "No, your friend is correct, sir. Éponine did just die. And Marius ends up marrying Cosette."

"Oh." He laughs and looks around, enjoying his moment in the spotlight. "Thanks for clearing that up, ma'am."

The Q&A session goes on for a few more minutes, but I don't hear anything. Just the pounding of my stomach and a ringing in my ears.

Mrs. Leonard eventually has the teachers in the audience dismiss the eighth graders to catch busses back to their school, and she then tells us that we'll start the next scene in a few minutes.

Since Éponine is already dead, I probably won't have to go back on just for the guys to carry me off.

So I have some time on my hands.

Recently, I've been hanging out in the dressing room during this Act II break, using the time to run lines with Sarah or to try to catch up on homework.

I don't think I'll be able to concentrate on either of these activities today, but I stand up with Eric and start to walk toward the dressing room anyway.

Before I can even make it to the left wing, I am stopped.

"Oh—Alexa and Collin, go see Mr. Croft and let him look at your microphones before we start again." Mrs. Leonard. "We've got to get this figured out before the next thing goes wrong."

I look over at Eric, and he motions for me to head to the back of the auditorium. His tongue is on his teeth again.

I start down the stage left staircase without looking over to see if Collin is coming too. When I get midway back the aisle, I see him...and Addison, out of the corner of my eye. They are walking back the right aisle, holding hands.

I look down and beg my eyes to just focus on the ground passing beneath me. I—

"Addie?" Mrs. Leonard again. I keep walking. "I need you to grab my clipboard from the band room. I left it in there between acts, and I have some ticket sale information I want to look over with you while we have a second. I need you to make a couple of calls tonight."

I hear no response. But I know she'll go. She doesn't really have a choice. She's made herself an assistant director.

I still don't look over. Or up. I get to the back and hand Mr. Croft my microphone. He tells me to wait, and then he turns back to the soundboard, fiddling around with different pieces.

A moment later, I feel Collin step behind me, waiting his turn to see Mr. Croft.

I stand, facing forward, staring at Mr. Croft's back...and breathing in Collin's cologne.

I feel his breath on my neck as he inhales to whisper.

"Meet me in our old spot during Javert's death scene. She'll be on the other side. I'll make some excuse to come over."

I don't turn around. Addison will be returning with that clipboard at any moment now. And she won't be pleased if she finds me facing him.

She also wouldn't be pleased to know that his hand is now resting on my side, making it almost impossible for me to hold myself up—to stop myself from falling back into him. I—

"Okay. Try this." Mr. Croft turns around, and Collin's hand disappears from my side. "This is a new microphone for you to use. It's an older model, but I'm hoping that it will give you less trouble than the other one did today. Wear it for the finale." I take the new, older, microphone from him and thank him.

As I move away, I can't help myself. I turn my head slightly, whispering "okay" before I walk back to the front of the auditorium.

I find Eric sitting in the hallway. He gets up as soon as I come out.

"You're blushing again, Lex." Then he pauses. "No, not again. Still."

I just shake my head and let him lead me to sit down beside him. Once we are seated as comfortably as we can be with our costumes on, he looks over at me, waiting.

"C'mon, Lex. I haven't seen *DAYS* all week. I need this."

"He wants me to meet him," I whisper as I move my eyes around to make sure that no one is in earshot.

Eric smiles, tongue back on teeth. "Excellent. Where? When?"

I raise my eyebrows and jab him in the side with my elbow. "It's risky. You know it is."

Eric sighs and pats my head. "It's like three days before the show, Lex. Really—what is she gonna do? Play all of the parts? Collin and I don't even have understudies—cause there is no one else to sing the songs."

"Sarah would do mine if I was kicked out," I say in a matter-of-fact tone. "And, I don't know, the Sparkles duo could take over for you and Collin if need be...they'd just have to carry scripts and be multiple characters or—"

"That is stupid."

"Yeah, but she might be that mad. You know that."

"Whatever. Take the chance. Meet him. You have to."

"I do." I look down at my hands. "I mean, I want to...and I told him that I would."

He turns toward me, hands gripped together in excitement. "Okay then. When and where?"

I tell him, and he starts to laugh.

"So, what, you two are gonna make out in a closet while Javert jumps off a bridge to his death? Oh, the romance." He sighs and laughs again.

And I jab him with my elbow again.

After Eric gets up to get ready for his next scene, I go into the dressing room and try to do some homework. I get nothing done, though. I just watch the clock and the people coming in and out to change for upcoming scenes.

I always leave before Addison comes in to put on her wedding gown, but today I leave early.

I head to the little prop closet for the first time in forever as Javert is just starting to sing his last song.

We arrive there at the same time.

Collin starts to pull me into his arms before he even twists open the closet door. His face is already a heartbeat away from mine, and he—

And he stops. And then he pulls his face back far enough to show me the turmoil in his eyes.

"It's locked." A pause. "Addison must've locked it."

I close my eyes in irritation. In frustration.

Before I can open them again, his lips are on my chin, his nose on my cheek.

"I can't wait anymore," he whispers.

My breathing stops as he slides his face up to meet mine.

"Lex." His lips brush mine as he says my name, and then—

"What exactly is going on here?"

We both pull back in shock, our limbs disentangling as fast as possible.

And standing right in front of us is Casey, who has a gigantic smirk spreading on her face.

I try to regain control of my breath to formulate an answer to her question, but Collin beats me to it.

"Casey." Words start tumbling out of his mouth. "You can't say anything to Addison. You just can't."

She crosses her arms over her chest, still smirking.

"And why shouldn't I?"

"Because...because I," he glances over at me and then back at her, "no, *we*, know that Addison really is fooling around with Michael."

Chapter 16

"Dog Eats Dog"

I didn't sleep at all last night. Not. At. All. And I didn't hear any of the words coming from my teachers' mouths during school today. Not. One. Word.

That moment from yesterday has been playing and replaying in my mind nonstop—like it is its own tiny little musical.

Except there is no singing. And I don't have any lines.

Somehow, it just keeps repeating.

So, Collin has brushed my name across my lips thousands of times, and Casey has said, "What exactly is going on here?" just as many.

The scene never changes much; it always ends with us getting caught. Then it branches off into new scenes, new scenes that play out different ways that this might turn out. Might turn out today...

After she caught us, Casey told us that she wanted to sleep on the whole situation, and there was really nothing else we could do but let her.

During the end of rehearsal yesterday, we separated and tried to stay away from each other. Collin even sat by Addison after the finale while Mrs. Leonard gave us instructions for curtain call. And when we ran curtain call like five times in a row, we didn't meet eyes even once.

After that, I left rehearsal with Sam and Eric. I walked to the back of the auditorium without looking back at Collin...or at Addison...or at Casey.

And now...now, rehearsal is about to begin today, and I'm ready to keep my head down, my eyes away from all three of them again.

Casey has other plans, though. She grabs me as soon as I walk into the auditorium. I follow her right back through the auditorium doors and back into the lobby.

"I've made my decision," she says as we stop walking and stand face to face.

I look her directly in the eyes. "Please don't tell her, Casey. Please—"

"I'm not going to tell her, Alexa." She makes a scrunched up face. "Gosh—chill out already." She pauses and puts a smile on her face. Not a friendly smile, or even a smile meant for me, but a smug, self-satisfied kind of smile.

"I sort of like that you two are sneaking around behind her back—just like what she's doing to me with Michael." She pauses. "It means she has more pain coming later...sometime in the future. I like that."

While this seems like a perfect example for the word "sadistic," another one of our new vocab words, I keep my mouth shut.

She's not going to tell her. She's not going to get us kicked out of the show.

Before I settle into complete relief, I remember that she said "more pain coming later." I ask what that means.

Casey smirks much like she did yesterday. "Oh, I have a plan. For today. I'll need you to help."

"Oh." I don't know what else to say.

She then pulls me further away from the auditorium doors and starts whispering her plan. I don't catch every word because she is talking really super fast, but I get the gist of it.

She repeats my part in it, my "job" in her plan, a few times so that I know where to be and when.

I don't tell her that I don't want to do it. I don't tell her that I think it all sounds pretty horrible. I wait and tell that to Eric when I replay the conversation about fifteen minutes later.

Right after I throw on my Act I costume, I make an excuse to Mrs. Leonard about having to run to my locker, and then I grab Eric and blurt out all of the information as we walk.

"Okay...so she's not going to say anything about Collin and me, I guess. And that's good. I'm grateful. But she has this plan to get Addison back for the whole Michael thing. Apparently, Casey liked Michael even before Mrs. Leonard convinced him to be in the show...and Addison knew that."

"And that should've made Michael off limits," Eric interrupts. "And I'm sure Casey didn't think she'd need to remind Addison about that—especially since Addison was so happily involved with Collin."

The last part of his sentence sends a punch to my stomach. Even though I know they weren't that happy. Even though I know they aren't together anymore. Even though he almost kissed—

"Okay—so what's the plan?" Eric stops in the middle of the endless dark hallway of lockers and turns to face me.

"Well, first, she will just break up with Michael. She said that losing her is enough punishment for him. Then she went into some disgusting details about the things he'll be missing." I scrunch up my face a little.

Eric scrunches up his face too for a moment, and then he shakes his head as though shaking off whatever thoughts had just crept in there. "Gross." He starts to talk again, "So what is the plan for Addison?"

I start to walk forward again toward my locker—even though I actually need nothing in there. Eric turns to walk beside me once more.

"Well," I start, "Casey is going to initiate another drinking party today. This time it will be in Practice Room I."

Eric nods and waits for more.

"She's going to call Addison's dad with a fake errand for intermission, and then she's going to get Addison to start drinking."

"A fake errand?" Eric questions. Just like I did when Casey first told me about it.

"Yes. I guess she'll tell him that Addison needs something from home—a leotard, a pair of shoes, or a school book or something. I don't really know what." I pause. "I don't really understand how Casey will come up with something that makes sense either."

Eric looks over at me, nodding his head. "Oh, she'll come up with something easily. Those two girls have pretty much lived at each other's houses since Casey's freshman year. She'll be able to describe a shirt or a necklace or something perfectly for Addison's dad to go find and bring in."

"And Addison's dad will drop everything to do that? Even if it's Casey calling and not his daughter?"

Eric's still nodding. "Of course. Casey is...or was, I guess, Addison's best friend. Addison's father would never let her down."

"Well, I guess that the plan is pretty well constructed, then. I kind of thought it wasn't going to work. I kind of hoped it wouldn't."

Now Eric stops again. "Why do you care if it works or not? She's been awful to you, Lex. Well, both of them have been, actually...Casey too."

"Yeah...but I don't want to be part of this gigantic fight. I only want Casey to not tell Addison about Collin."

"But Casey said you have to help?"

"It sounds like it. It didn't seem like a request...I didn't get the opportunity to say I didn't want to be involved or anything."

Eric puts his hands on my shoulders and spins me around so we can start our walk back down to the auditorium. "Okay. What do you have to do?"

"I have to stand in the hallway outside of the practice room and make sure Addison doesn't try to leave. Casey wants her dad to see her physically in the same room as the alcohol...not just drunk. She thinks that Addison would somehow otherwise explain seeming drunk as not feeling well or as just being really excited about the show or something."

"Well, that's always what she's done in the past when she's been drinking," Eric reminds me. "You'd think her father wouldn't be buying that crap anymore, but he does."

I just shrug my shoulders.

"But, Lex. It's not that bad. So you have to stand in the hallway? What's the big deal? It's—"

"What if she comes out? What am I going to say to her? How am I supposed to—"

"She probably won't even come out, Lexi. Seriously. When they have those little parties, they normally don't come out until they've finished drinking." He stops. "Wait. What about Casey? Isn't she worried about being caught in there as well?"

"Well, no. She plans on leaving. Another fake errand. And she's gonna leave Addison alone with Michael. She thinks that will keep Addison occupied and unsuspicious."

Eric nods. "So Michael will also get caught?"

I shrug. "I guess. She didn't say much about that. She doesn't seem to care what happens as long as Addison gets into trouble." I shake my head a little, trying to remember the last parts of my conversation with Casey. "She doesn't even seem to mind if she somehow gets caught during all of this. She doesn't care if she gets kicked out of the show. She said something about there always being next year for her."

"Well, yeah, if Leonard still casts her after all of this goes down."

"But what if the whole show gets canceled?" I change the subject and spit out the question that's been pounding in my head since I talked to Casey.

"Oh, it won't," Eric assures me right away, now casually walking down the staircase to the auditorium lobby. "It can't be canceled now. It's too late. The set and costumes and props have been paid for. Programs have been printed. People already have tickets, and ads have been running in the newspaper for weeks." He looks at me with a serious face. "Leonard can't cancel the show." A pause. "Neither can

Addison's father. He doesn't have that kind of control...especially now that the checks have already been cashed."

"But—"

"Lexi—Addison and her father might be able to make some decisions...or get a person kicked out of a show here and there...but they can't stop the whole thing two days before opening night. Can you imagine the irritated phone calls from parents and ticket holders and...and...this is *Les Misérables*. It's never been done anywhere around here. People would FREAK if they shut it down."

"Okay...so even if Addison's dad sees that there is drinking going on during rehearsal..."

We are now at the auditorium door. Eric pauses in front of it.

"There is no way that he is gonna believe that Leonard okayed that." He pauses. "I think Casey's plan might work. It'll get Addison into trouble...and maybe Michael. But that's it."

"I still don't want to be involved, though."

"I know." Eric smiles. "But that is your punishment for getting all heated and breathy with Collin."

I just roll my eyes and reach around him to open the auditorium door.

And rehearsal is about to begin. The lights are already down, and there are only two people left in line to get microphones with Mr. Croft. Eric and I jump into line behind them. Minutes later, we approach the hallway just as Mrs. Leonard is asking everyone to gather in the band room.

Good thing there's no audience and we aren't doing full makeup today. Eric and I never would've made it on time.

We walk into the band room, and my eyes begin to roam around. I can't help it. Before I even get the chance to find Collin's face in the crowd, though, Eric nudges me and tells me to stop.

We sit in the first seats we can find, and I focus my gaze forward, on Mrs. Leonard.

She talks about yesterday's microphone issues a little and says that she thinks the problems have been solved. I already know that. Mr. Croft gave me my original microphone to try again today, saying, "It should work for you now."

Mrs. Leonard discusses ticket sales. Apparently, we only have one hundred more to sell for Thursday night.

I lean over to Eric and whisper, "You should ask Lance to come."

He whispers back, "But who would he sit with?"

I shrug. "I don't know. I think my mother is coming. She wouldn't care."

He smiles and puts his tongue on its spot on his teeth. "I don't know. It's probably too soon for him to meet my hag-in-law. I haven't even met her yet!"

I keep myself from laughing and check to see if Mrs. Leonard is looking our way. She's not. And she's still discussing ticket sales.

"You will," I whisper again. "I think she's taken off for each show. Dad is even going to make it to a couple of the performances."

Eric smiles. "Isn't their firm gonna fall apart or something? Or won't all the guilty people start running free?"

Jabbing him with my elbow, I tell him, "I think it'll be okay if they take off one weekend out of the year." Now I smile. "And I'm sure Mom would love to spend part of it sitting with Lance."

Tongue back on teeth. "Well, who wouldn't want to get to sit close to him in the dark for a few hours?"

I smile back. And then I raise my eyebrows and put my own tongue up on my teeth. For the first time ever.

He nudges me. "Hey—this one's mine. Don't get any crazy team-changing ideas about Lance. It didn't work for Collin and it doesn't work the other way around either."

I shrug my shoulders with a smile, and we both turn back to Mrs. Leonard, who has just started to announce call times for the nights of the show. I wait for my name to be announced as she reads down her list.

But before she gets to me, the band room door opens behind her. Casey walks in first, and Collin is only a step behind.

His eyes knot with mine the second he walks in.

In an instant, I'm back in that moment with his arms around me, his lips saying my name as—

"LEX." Eric is nudging me as he whispers me out of my daydream and away from Collin's eyes. I push my head down and just stare at my hands on my lap as Mrs. Leonard continues to call out names.

I don't know where Casey and Collin go exactly, but I'm pretty sure they've found seats somewhere close to me. Casey's shoes definitely clicked over this way.

I start to wonder what Addison thinks about Casey being alone with Collin. I wonder if—

Now I am being poked on the back. I turn around and see that April girl, the one who overheard Addison and

Collin's argument about me during callbacks. She's never talked to me.

And apparently, she's not trying to talk to me now. Without even catching my eye, she hands me a little folded up piece of paper. I take it and turn back around in my seat.

Eric looks over with questioning eyebrows, and I just shrug. I don't know what it says. Or who it's from. All I do know is that it has "ALEXA" printed on it in large loopy letters.

Before I can open it, Mrs. Leonard calls out my name on her list. I make a mental note of my call time, and then I unfold the note.

More loopy writing.

Intermission

Be at your post three minutes after the curtain closes.

-*Casey*

I move the paper over so Eric can read it too. Mrs. Leonard starts to give individual notes to different cast members—mostly to members of the revolution.

"Her dad is gonna make her drop the show. Isn't he?" I whisper another question that's been circling in my head.

Eric shrugs as if to say, "What does it matter?"

And I guess he's right. I mean, Sarah could play her part, I guess.

"It's a little over the top, though, isn't it? Getting her into this much trouble?"

Eric raises his eyebrows and lifts his shoulders again before whispering, "It has to be this extreme, though, if Casey wants to get back at her. If it wasn't this harsh, Addison would talk herself out of it somehow." He pauses. "Don't you want to get back at her a little too? She's been such a bit—"

I shake my head.

"Really, right now, I just want her to not know about Collin and me...and I'd like her not to ruin what might happen there."

He puts his tongue back on his teeth for like the seven thousandth time this week. "Oh, we're getting back to a heated and breathy discussion, aren't we?"

Another shake of my head and a roll of my eyes, and then I lean back into my chair.

It looks like Mrs. Leonard is wrapping her notes up. She seems to be on the last index card from the stack she is going through.

Her last note is for the girl playing Gavroche...something about slightly adjusting her position as she dies.

No notes for me today...probably because no one could even hear half of the stuff I did on the stage yesterday.

When Mrs. Leonard finishes talking, a sparkle of blonde hair catches my eye as it moves past me. Addison, who doesn't have her Cosette wig on yet, walks up to the front to talk about Casey's party again, which, well, shocks me at this point, but I try not to react. Obviously, Casey is keeping her little intermission plan very well hidden.

Addison complains a little about the fact that not many cast members have signed up to go. A few raise hands to ask questions about how to get to Casey's house and where to park. Others make excuses about not being able to go...family being in town...homework to do...wanting to be in bed since it's on a school night...

Addison tells these people that they need to prioritize, especially seniors, because this could very well be their last opening night ever.

As this is going on, I have to stop myself from looking around to find Casey's face. How is she reacting to all of this discussion about a party that she might not even end up having...or at least that her blonde event coordinator won't end up attending?

I instead watch Addison while she finishes up her little speech. As she says her final sentence, something about all of the fun we'll have at Casey's...all of the memories that will be made, she looks directly at me with a smirk, no doubt wanting me to think about her message to Collin.

Disgusting. I move my head down quickly to avoid her.

I get it, Addison. But I also know it's all a lie.

Somehow, it still makes my stomach hurt and my throat a little dry, though.

I just keep my head down until I hear Mrs. Leonard's voice as she calls for Act I places.

Eric grabs my hands to stand me up out of my chair, and we then walk to the stage together, not turning back to look at any of the other cast members behind us.

Act I starts smoothly. No one misses a cue, the sound system seems to be behaving, and no crew members drop any props or scenery. We are definitely in that almost comfortable groove where scenes change like clockwork and lines bounce from one person to the next. Mrs. Leonard said something yesterday about this being potentially dangerous because with a comfortable routine might also come a lack of excitement or intensity on the stage...but she also then said that this is all cured in front of an audience.

I, for one, don't feel any lack of intensity or excitement during the Marius, Cosette, and Éponine scenes. I'm pretty sure the tension on the stage is at a higher level than ever before. Mrs. Leonard even cheers after a couple of our scenes.

Collin and I do nothing that should cause any questioning. Sure Marius might have a couple of unblocked glances at Éponine, and, yes, sometimes a hand grab or a shoulder clutch might last a few beats more than normal, but these should be going unnoticed by anyone watching.

Unnoticed by everyone but me. And him. And maybe Addison under normal circumstances, but she has been drinking since the middle of Act I, so she's a little off her game.

Now she's on her way to start drinking again. It's intermission.

And I have a job to do.

Casey passed by me a few minutes ago, handed me my cell phone (which she must've taken out of the phone box in the band room), and told me to report to my spot in three minutes.

So I'm on my way off the stage, away from my end of the Act I finale position. And I'm alone—just like Casey told me to be.

Eric and Sam and many others are passing me on their way to the band room to listen to Mrs. Leonard's mid-show speech.

I think Casey made some excuse to get Addison and Michael and her out of going to the band room...something about the girls trying to fix a tear in Michael's costume.

I doubt she said anything to get me excused. Hopefully Mrs. Leonard will just think I ran to get a bottle of water or something...or, better yet, maybe she won't even notice that I'm not there.

From what I can tell, Collin's job is just to be in the band room like normal. Since he completely avoided Addison's drinking parties in the past, it only makes sense that he isn't around this time, I guess. That would definitely make Addison suspicious.

But won't she also be suspicious if she sees me in the hallway? That, of course, was my question to Casey earlier.

Casey's answer? Addison won't even see me. She'll already be in the practice room and drinking before I report to my spot...and then, well, she probably won't even come out of the room. That's what Casey thinks, anyway.

I'm still worried.

And now, the entire cast has passed me as they've walked to the band room. Where we're supposed to be. The one person I've been waiting to see hasn't passed me— Collin must've gone into the band room early, doing his job in this whole plan.

But hopefully I'll get to see him soon.

As for now, the hallway is empty. I can hear some laughter coming from the closed practice room, but otherwise it's quiet.

I stand at my post and click on my phone to find Casey's newly listed number. I leave it up on the screen. Ready. Just in case.

At least five minutes pass, and then Casey slips out of the practice room. She holds up her cell phone and says, "Text me if she tries to leave" as she passes me on her way back to the auditorium. "I'm gonna wait in there until her dad gets here." She pauses. "And I guess I'll just tell him that Addie needs to talk to him or something. I will somehow get him to come back here."

And then I'm supposed to just start walking to the band room, pretending that I was just passing through the hall. Yes, I remember.

I just nod at Casey as she disappears through the left wing entrance doors to the auditorium.

More time passes...a couple of minutes that seem like decades.

And then my phone buzzes with a text from Casey.

He's just walking through the back auditorium doors now.

Great.

I don't write back. Nothing new to rep—

The practice room is opening.

I freeze in my spot as Addison's head pokes out of the door. Her eyes land right on mine.

A lazier than usual smirk spreads on her face, and her eyes dance around a little.

"Shouldn't you be in the band room, Alexa?"

As I open my mouth and try to come up with a reply, my phone buzzes again. I don't move to check it.

Words just fall out of my mouth.

"Your dad is here."

Her eyes stop twinkling as she steps out of the practice room, shutting the door quickly behind her.

"What?" Her smile is gone, and her face is as panicked as I've ever seen it.

And then I hear the left wing door creak open.

"Addie, honey?" A deep male voice.

All of a sudden, her dad appears in a black pinstriped suit. Her dad—just standing in the hallway with us.

I pry my feet off of the floor and start to move toward the band room, trying my best to make it seem like I was on my way there all along.

I hear Addison say, "Hi, Daddy" as I hit DELETE on my phone, getting rid of the message that Casey sent while I was talking to Addison. I don't even read it. I send Casey a new message instead.

She just came out of the room.

I send the message, already dreading the response I will get, and then I open the band room door.

A few faces turn to meet me right away. Eric and Sam both have questions and some amusement in their eyes. Collin, though, looks much more serious, rather distraught. Worried. Anxious. A little like he just wants to get up and hug me.

A small part of me just wishes he would. Just hug me. Kiss me. And we'll work through whatever happens afterward together.

"Alexa—is everything all right?" Mrs. Leonard has now turned to look at me...probably because I'm just standing motionless in the doorway, looking ridiculous.

I clear my throat and shake my head, shaking my eyes away from Collin's.

"Yes, um, I just couldn't get rid of the hiccups, and I needed to go have some water."

"That's fine, Alexa. Why don't you join us now?" She doesn't look entirely convinced by my story...but she doesn't look mad either, at least.

I hurry over to where Eric is sitting. He moves over in his chair so I can have half, and he grabs my hand as I sit down beside him.

"What happened?" He whispers, still looking straight ahead.

"I'm not even sure," I whisper back truthfully, also not turning my head since Mrs. Leonard's eyes keep flickering over to me as she speaks. She begins to look over so often that Eric doesn't even try to get more out of me. We listen as she gives some notes, some more details about ticket sales, and—

And the band room door opens again. This time it's Casey. Her eyes fly right to mine. And they are just one shade below murderous.

Eric squeezes my hand. Mrs. Leonard stops speaking to turn once more to the door.

"Did you fix Michael's costume? Where's Addison?"

I gulp back all of the nervous lumps that have risen in my throat.

Casey, still looking at me, responds with, "Well, I tried to take care of things on my end. Addie is—"

"Right here." Cosette's wig, Addison's face…Addison appears in the doorway. She looks pretty sober for someone who just got caught drinking. Well, someone who was supposed to have been caught drinking.

"Okay girls, have a seat. I'm almost done here."

Casey squints her eyes at me in a final little assault, and then she goes to sit with Addison…who, I'm pretty sure, goes to sit near Collin.

I glue my own eyes on Mrs. Leonard, hoping that she is done soon, but also hoping that she isn't…the longer she talks, the longer no one can come talk to me.

She finishes up with her usual pep talk where she refers to us as "blossoming stars" and "lovely young people." Just as she tells us to "make something beautiful out there," the band room door opens yet again.

It's Michael this time. He looks, well, like he always does. Rather calm. Unfazed. He heads in the general direction of Casey…and Addison…and Collin.

Eric just tightens his grip on my hand even more, trying to make me aware that he wants to know what happened.

So. Do. I.

Just as Mrs. Leonard calls for places, I feel a buzz on my lap.

I look up to make sure Mrs. Leonard doesn't see that my phone is on my lap…that it isn't in the box with the rest.

She isn't looking. I release Eric's hand to open the text.

Stay here. Alone.

Casey again.

Eric leans over to read the text and then asks what he should do. I tell him to go. No need to make Casey even angrier.

Eric kisses me on the cheek, gives me a sympathetic look, and heads out with Sam and Sarah. I then cover my phone with my hand so no one else sees it, and I wait for the band room to clear out.

The sound of Addison's voice reaches me before I see her walking toward the door, hand in hand with Collin. She's talking about Casey's party again.

I push my head down as far as it will go, trying to be invisible while I wait for Casey.

A few moments later, we must be alone, because Casey comes over and stands above me.

"What did you do?"

I raise my head a little, but I don't meet her eyes. "I did what you asked. I sent you a text right after she came out, and then I had to go to the band room because her dad arrived like a second later."

"That's all you did? You didn't, I don't know, knock on the door to warn her or something?"

I shake my head. "No."

She leans down so that she is right in front of my face. "That better match up with the story Addison tells me when I talk to her about everything tonight." She sighs heavily with a small groan. "Now I have to go clean up after my stupid excuse about why her dad was even here."

She stands up and hovers over me again, now in thought.

"Once she sobers up a little more, she's going to have a lot of questions."

I don't understand how Casey explained the whole situation well enough that Addison actually sat with her in the band room, but I'm not going to ask Casey to explain. I don't want to be more involved. And I doubt that she'd tell me anyway.

Casey is now holding her hand out to me. I hand her my phone and watch as she places her phone and mine back in the collection box before starting to exit the band room.

At the door, she turns around.

"Your story better check out, Alexa. Otherwise, Addison's going to hear about you and Collin. Tonight."

Then she leaves...and leaves me frozen in my chair.

Chapter 17

"One Day More"

Needless to say, I didn't sleep again last night. Now it's been at least fifty-some hours since I've been able to dream...to just escape my thoughts for a little.

I did pointlessly crawl into my bed around midnight last night after spending hours listening for the phone, or the doorbell, or pebbles on my window or something.

I just assumed some sort of information would come— that Mrs. Leonard would call or come over to kick me out of the show...or that Casey...or Addison...or both of them...would stop by to deliver the information.

I even checked my email like a hundred times just in case.

But no information came.

Eric and Sam both called to check on me and the situation, but those conversations were short. None of us had anything to report. No news.

And I wanted to call Collin. Or to go see him. Or to have him throw pebbles at my window to try to secretly meet me. But I think we both knew that any communication between the two of us would've been a terrible idea.

We were really careful during our Act II scenes yesterday. We stuck to the blocking. Our faces weren't abnormally close during my death scene. No extra touches or glances at all. Nothing really out of the script.

If Addison and Casey were watching us, they really should've had nothing to complain about. Well, nothing new to complain about.

But I don't know why I haven't heard anything yet. Even in school today, I heard nothing. Like the whole issue didn't exist beyond every second of thought running in my mind.

Like it doesn't exist now as I'm about to walk into the auditorium...just like I do every day...

I don't know what to expect as Eric opens the door and nods for me to go in first. But I go in anyway.

I take two steps in and then freeze. Coming toward me is a man I've only seen a couple of times before, but one I'll never forget.

Addison's father.

My feet won't move. Neither will my eyes, even though I know I'm rudely staring. Fortunately, he keeps walking and looks right through me as he passes.

I stay right where I am, unsure of what to do. Perhaps it would be easiest just to leave now and not face whatever is coming.

Eric doesn't let that happen, though. I hear him say, "Good afternoon," and then I feel his hand on my back, pushing me to walk down the aisle of seats. I stare straight ahead and pick up one foot and then the other.

Mrs. Leonard is standing right below the stage, and she asks us to sit down as soon as she sees us.

Something is clearly wrong.

Eric and I sit quietly in the middle section of seats, not even looking at each other.

A few other cast members are already seated. One yells out, "Shouldn't we get into our costumes?" She asks as though she thinks Mrs. Leonard has somehow forgotten her routine of getting us into costumes and makeup before talking to us...like that somehow slipped her mind. Mrs. Leonard looks at the girl and shakes her head, her face more serious than I've ever seen it—even worse than when she fell down the stairs. Nothing has slipped her mind.

Something is wrong. Very wrong.

More cast members filter in, and Mrs. Leonard just has them sit. A few more ask her about costumes, and she gives them the same shake of her head that she gave the first girl.

When Casey shows up, I catch my breath, just waiting for her to come sit beside me and tell me that Mrs. Leonard is about to publicly remove me from the show or something, but that doesn't happen. She doesn't even look over at me.

Eric nudges me. I shrug. I have no idea what is going on.

More students file in. Michael shows up and sits with Casey.

The auditorium is pretty much silent...the exact opposite of the usual atmosphere when opening night is just one day away.

Collin still isn't here. Neither is Addison.

"Alexa Grace." Mrs. Leonard is looking around for me. I hesitate, but then realize there is no point in delaying this anymore. I wave my hand a little to catch her attention. When she finds me, she says, "I need to talk to you for a minute before we begin." She motions for me to come to the front of the auditorium. She isn't smiling.

I give Eric a brief, panicked look, and he tries to come up with a reassuring smile for me.

"Do you want me to come with you?" he whispers.

I just shake my head with a small, closed mouth smile. She only asked for me. Maybe Eric and Sam will be left out of this. Maybe they'll get to keep their parts.

The auditorium is now all the way silent as I make my way to the front. I wonder how many cast members already know what is going on, what Mrs. Leonard is going to say to me.

I avoid the stares I'm getting as I pass each row of seats. I walk as fast as my heavy feet will allow.

As soon as I reach Mrs. Leonard, she tells me that we should talk in the hallway, so I follow her up the stage left staircase and through the left wing. It takes forever since she is still walking with crutches. And because everyone is looking at me.

We end up right outside of Practice Room I. Right where I was standing about twenty-four hours ago.

Mrs. Leonard maneuvers herself so that she faces me. She looks like she hasn't slept for as many hours as I haven't. Even though she never wears makeup, today she looks even less made up.

Still not talking, she rubs the palm of her hand over her forehead and then her eyes.

I just wait.

Eventually, she speaks.

"Alexa. I can't believe I'm having this conversation with you now—the day before the show."

Here we go.

"I just spoke with Addison's father."

I cannot believe this is happening. My hands are starting to sweat. I shove them into the front pocket of my hoodie and lower my eyes from her frazzled expression.

"Alexa, Addison is no longer going to be in the show."

What? My head jolts up to meet her eyes.

"I know," she continues, "it's very difficult to believe this when here we are with one rehearsal left before opening night."

"But—what is going on? Why?" I manage to get some words out.

Mrs. Leonard shakes her head slowly. "Her father made the decision just a couple of hours ago." She pauses. "And I have to respect a parent's right to do what seems fit."

My eyebrows scrunch together in confusion, but I don't ask any questions.

"But enough about what happened. We've got to talk about how we're going to fix it."

My eyebrows are still bent in question, but I nod, grateful that she just said *we're* going to fix it and not that she'd like me to also be out of the show.

"Alexa...would you like to be Cosette?"

"What?" I know that my eyes are wide, and I can feel my mouth hanging open. "What about Sarah?"

She smiles a small smile. "Well, Sarah, of course, can play either of the parts. Cosette or Éponine." She pauses and clears her throat. "It's just, well, you auditioned so well for Cosette, and I'm rather sure that you have her whole part pretty much memorized." She smiles again. "I remember reading your audition form. You put that down for your 'fun fact' response. You have been running Cosette's lines since you were a little girl."

I nod. I did write that back on audition day. About a lifetime ago.

"And you are in a lot of scenes with Cosette, so I'm sure you know the blocking."

I tilt my head back and forth to suggest that this is sort of true.

"Alexa, this is your choice. You just—you deserve the chance to decide. I can give you a few minutes."

She turns around to go, to give me some space to think.

But I don't need it.

"Mrs. Leonard." I call her back, and she turns around to face me once more.

"Yes, Alexa?"

"I want to play Éponine. Sarah will play a wonderful Cosette."

"Are you sure?"

"Positive. Sarah knows all of her lines and blocking backward and forward." I pause. "And I'm actually rather attached to Éponine."

Mrs. Leonard smiles. "Okay. But Sarah is going to need a lot of help over the next few days. Costume changes, entrances, everything. Will you help her?"

Now I smile. "Of course."

Mrs. Leonard nods and then motions for us to go back into the auditorium so that she can speak to the full cast. Well, full minus one. For some reason.

As I start to walk back through the left wing, I wonder if—

Yes. He's here now. In the third row.

Looking right at me.

And he's smiling—a relaxed, full-mouthed, bright-eyed smile.

It's fantastic.

But I don't know what to do with it. I don't know what I'm supposed to do...or allowed to do.

So I glance over to make sure that Casey or, I don't know, someone else, isn't watching in a way that suggests that he or she is trying to get me kicked out of the show. As far as I can tell, no one's watching, though, so I stop holding back the smile behind my straight face for a few seconds before I blink away from him and head to take my seat beside Eric.

Eric is more wound up than the jumping monkeys on his long-sleeved t-shirt.

"What happened? What did she say? Are you in trouble? Should I—"

I cup the palm of my hand over his mouth to stop him.

"I think it's okay," I whisper. "It's going to be okay."

Mrs. Leonard starts ringing her bell. I give Eric a "be quiet" look and then slowly remove my palm from his mouth.

Then we both look forward to listen.

"Okay, my lovely people." She looks around. "You have all worked so hard, and I couldn't be more proud of you. And tomorrow, your parents and friends and community members will feel the same, I'm sure."

She pauses and takes a long breath in.

"With that being said, let me remind you that doing a show always comes with a little drama on the side. And this show is no different than any other...so I'm just going to come right out and say this."

She pauses again, and Eric looks at me with scrunchy eyes.

"Addie, um, Addison, will no longer be in the cast."

There are some gasps, some comments, and some people looking around, just now noticing that Addison isn't here.

I really only watch one of the heads in front of me—the one with the dark tousled hair in the third row that hasn't moved at all during this announcement.

He already knew.

And he probably knows what is going on.

"She already told you this," Eric whispers beside me with wide eyes.

I just nod, even though he didn't really ask a question.

He looks even more confused than before. "But why did she have to talk to you fir—"

"Shh." I cut him off. Mrs. Leonard is trying to quiet everyone so she can continue.

"Now, fortunately, we had some very talented people try out for Cosette." Her eyes land on me for a beat before she looks over to Sarah, who is sitting in the front row. "And Sarah, our understudy for two of the leading females, will now be playing Cosette."

Sarah makes a surprised little shriek, and different cast members begin to clap slowly, still a bit stunned, while others go over to congratulate her.

Eric does neither, however. He whips his head around to me and then pushes my chin toward him.

"Oh my dear Madonna. She asked you if you wanted to be Cos—"

I fling my palm back over his mouth, grateful that Sarah and Sam are sitting together in the front, away from us.

Eric tries to talk through my hand. "BUT WHY DIDN"T—"

I put more pressure on his lips.

"It wouldn't be fair," I whisper. "Sarah is the understudy. And she has been working nonstop on her lines. She and Sam were even running them now, before Mrs. Leonard started to speak." I pause. "Honestly, I can't believe that Mrs. Leonard would even think to make an unfair switch like that."

Eric bites my hand and, in surprise, I move it.

Fortunately, he whispers what he says next. "What—you are surprised that Leonard would make an unethical casting call?" He smiles and puts his tongue on his teeth. "How could you think that with her track record?"

I smile too. I can't help myself.

But then I turn back to him once more.

"Promise me you won't tell Sarah. Or anyone. She'd be so upset if she found out."

Eric tilts his head toward me. "I won't, Lex." He pauses. "For you."

"Promise me."

He places his right hand across his chest. "I swear to you on this pile of jumping monkeys."

I shake my head. I guess that will have to do.

He moves his hand from his shirt and now grips my arm.

"Okay, Lex—now tell me why Addison is out of the show."

I shake my head back and forth slowly. "I don't know what happened. I really don't. Mrs. Leonard just said that her dad was pulling her out."

Eric smiles. "Well, I guess I have my work cut out for me today. I'll find out." He grips my arm harder. "You should help me."

"I might not have the time. Mrs. Leonard wants me to assist Sarah like twenty-four seven."

He moves back in his seat and pouts a little. "Maybe Sam will be able to help me investigate."

"Just be careful, Eric." I look over at him. "Seriously. I don't know that I'm in the clear for sure."

He shrugs and rolls his eyes. "Of course you are, Lex. She's gone. She's done." His tongue travels back up to his teeth. "You could just go jump on Collin's lap right here in front of everyone if you wanted."

Now I roll my eyes.

"Or I could do it...and take one more stab at pushing him over to my team."

I just keep my eyes rolling, and then I turn forward as Mrs. Leonard tries to talk to all of us again.

She announces that we all need to help Sarah today, and then she tells Sarah that I will be her go-to person to help with cues, costume changes, etc.

Sarah turns around to smile back at me. She looks radiant. Like she's just landed the role of her dreams.

I smile back and then listen as Mrs. Leonard gives notes and instructions for today and tomorrow.

When she tells us to get into costumes, Sarah and Sam start back to join us. Before they arrive, I look up and right into that brown pair of Marius eyes. Smiling eyes again.

He is alone, standing up beside his third row seat. His eyes move around a little as Sam and Sarah show up beside me. When he settles his gaze back on me, he mouths the word "later" slowly before giving me another smile.

I nod. And smile. And smile. And smile.

Then we go our separate ways to get ready for our final dress rehearsal.

The beginning of rehearsal is a whirlwind; I've never been so crazy busy during a practice.

I've been backstage with Sarah almost all evening, running blocking and lines, straightening her costumes and wig, and really just being ready to do whatever else comes up.

Eric has come to find me two different times with two different pieces of information.

First, during "Castle on a Cloud," he had information from that April girl, who somehow again seems to be in the know.

"Addison was drinking again today, Lex. She was in some bathroom or something during third period with some non-cast members. They were all drinking the leftovers from yesterday's little practice room party."

A scene or two after telling me this, Eric caught me again, this time with information from Justin.

"Guess who turned her in, Lex! Miss Price. She found her all trashed in the bathroom right outside of her classroom."

It's been a bit since his last update, but Eric is now heading toward me again. I have to be on the stage in a few minutes, so he talks quickly.

"Hey—Lex, I just overheard Casey telling Michael—"

I stop him with a stunned face.

"Yeah, I know. It's weird that they're talking. It's even weirder that I saw them kissing a few minutes ago—but we'll have to dissect that info later. For now, focus."

I nod and push aside the questions I have about Casey being back with Michael.

"Casey talked to Addison late last night. She told her about seeing you with Collin."

He has my full attention now.

"Addison planned to see Mrs. Leonard during her study hall after lunch. She planned to get you into trouble. I think she was going to tell Mrs. Leonard that *you* were drinking during yesterday's rehearsal."

My mouth opens in shock.

"I think Casey was going to go along with Addison's story."

Wow.

"But, Lex—Addison screwed it up for herself just in time. It's over, Lexi. It's—"

It's time for a new scene to start.

I plant a kiss on Eric's cheek and then step out into the darkness as the scene switches behind me. My stomach cartwheels with nerves. And with some anticipation.

I haven't seen Collin since Mrs. Leonard's opening meeting. Somehow, we haven't crossed paths...even though he's crossed my mind approximately every five seconds since I last saw him.

The lights rise for the scene, and before I know it, he's there. He's here.

He's Marius. And he's calling me Éponine. But our alter egos (or real egos—if a person can say such a thing?) are communicating too...with brushes of our hands as we pass each other in our blocking...with searing gazes that hold layers of meaning...some for Marius and Éponine...some for us.

It's intoxicating. Being with him...having him so close...knowing that we are finally both free...free to talk, free to look at each other...free...but still not able to do anything about it as we move Marius and Éponine around on the stage.

When our early scenes together end, I walk off the stage in a smiling daze, and Eric grabs me on my way to the dressing room.

"I can't stop watching the two of you trying not to just fling yourselves into some hot make out session."

I crumple up my nose at his description.

"*DAYS* has nothing on the chemistry between the two of you."

I roll my eyes and head to the dressing room to check on Sarah. Before I go in, I ask Eric if he's gotten up the nerve to text Lance yet.

"I wrote the text. I asked him to come tomorrow night."

He looks at me rather sheepishly for Eric.

"What is it?"

"I haven't gotten up the nerve to hit SEND yet."

I don't say anything. I push past him and head to the band room. He follows.

I fling open the band room door and walk right over to the phone collection box. It's not difficult to find Eric's phone. It's the only one with a purple sparkly case.

I find his text, look at him with what I hope is a reassuring smile, and hit SEND. Then I place the phone back in its spot and grab Eric's hand to leave.

We just make it back to the door when we hear a vibrating sound.

And even though there are like fifty phones with Eric's, fifty different people who could be getting a text message right now, we both bolt back to the phone collection box.

I grab the sparkly purple phone once again.

And he has a text from Lance. I jump up excitedly and then open it.

I'll be there.

I read it to Eric, and his slightly nervous eyes immediately start to shine just as his tongue makes its way to his teeth.

We leave the band room trying to decide what Lance might wear, what we should do after the show with him, what Eric should wear after the show...

I check on Sarah in the dressing room, and then the three of us go out to the stage for the Act I finale.

As we sing our final notes of "One Day More," Mrs. Leonard claps and claps. She's obviously quite pleased. And relieved. She tells us to be ready for Act II in fifteen minutes.

Sarah and I start to walk off of the stage. My heartbeat gets crazier and crazier with every step that I get closer to Collin.

Then it skips like seven beats when I finally do get to him. He meets my eyes. And then he catches my fingers in his. He pulls my hand up to his face, putting it right on his cheek. Then he blinks me a soft smile and turns to kiss the bottom of my palm before releasing me to follow Sarah.

I resist the urge to reach my hand back up to his face, his lips. Instead, I return his smile and make my body turn to catch up with Sarah.

After intermission, Marius and Éponine meet onstage once again. Marius sends Éponine on her way with a cream-colored envelope to give to Cosette just as Collin sends me off the stage with a grasping of my arm, an intense look in his eyes, and a note slipped into the front pocket of my trench coat.

I have a quick chance to look at his note after my part in the next scene with Jean Valjean. When I exit the stage, I stand on the very edge of the right wing, using the light on the stage to pull my note out and read.

I can't stop thinking about you...or about picking up where we left off a couple days ago...

I know you are really busy helping tonight, though.

So how about tomorrow?

Meet me in our spot after the show.

I'll be there waiting for you.

-Collin

Lightheaded, shivery, and, I'm sure, flushed, I fold the note back up and return it to my pocket. I'm in no way ready to wander onstage to lament about being lonely.

But it's just about time. The scenery is almost ready. So I quickly assume Éponine's face and walk onto the stage— miserable, distraught, and alone.

At least that's how I look. How Éponine looks.

Mrs. Leonard claps as I finish my song, and, really, before I know it, it's time for my death scene.

Only a second after the gunshot rings out, Marius is there to catch Éponine.

Collin wraps his arms around me and lowers me to the floor, crushing my back into his chest.

His heart is beating so quickly. Mine is pounding.

Our position is off. Our blocking is off.

Both of his arms are wrapped tightly across the front of me, and I clutch both of his hands with mine. He nuzzles his cheek back and forth across my hair as I sing.

When he sings, I feel his lips move on my skin.

Éponine gets weaker and weaker, but instead of falling further down toward Marius' lap, she falls further back into his chest, her head leaning further into his body. When she dies, her head falls down into him as her hands lower to the stage. Marius rocks her back and forth as he sorrowfully finishes her song.

The orchestra pit plays the final notes. And then there is silence. Complete silence.

I don't move, but I feel as though my head and body are swirling in circles. I breathe in his cologne. I feel the weight of his head as it rests on mine. And my ears explode with the pure stillness of the auditorium.

I don't know how long we sit there. Not long enough.

Eventually, Mrs. Leonard's clapping hands break through my daze.

"I—" she starts to speak, but then stops.

"I'm almost speechless," she says a moment later. "That was perfect."

We each mumble a thank you and move our heads to look at her. She then tells me to run back and check on Sarah to see if she's ready for the next part. I'm supposed to do this instead of just lying on the stage and waiting to be carried off.

I nod. And we begin to disentangle ourselves. Our bodies don't make it easy for us, though. With seemingly every move we make, we manage to brush up against each other. A graze of an arm. A touch of a hand.

Each time, a new shudder flows through me.

When I eventually get myself to a standing position, an unbalanced and shaky standing position, I somehow manage to make my way off the stage to the right wing.

I only get two steps into the wing before I hear footsteps rushing toward me.

Collin. I know it's him.

In an instant, he flings his arms around my waist, spinning me around to face him. I can't really see him in the dim blackness of the wing, but I can feel his breath on my lips.

"Tomorrow is too far away," he whispers.

I don't have time to say anything back. Or to breathe.

His lips crash against mine as he tightens his arms around me, pressing the palms of his hands into my back. I pull him even closer, circling my arms around his neck and losing my hands in his hair.

Our lips move together in a hungry, pulsing rhythm...over and over...wasting no time for air.

We don't stop until we have to...until a shout from the stage breaks in and makes us all of a sudden focus, all of a sudden realize that Collin is still supposed to be out there.

"Marius is still in this scene," I whisper frantically.

He rests his forehead against mine and groans.

"I know. I wish he wasn't."

He places one last soft kiss on my mouth and heads back out.

Chapter 18

"Who Am I?"

So here I am on opening night, standing in the dressing room.

And I'm Éponine. Not Cosette.

But I couldn't be happier.

I zip up Sarah's dress and give her a hug. Then I walk with her to the band room, where we meet up with Sam and Eric.

As soon as he sees me, Eric grabs my hand and pulls me down to sit next to him.

"Lance just texted me. He's here. Third row. Left side. Center aisle. By your mom."

I smile with him excitedly. We agreed that this arrangement would be okay after I introduced Eric to my mother last night.

Casey, who is sitting on Michael's lap, yells to get everyone's attention. She talks about her party after the show. I tune her out. I'm not going. And I still can't believe that she's back with Michael.

As she continues to talk, I see the band room door open behind her.

In walks a football player-looking guy with intense brown eyes.

He looks right at me.

My heart begins beating faster as he walks over to take the seat on the other side of me.

He starts to put his arm around my shoulder, but then stops, his arm hanging in midair.

I watch as he turns his gaze to Eric, a question in his eyes.

Eric squeezes my hand and nods to him.

"We can share her," he whispers before lifting his tongue up to his front teeth.

Collin wraps his arm around me, and I lean my head in against his neck. We get a few curious looks. And a few people whisper. But I don't care.

Soon, Mrs. Leonard crutches in and begins her announcements for the evening.

"My beautiful, inspiring cast. I am once again so very proud of all of you. I wish you a wonderful opening night." She pauses and looks around the room with a smile. "Now, you have a sold-out audience out there tonight—so don't forget to wait for applause, to be on top of your cues, and to keep going if something unplanned happens." She smiles again. "But enjoy yourselves too."

When she pauses again, the room becomes noisy with chatter, cheering, and general excitement.

But then Mrs. Leonard puts her palm up in the air to quiet us once more.

"Oh—and Marius," she grins and looks right at Collin...and me. "Try not to leave in the middle of a scene tonight."

I feel my cheeks start to flush.

Mrs. Leonard's smile is even bigger now. "See if you can make it until after the show to be with Éponine."

I bury my head further into Collin's neck as Eric squeezes my hand rapidly.

"I'll see what I can do," Collin replies with a laugh.

Then he tightens his arm around me and plants a kiss on the top of my head.

A nd the show begins.

Most of my interactions with Collin are between Marius and Éponine...except for an occasional clench of hands when we pass backstage...and the slight shift of our eyes when we cross on the stage...and the way he caresses my hand for a moment after Éponine dies...nothing that should even be noticeable to anyone but him, and me—and my dizzy stomach.

Hopefully everyone else is concentrating on the show itself.

That seems to be the case. The audience claps enthusiastically after each song. They stand for most of our curtain call. And when we go out to the lobby at the end, we are surrounded by compliments and hugs and flowers.

I spend some time with my mom before heading over to where Eric is standing with Lance. When he sees me, Lance gives me a smile and points his eyes to the purple gift bag in his hand.

I give him a quick nod, glad that he's waited for me.

Eric catches our exchange and looks at me questioningly.

I just shrug and let Lance take over.

"I was going to get you flowers tonight, but I heard that you might like this better." He holds the sparkly purple bag out to Eric.

Eric gives both of us a confused look as he takes it.

"Come on. Open it," Lance encourages him with an excited smile.

Eric does as he is told. He digs through the glittery tissue paper and pulls out his present: a rather large, golden trophy.

He looks at me first, his eyes sparkling. Then he turns to Lance and thanks him.

Lance smiles. "Obviously, I had a little help." He nods toward the trophy. "More than a little."

Eric takes the time to examine the award in his hand, running his fingers over the little French *Les Mis* flag now affixed to the trophy figure's raised golf club and examining the drab looking, Thénardier-inspired costume the golfer is wearing. Eventually, he raises the trophy to read the little gold plaque at the bottom, which reads his name (just Eric— like Madonna or Björk) and then BEST SUPPORTING ACTOR IN A HIGH SCHOOL MUSICAL.

When Eric looks up again, his eyes are a little misty. He squeezes my hand and then hugs Lance. When he pulls back from the hug, he has an excited gleam in his eyes.

"I'm gonna go show my brother." He grabs Lance's hand to take him along and then looks back at me. "Guess you can't come." He smiles. "I'm pretty sure you have other plans about now."

I smile back. I do.

I tell him that I'll catch up with them at the little coffeehouse on the corner in a bit.

Then I head to that little prop closet once again.

I open the door, and I am immediately showered with light. Fiber optic light...coming from dozens upon dozens of roses surrounding the little room.

Collin sits in his normal spot. Back against the wall. Knees up. Hand stretched out for me.

I grab it and sit down beside him, my shoulder pressed to his. He turns his head to face me and brushes his hand over my forehead before resting his fingers in my hair.

"Lexi," he whispers, our faces only seconds apart. "You know, one of the very first times that I saw you, I made a comment about how pretty you are."

I blink a smile, my face getting warm.

He smiles now too. "I got myself in quite a bit of trouble for that."

I nod slowly. "Yes—so I've been told."

He moves his mouth even closer to mine.

"Best trouble I've ever been in." He brushes my lips with his for a moment and then pulls slightly back. "Look where it's gotten me."

This time when he meets my lips, he is in no hurry to move away.

He kisses me at an achingly slow pace, pulling me into his arms and rubbing my back gently.

It's a kiss that reminds me that we have nowhere we need to be right now and no one about to barge in on us.

A kiss that promises many more kisses to come.

A kiss that knocks every thought and every breath...everything...right out of me.

Epilogue

"A Heart Full of Love"

The play went well. Amazingly well.

Sold-out crowds each night. Standing ovations. Lots and lots of flowers.

We, of course, weren't completely perfect. As Mrs. Leonard has told us over and over again, an entirely clean performance isn't to be expected with live theatre.

Gavroche was late on a cue during opening night, but one of the bribed revolution boys on the stage covered it up pretty well.

The bottom hem of Sam's dress ripped out a little during Friday night's "Master of the House," but we fixed it so she didn't have problems during our next two performances.

The most talked about mess-up also happened on Friday night. Mr. Fiero was a couple of seconds late during the "Who Am I?" scene. Rumor has it that he was backstage...with his arms around Miss Price. And she was the one who was so afraid of seeing any backstage embraces!

I'm pretty sure she won't make that announcement again if she ever does another show with Drama Club.

As for me, I did make one noticeable mistake. On Saturday night, I accidentally dropped the cream-colored envelope just as I took it from Collin. He covered for me, though.

Marius held up his palm to show Éponine that he would bend down to get the letter. He then picked it up and placed it carefully in her hands before sending her on her mission.

He might have also given Éponine a non-scripted, reassuring look when his back was turned to the audience...

One other "mistake" was made during each of our four performances.

Each night before Sarah got ready to sing "Castle on a Cloud," the backstage crew ran around frantically, trying to find the cloud castle scenery. They really freaked out when they didn't find it on time during the opening night performance. And they still were a bit distraught on Friday night when they couldn't locate it.

However, on Saturday and Sunday, they really only appeared to look for about thirty seconds before giving up and just letting the song run without it.

Mrs. Leonard never said a word.

The show has been over for about a week now. The set is gone. The costumes have been shipped back, and the scripts have been erased.

Only a couple of last rituals to go.

The cast party is tonight.

Addison's father offered to keep it at his house—even though Addison wouldn't be there as she is still staying at a rehab center for another few weeks.

As a cast, we decided not to go that route. We did send him a really big thank you note, though. For paying for our show. For recently telling Mrs. Leonard that he still wants to donate money to Drama Club in upcoming years. And for offering to throw the cast party.

The party will be held at Sarah's house tonight, though. We helped her decorate and set up last night.

Collin will be here soon to pick me up. I'm almost ready to go, but my phone keeps slowing me down.

Eric keeps texting me. He's nervous about tonight. Lance is going to the party with him, and Eric is counting this as their first official date. He keeps sending me pictures of different shirts, belts, shoes...not sure of what to wear.

He also is sending messages about what I think has to be the last ritual of Drama Club season: the yearbook reflections.

Apparently, every year, senior cast members answer questions to be published alongside Drama Club yearbook pictures.

Eric is pretty sure that Addison started this ritual during her freshman year. It's weird that she won't even get to do a reflection now.

I don't really want to write one either.

The questions aren't bad, but I really don't like to think of my answers being published for everyone to see.

Years in Drama Club, past parts in shows, experience in singing and dancing, plans for college, etc. I have already recorded all of this information.

Eric just texted me all of his answers for his reflection—just in case some of them will help me think up my own answers...and probably also because he is super excited about his spot in the yearbook.

I scroll down on my phone to find his response for the last question—the only one I haven't answered yet.

Dream role.

I laugh as soon as I get to his answer.

ANY CHARACTER ON *DAYS OF OUR LIVES.*

Perfect response.

I put the phone down and sit for a few minutes, pen poised to write...but not writing.

And then the doorbell rings.

Collin's here.

I slowly put my pen down and leave the last question as it is. Blank.

Dream Role:

I'll probably never get the chance to audition for *Les Misérables* again.

So I'll probably never be Cosette.

And...I'm pretty okay with that.

Much more than okay.

I fold up my paper, seal it in its envelope, and run downstairs to open my door.

*Most chapter titles are song titles from Alain Boublil and Claude-Michel Schönberg's musical adaptation of *Les Misérables* (A Cameron Mackintosh production based on the novel by Victor Hugo). Many of the song titles are also mentioned throughout the book. These song titles are in quotes. Characters from Victor Hugo's novel and Alain Boublil and Claude-Michel Schönberg's musical adaptation of *Les Misérables* are also mentioned throughout the book.*

Books by Jennifer Jamelli

Checked

Checked Again

Drama Unsung

www.facebook.com/jamellijennifer

Made in the USA
Lexington, KY
15 October 2014